B-MINE

MM ROCKSTAR ROMANCE

WAYWARD LANE

AVA OLSEN

B-Mine: MM Rockstar Romance

(Wayward Lane 2)

Copyright © 2024 by Ava Olsen

http://avaolsenauthor.com/

Beta-reader: Jennifer Sharon

Editor: Devon Vesper

Proofreader: Jennifer Sharon

Cover Design: Covers by Jo Clement

Warning: Mentions of anxiety, addiction, depression and mental health issues, death of a loved one.

Copyright and Trademark Acknowledgments

The author acknowledges the copyrights, trademarked status, and trademark owners of the trademarks and copyrights mentioned in this work of fiction.

CHAPTER 1

DAWSON

"Holloway's disappeared."

The voice of my colleague, Lennie, crackled in my earpiece.

Fuck, this was getting out of hand.

I loved being a bodyguard, but some primaries made my life a living hell. And Iain Holloway was one of them.

Or, rather, he was it.

Join a security team for a popular rock band, they said. *It'll be fun.*

Fun, my fucking ass.

The past four years had been a never-ending cycle of yanking the bad boys of Wayward Lane out of one rockstar fire and preparing for the next one.

"What do you mean he's disappeared?" I barked in response. "You accompanied him from the dressing room directly to their VIP room. How could he have disappeared?"

A year ago, I'd asked my boss, Regan, to take me off Iain's detail. I couldn't handle the lead guitarist's Houdini hijinks anymore. Or his endless flirting. Not that I minded much of the latter, and hell, he flirted with everyone. But it wasn't smart or professional.

So, I switched to guarding the band's singer, Brodie James. At least Brodie had grown some common sense. Of course, that could be because he was recently married to his former manager, Ivan Cross. To say Brodie was protective of his husband was putting it mildly.

For a while, my work stress had lowered. Iain was someone else's problem.

But a month ago, there was a break-in at Iain's Nashville home, and Regan put me back on Holloway duty. My blood pressure had never been the same. Lately, my face was as red as the hair on my head.

And I had red fucking hair.

Iain was a free-spirited imp who chafed at any kind of authority figure. Rules and safety protocols? Iain ignored—and fought against—most of them.

What he needed was a good, hard spanking to put him to rights.

Not that I would ever say that out loud, or my boss would kick *my* ass.

And I was still working out how to get through to Iain. He didn't take me or any of his security staff seriously, and as the band's popularity rose, the stakes got higher. It wasn't just a matter of being unexpectedly approached by one rabid fan for an autograph. It was getting swarmed and injured, or worse.

It happened at a nightclub in New Orleans back in October when a drunk hit Iain in the face. I'd been guarding Brodie and Van, but when I heard my boss's SOS call, my blood turned to ice. Just thinking about it now, about something bad happening to Iain, had me sweating like a marathon workout.

All a perp needs is a split-second opportunity to get close. To inflict harm.

And my job was to anticipate those threats.

Even if the biggest one came from the person I was guarding…

"He found a way to sneak out again, boss. None of the guys in the band know where he's at. I swear, I only turned my back for a second."

I had a good idea where Iain was at. He was getting sucked off by some groupie backstage or just outside the building. I'd found him in that same scenario so many times that if you asked me what Iain looked like, I could accurately describe his dick and balls to a sketch artist.

And yeah, he had a pretty cock. And balls.

Not that I paid attention. Or that I should be thinking about that.

Ever.

The band members were told that when they hooked up on a venue site, they needed to pick a place where security could be on standby, like a closed dressing room, but no.

Not Iain.

And I was done playing his fucking cat and mouse game.

"I put you in charge of him while I was doing the last rounds. Your job is ensuring he stays within the building and the rooms we set out! If you can't handle being my secondary, I'll assign someone new," I snapped.

"Sorry, Daws. It won't happen again."

As irritated as I was at Lennie for losing Iain, I also knew how difficult the job was. Not to mention, I was worried. The thought of Iain getting hurt made all my protective instincts kick into overdrive.

Maybe it was also the single dad in me. Protectiveness came with the territory.

I was concerned about all my details but Iain most of all. Not every fan had good intentions. And he was taking unnecessary risks. One of these days, he was gonna find himself in a situation he couldn't joke his way out of.

But even though Iain was always playful, I didn't buy his

flippant act for one minute. Sure, he loved what he did, and he enjoyed himself, a lot, but no one was that happy-go-lucky all the time.

I'd been around the boys in the band long enough to know that there was more to Iain Holloway than long blond hair, lightning-quick fingers, and salty quips.

"Scour every inch of the hallways behind the VIP room," I directed. "I'll check the exterior."

"Will do."

"Notify me as soon as you have an update."

I tapped my earpiece again and hung up. Then, I made my way from the stage to the nearest exit.

I encountered several tech crew members, including our chief engineer, Ace. He was getting the last-minute technical glitches resolved.

Everyone stepped out of my way.

People usually did when they spotted me. It was a fact that most bodyguards were hired partly because of their size. It wasn't the most important factor, but being a big guy (I was just shy of six-four) had its advantages. And everything about my manner told people to back off. Throw in the red faux-hawk, redder face (thank you, Iain), and the steam that was now coming out of my nose, and there was a reason my colleagues gave me the nickname 'Rampaging Viking.'

I walked past the VIP room and spotted all the guys in the band—Brodie, Ronin, the bass player, and Faisel, the drummer—talking with Van and their invited guests. They were offering everyone celebratory shots and amping up the atmosphere. Nothing unusual there, but still fairly tame compared to how they used to party. I'd noticed a shift ever since their last concert on Halloween. With Faise's brother in drug treatment and Brodie's relationship with Van, they partied less but hung out with each other more.

The guys were growing up.

Everyone except you-know-who.

They'd been in the recording studio this past month, finalizing their next album, and tonight, they were hosting an LGBTQ+ community charity event in Nashville. And while the rest of the guys were doing their bit, Iain was nowhere to be found.

I headed down the hallway and spotted the exit sign to the back alley of the building. When I got up close, I noticed the door had been propped open—a breadcrumb leading me to my target.

"Jesus Christ!" I yelled out, then tapped my earpiece. "Xavier, Lennie, I'm on to him. He's out back. He propped the exit door, and I don't have to tell you how dangerous that is."

"Shit, you need backup?"

"I can handle him."

Oh, I was gonna handle him all right...

Stepping out into the alleyway, I spotted Iain not five yards down, leaning against the brick wall, a man kneeling at his feet. The guy was giving him a hand job and a piss poor one at that.

At least, that's what I assumed. Iain looked bored as fuck, which was not like him at all.

"Holloway, get your ass in here!" I yelled out.

The man on the ground startled.

"Ow, careful!" Iain snapped at the guy. "That's my dick, not a squeeze toy."

The guy dropped his hand and stared at me with wide eyes. "Sorry, he scared me."

"Yeah, Dawson has that effect. On some people," Iain replied, looking right at me. Then he gave me his favorite finger and turned back to his fuck buddy. "Keep going, hot stuff. I need to come before I take the stage."

"No!" I barked and stalked toward them. "Inside, now! I'll find you a dressing room if you need to finish up, but not out here."

I pointed to the end of the alley and the busy downtown

street where people were strolling by. It wasn't just that random strangers could see what Iain was up to or take his photo (which was a nightmare for PR); anyone could walk right up to them.

Unreal.

Iain tucked his pretty cock back inside those skintight leather pants he favored and shook his head.

"Move it!" I commanded.

Mr. Squeeze jumped to his feet and bolted past me.

At least one person was listening.

Iain sighed and ran a hand through his wavy blond hair. "You had to ruin that for me, didn't you?"

"This is just the type of situation I've warned you about. Do you not care that you're putting yourself at risk?"

"For what? STDs?" he quipped and pulled out a pack of cigarettes from his denim jacket.

"You're smoking? Since when?"

"If I can't come before a show, then a cig will do. I don't smoke regularly. Just when my nerves hit. Is that okay, *Daddy*? Or do I need your permission for that, too?"

"You're the one acting like a child, so—" I gave him a finger in return.

It wasn't my most mature moment.

But it was better than taking Iain over my knee like I wanted.

Then I noticed his foot tapping the ground and the way he bit his lower lip.

"What are you nervous about?"

Iain rolled his big brown eyes. "Believe it or not, even experienced musicians get nervous before heading out on stage."

That wasn't it. This was a charity concert, not a stadium tour. And I'd seen him before shows plenty of times. He was never like this.

There was something he wasn't telling me.

Surprise.

"It's nothing," he continued, pulling out a cigarette and sliding it between those cocky lips. "Can I smoke now?"

I nodded, our gazes clashing.

"Make it fast. I want you inside."

"Really? I didn't take you for a bottom."

Instead of reacting, I stared at him silently.

He pulled out a lighter, lit up the cigarette, and took a deep inhale. Then he looked up at me and let out a long plume of smoke. Right in my face.

My hand itched to show Iain—specifically, his ass—exactly what I thought of his rebellious routine.

If only.

CHAPTER 2

IAIN

ockblocker.

    Dickhead.

    Asshole.

I took my time smoking, enjoying the last puff of freedom I'd have for a while.

Until I could sneak off again.

After four years of touring with security personnel, I'd become skillful at finding ways to distract them, leaving them behind in the dust.

Just like poor Lennie tonight.

Don't get me wrong, I liked the guy. Hell, I liked everyone I worked with. But this constant shadowing was fucking annoying. I couldn't take a piss without someone looking over my shoulder. And I wasn't one to just give in to other people's rules, especially when they were ridiculously constrictive.

All I wanted was five fucking minutes alone.

Or, five minutes with a hot guy.

An orgasm was beneficial before a show and more enjoyable when someone else was doing all the work. Like the catering guy I'd snuck out here with. Ron? John? Whatever.

He was sexy and eager, and I was happy to leave myself in his hands.

Not that I'm always a selfish lover, but hey, I'm a guitarist. I gotta rest the fingers in between shows.

And I wanted, no, I needed, one goddamned moment where no one was asking me about work or peppering me with invasive questions about every aspect of my life. I just wanted my brain to shut down and pleasure to take over.

Sex was my main vice since I wasn't one for taking drugs, other than pot. And I needed sex on the regular. It was a wanted diversion.

And I needed distraction now more than ever.

I didn't want to think about the disturbing messages that kept popping up on my phone over the past month. No, I didn't dare think about it, let alone mention it to anyone. Also, my home had been broken into the day after New Year's. Add those two things together, and I just knew that if I told Dawson, he would confiscate my phone and lock me in my house. And then I'd be climbing the walls. Trust me, you didn't want to be around when that happened. I was an easy-going guy, but corner me and watch out.

Look, I knew early on that signing up to be a rockstar would basically blow my private life to hell. But still, I needed some freedom—a sense of normalcy.

But not lately.

I couldn't even enjoy a random hand job anymore, thanks to my cock cage of a bodyguard.

My protective detail was fucking gorgeous but a ginormous pain in my ass.

Not the kind I liked.

When I didn't bicker with him, I flirted. For two reasons. One, like I said, he was hot as hell with those dark green eyes and that ripped body of his, and two, I tried anything to throw him off my scent.

But the guy was like some wall of steel or something. Immune to my quips. Immovable.

Irritating as fuck.

And I'm not gonna lie; it ticked me off that I couldn't charm him the way I could everyone else. I knew he was bisexual because he was open about it from day one with the band and his coworkers. And, not to sound egotistical (but I will), with most queer guys I met, all it took from me was a stare and a smile.

The rockstar effect is not a myth; it's my life.

But not him.

Dawson was a locked puzzle, and I'd yet to figure out just how to work his goddamned key.

The only other thing I knew about him was that he was a single dad. There were a few times he had to leave his post due to family reasons—his eight-year-old son, Jaxon—and while I was itching to know more, I never asked. Dawson drew a clear line between work and personal, and no one, not even the security staff who worked with him day in and out, knew that much about his private life.

Not that I should be curious about him or anything, but you know, I was a naturally curious person.

I took the last drag of my cig and dropped the butt on the ground, grinding it under my boot.

I wished it was Dawson's foot.

Kidding. I'm not violent.

But my balls were aching, and my tension was higher than ever, thanks to his interruption. So, yeah, I was cranky as fuck.

Given Dawson's size vs mine, it would be no contest anyway. Besides, there were more effective ways of getting my revenge. I just needed time to think on it.

My phone buzzed again, but I ignored it. A sense of panic threatened to overwhelm me, but I didn't dare ruin my concentration right before a performance.

"Aren't you going to check your phone?" Dawson asked as he motioned to the door.

I shook my head as we wandered down the alleyway and back inside the building.

"It's not urgent."

"How do you know?"

"I just do, okay! Back off!" I snapped, my body shaking.

Fuck, fuck. This was not good.

I needed to find some way to calm myself down.

"What the fuck is going on with you, Holls? And don't try to bullshit me. I see through your act."

Dawson moved to stand in front of me, blocking my path. He was four or five inches taller than me, so I had to look up at him, at his dark green eyes that saw much more than I was comfortable showing. It was on the tip of my tongue to tell him about the texts.

But I didn't. I just…couldn't.

"It's nothing. I'm just wound up. We've been in the studio recording for a month, and I'm itching for the road again. You know me, I can't sit still. And sex is my outlet. Or it should have been, before you interrupted me."

"Iain," he sighed in that exasperated tone I knew all too well.

I readied myself for his lecture. He'd been using my first name a lot lately, usually when he was about to ream me out.

"What?"

"I know it's not easy to have someone always hovering over your life, but we're here to help you. And I can't do that if you're not honest with me. Like I said before, you can fuck around with whoever you want, but you have to let your detail know, and we have to be nearby."

"I thought it was just rockstars who were into the voyeurism thing," I teased.

"Can you be serious for one moment?"

"Can you lighten up?" I countered.

Dawson ran an agitated hand over his spiky red hair, his massive biceps bulging under that black T-shirt he always wore. Black jeans, T-shirt, motorcycle boots. That was his uniform. Except for our high-profile events, where he added a blazer.

In black, of course.

Imagine a bodyguard version of Chris Hemsworth but with redder hair. And fuller lips. And stunning green eyes.

Too bad Dawson was wound so tight.

He let out a loud groan that meant total frustration. On that one item, we agreed.

My phone buzzed again. Shit.

"Who's calling you?"

"How the fuck should I know? I'll check it after the show."

I walked around him and started down the hallway to the VIP room. There was still time to check out the scene and find someone to hook up with. This time, however, I'd be a good little rockstar and let Dawson watch.

I sauntered into the room, with Dawson at my back, and spotted my bandmates downing shots. They were surrounded by a group of VIPs, several of whom were sexy as hell.

My luck was changing already.

"Hey, what's happening here? The party can't go on without me," I declared as I reached my friends.

Faise rolled his eyes, and Ronin mimed jerking off.

"Are you under some delusion that we're your placeholders?" Brodie snarked, and I gave him a playful swat on the shoulder.

Then Brodie motioned to the bar staff for another round. "We assumed you were getting your pre-show ritual on."

Another tray of shots appeared, and I grabbed two of them, downing them in quick succession.

Top-shelf tequila, my favorite. I reached for a third.

"The hand job got interrupted by my jailer." I pointed over my shoulder to Dawson. I could feel his angry glare on me like a spotlight. "But I'm ready now. Introduce me to our new friends."

It turned out the guys didn't have to say anything.

A handsome man in a fancy suit, maybe late twenties, stepped forward. He had a confident air, a perfect smile, and held my gaze for a long time.

He'd do.

Pretty Boy reached out his hand. "I'm Frankie Salich, a friend of Zoe's. It's very nice to meet you, Iain. I've heard good things."

Zoe Nord was our PR rep and dealt with our shenanigans for the past three years. 'Good things' was probably her PR code for horror stories about our antics.

"Holloway," I corrected him when I shook his hand.

I didn't like strangers calling me by my first name. Too personal and tied to my past. Only my closest friends were allowed to use it.

And a certain bodyguard who shall remain nameless.

"Sorry, Holloway," Frankie repeated and gave me a thorough once over.

He had a firm grip. I could work with that. "Nice to meet you, too."

For some strange reason, though, my dick was not with the program. I wasn't getting turned on at all.

What the fuck? Maybe I needed another cigarette.

"You want to have a drink in private?" he asked with a flirty grin.

Still nothing. Fuck.

"I'd love to, but we go on in thirty. And I have to talk to my boys beforehand."

"Cool. Afterwards?"

"Meet me back here." I turned around and waved Dawson over. "Daws, see that this man gets a pass to come on back to my dressing room after the show."

"ID," Dawson barked at him.

"He's a friend of Zoe's. And he already made it in here, so he must have passed a security checkpoint. Chill."

Dawson shook his head. "I don't care. ID."

Frankie pulled out his wallet and showed him his driver's license. Dawson took it and nodded. "I'll be right back."

As soon as Dawson stepped away, the air lightened. The vortex of rules was gone. Temporarily.

"He's intense," Frankie commented.

"He's something all right. Sorry about that."

"No worries. I work in this business, so I get it."

Frankie's phone buzzed, and he pulled it out of his pocket. "Sorry, I have to respond to this. I'll see you later?"

"Looking forward to it," I replied before he turned and walked away.

Hopefully, my cock would cooperate by then.

I grabbed another shot and let the alcohol burn away my nerves. Until my phone buzzed, and my anxiety kicked up again.

"You okay, bud?" Brodie whispered as he leaned into me, eyeing me with concern.

That was the one problem with working with someone who knew you all your life. Brodie realized something was up without me saying a fucking word.

For a second, I felt guilty as hell for not telling him about the messages. We'd been best friends since we were kids and shared everything.

Well, everything except Brodie's husband, Van.

"I'm good. You know me, once I get out on stage, everything will be all right."

It would be. And my mojo would be amped up by the time the show was over. It always was.

A quick release prior to showtime and a longer one after made for a relaxed rockstar.

And for tonight?

I'd take one out of two.

CHAPTER 3
DAWSON

Frankie's ID didn't raise any flags, so I gave him a pass and a long list of strict instructions on where to go after the show. And what not to do.

Like sneaking off with Iain without informing me.

Then I handed him my phone to e-sign the NDA.

The guy smiled and chatted with me through the whole thing. Which was usually the case. Most guys were so eager to fuck around with a rockstar, especially one as magnetic as Iain, that they would sign away their life without realizing it.

Personally, I found Frankie to be far too smooth and polished for Iain's usual taste. Then again, he was a friend of Zoe's and probably worked in PR, so that was his persona. Charming, pretty, effortless.

Everything I was not.

For some reason, Frankie irritated me, but I didn't have time to stop and think about why. It didn't matter. Iain could fuck whoever he wanted. As long as the guy didn't encourage Iain's subterfuge, I didn't care.

Once I finished warning Frankie, I escorted him to his seat. The hall was filling up fast now that showtime was only ten minutes out.

Then, I made my way backstage again. The curtain was still closed, and the guys were in place, chatting and getting ready for their opening number. Iain sounded like his usual jovial self, but I could tell by his pacing back and forth that he was worked up. I could've sworn that earlier, he'd been about to tell me something important. But he refused. The guy could talk and joke for days, but ask him a serious question, and he evaded it as he did with every security measure I put in place.

"Do you think they're okay?"

I turned to find Van, Brodie's husband, standing behind me. Van was a forty-four-year-old songwriter and the band's former manager. There was a fifteen-year age gap between him and Brodie. Not that it made any difference, given their intense chemistry both on and off the stage. I'd been a first-hand witness to their love story. It made me a bit envious, if I was being honest.

I've never been in love like that.

Not that I wanted or needed to fall in love.

Putting that ridiculous thought aside, I wondered how Van had gotten the drop on me. I hadn't heard his footsteps, and the floor of this venue wasn't exactly soundproof.

"What do you mean?" I asked, startled not only by Van's stealth but by the question.

"The guys. They seem subdued compared to usual."

"Your husband sounded like himself in the VIP room earlier."

"Oh, the snark is still there. That hasn't changed." Van smiled, and the crinkles at the corners of his eyes deepened. "Don't mind me. Maybe it's my imagination or something."

"I don't think so. You've been around them as long as I have. What's up?"

Van sighed and crossed his arms. "Ronin and Faise have been quiet since they got back from visiting his brother in California."

"Well, dealing with a family member in crisis puts a huge strain on anyone."

"True, but Faise has been more silent than usual. He never wants to go out or even stop by our place. He wasn't like that even when he was fresh out of rehab himself."

I took that information in. "He still looks tired. Or perhaps being in the recording studio nearly every day for the past month has worn them out."

Then I thought about Iain and my instinct about something being off.

"But you're right," I continued. "Something's going on, at least with Iain. Look at him pacing. He's been acting nervous these past few weeks. But naturally, he won't tell me what's going on."

Van looked around, stepped back into the farthest corner of the wings, and motioned for me to do the same.

"Iain's phone was buzzing non-stop in the studio. Even when he turned the notifications off, he checked it every five minutes. And when he's not playing, he's always staring at his phone."

"Maybe an ex is harassing him?"

Van shook his head. "That's not likely. Iain doesn't date."

"What about before they hit the big time?"

"He's never mentioned anyone."

"I'm keeping a close eye out. If you notice anything off, you tell me."

Van grimaced.

"I'm not asking you to break any confidence, Van. Only if you think they're in danger."

Van nodded and placed his hands on his hips. "All right. Hopefully, I'm wrong, and they're just working through some things."

I gave him a nod. "I've gotta do my rounds. See you in a bit."

Lennie was standing nearby, and I pointed to the stairs when I passed. He nodded in return.

As I wound my way downstairs to the dressing rooms, my phone buzzed.

I glanced at the screen, but it was an unknown number. I swiped to answer.

"Dawson Everly."

Silence.

"Hello?"

I could hear background noise but that was all, no voice, then the telltale beep of the line dropping.

"Okay, then," I said aloud to myself as I placed my phone back in my pocket. "Wrong number."

I knocked on the first dressing room, the one Brodie and Iain shared, and entered.

"Hey, Daws."

I was greeted by Brodie's assistant, Bibi. She was also a redhead, but unlike me, her personality was just as fiery. Bibi was fun, hyper-organized, and fiercely protective of all the guys.

"Just a quick room tour, and then I'll be out of your way."

"No problem."

Then I remembered that the guys handed over all their personal belongings, including phones, to her safekeeping while they were on stage.

"Have you noticed Holloway's phone ringing more than usual?" I asked.

Bibi shook her head, her ponytail sliding over her shoulder. "I don't think so. But he did turn it off before he gave it to me."

"Does he normally do that?"

"No, but maybe he was expecting a message or call that he doesn't want anyone to see. If Brodie's rings, I answer it, but everyone else, I leave alone."

"That's what I thought, thanks."

"Why the question about his phone?"

"Call it bodyguard intuition. He's getting more calls than usual but he won't answer his phone. And he got testy when I asked him about it."

"That's because you don't know how to ask."

"What?"

"Come on, Dawson. You order him to do stuff, and you know he hates that. Instead, try talking to him. Person to person, not bodyguard to client."

"I have. I do."

"No, you don't. Look, you're great at what you do, and no one can fault that. But you don't share much of anything personal with anyone."

"I have a line when it comes to work and—"

Bibi held her hand up. "I know, I get it. But to build trust, especially in this environment, you need to open up. We're not just dealing with the band's work schedules. We're a part of their everyday life. We see stuff no one else does. And I speak from experience. I mean, Jesus, Brodie probably knows more about my personal life than some of my family at this point. And vice versa. It's necessary. Because without that, he wouldn't trust me to help him manage every aspect of this crazy-ass world he lives in."

"And so, what, I should take Holloway out for a beer?" I quipped.

"No. Just talk to him like you would a friend. It's the only way you're going to get through."

I digested Bibi's advice even though it didn't sit well with me. I'd never had a problem with other clients doing as I said. It was always with their best interests in mind. But maybe Bibi was right. Even if the thought made me somewhat uncomfortable. I tended to keep myself to myself, even in my personal life. It was the complaint of past girlfriends and boyfriends. Fucking hell, it was the reason I was still single.

The only person I'd ever opened up to was my son, Jaxon.

After my ex-girlfriend Nadia—his mom—passed away two years ago, I'd become both parents to him. And he was still healing. No way was I going to let him down and not be the father he needed.

But it still wasn't easy.

"I'll take your advice into consideration," I finally replied with a nod.

And I would. Even though it made my stomach flip over.

I checked the remaining rooms in the basement and then headed back up to the wings.

The guys were into their first set, and the crowd was lapping it up.

As usual, I was mesmerized by the way Iain played his guitar. It seemed effortless, even though I knew it was anything but. His fingers were so quick and nimble, and the way he held his guitar? It was like another extension of his body. When he got in the zone, with his blond hair thrown back and that look of pure joy on his face, everyone in the crowd went wild.

He and Brodie played off each other, sharing the mic at one point as Iain sang back up. The crowd loved it and screamed his name as loud as Brodie's.

Of all the guys in the band, Brodie was the most popular for sure. He was a talented singer with an intense performance style and a demanding charisma that drew the crowds. Iain came a close second with the fans.

But it was Iain who always commandeered my attention. On and off stage.

Even though he wasn't shy or humble when it came to his sex life, his self-deprecating jokes about his talent were telling. And surprising. He was a curious mix of guitar genius, celebrity ego, and, shockingly, imposter syndrome. You wouldn't know it to look at him, but Iain Holloway wasn't just another cocky rockstar. He played up the image, and most of the time, people bought it.

But underneath that glamorous veneer, Iain had layers. And secrets.

Of that, I was sure.

As sure as I was that as soon as he was done on stage, he'd be sneaking out of the venue with his man of the night…

Iain suddenly spun around, playing to Faisel on the drums, and caught me staring.

Instead of blinking and looking away, I didn't move a muscle.

An electric throb of awareness pulsed between us.

It's just animosity, I reasoned. Keep your enemies closer and all that.

I had no idea what I was trying to prove, but I wanted him to know I saw him. I recognized the fear in his eyes earlier. All my training and my sixth sense told me to keep pushing him for answers. Or that I should try Bibi's method.

No matter what, I wasn't letting him out of my sight.

Iain stuck his tongue out at me, and that's what finally broke my trance.

Christ.

I wanted to laugh and spit nails at the same time.

Clients often irritated me, but not to this degree. Iain was making me restless in a way I'd never been with any detail.

Thankfully, he turned back to face the audience and finished his guitar solo.

"He's incredible, isn't he?"

Ace's sudden voice startled me.

Shit, that was twice in one night I'd been taken by surprise. What the fuck?

Head in the game.

"Hypnotizing. Every time. He makes it look so easy."

Ace chuckled. "That man is so talented, and the funny thing is, he downplays it."

"I was just thinking the same thing."

"Between you and me, he loves hearing the praise. Lives

for it. Some musicians need that feedback more than others. No matter how famous they are or how good a player, they need the attention."

I made a mental note. A strategy was forming in my mind.

A way to finally get Iain to see reason.

And if he didn't?

Sometimes, you just have to fight dirty to get what you want.

CHAPTER 4

IAIN

eing on stage was being home.

The intense lights, the screaming fans, my closest friends beside me.

My baby in my hands. The one true love of my life.

My guitars weren't just instruments. They were my heart and soul outside of my body. Playing had been my salvation since I was a kid. It distracted me from the mess that was my childhood and soothed me from the pain of losing my mom.

It brought me to Brodie, and Faise, and Ronin. It gave me a career that was hardly work at all.

Even if I had never made it to the biggest stadiums in the world, I'd still be playing.

Probably in some dive bar.

But I'd still be me.

I could live without the accolades and awards.

But I could never live without music.

I was so into my performance that I almost didn't realize when our first set was done. An hour and a half flew by when you were in the zone.

We took several bows and headed for the wings to

hydrate. Tommy, one of our road crew, threw us towels and then headed on stage to change my guitar.

I wiped down my face and neck and pulled at the T-shirt sticking to my sweat-soaked body. Sometime in the second set, my T-shirt would get thrown off and into the crowd.

I spotted Dawson talking with Van near the catering table. The nerves in my belly kicked up the closer I got to him. I stopped and grabbed an electrolyte drink, my hand starting to shake again.

I'd nearly flubbed my guitar solo earlier when I turned around and saw Dawson staring at me from the wings.

I had thousands of eyes looking at me on any given night. I should be used to it. But that was different. The fans wanted us, admired us; hell, they wanted to be us.

Dawson, on the other hand, didn't seem to be admiring me. In fact, I was pretty sure he was trying to intimidate me with that glare of his. No fucking way.

"Don't you have rounds to do or something?" I asked Dawson between sips. "No one's going to get to me here. I'm safe."

"Stick to playing music instead of telling me how to do my job," he snapped back. "Oh, by the way, I cleared Frankie."

"Who?"

Dawson smirked.

Oh shit. I forgot all about the guy from the VIP room.

"Your new friend, remember?" Dawson replied, his green eyes sparkling.

"Oh yeah, well, that's great." I nodded and took another sip of my drink. "But instead of the dressing room, I'd like to take him back to my place."

Dawson's eyebrows nearly hit his hairline. And with good reason.

I rarely brought guys home. I preferred to fuck in hotel rooms, dressing rooms, tour buses, everywhere but my sanctuary. Only my family—and by family, I mean the guys and the people we worked with—were allowed in my home.

I know, I know, for a guy who hates rules, I did have a few of my own. Don't use my first name, and don't ask to come home with me.

Tonight, though, I felt like breaking one of them.

"All right," Dawson sighed and tapped his earpiece. "Lennie, I'm gonna be on night watch at Holloway's. You'll switch over tomorrow at ten to take them to the studio."

"Is that really necessary?" I asked.

Dawson crossed his arms. "By night watch, I mean, I'll check the house, see you guys inside, and wait on the premises."

"That's ridiculous. There's no need for you to stay on the property overnight. I'm perfectly safe in my own home."

"New rules since the break-in. If you bring any overnight guests to your house, and I mean anyone that isn't the band or members of our crew, security is to remain on site. Text Regan if you don't like it."

Regan was Dawson's boss.

"I will. As soon as the show's over," I replied and looked around. "Where is she, anyway?"

"She's in Paris, scoping out the venues."

Normally, we'd do our European concerts at the end of the year, but Brodie wanted to try something different. Break up the schedule. So, in a week, we were flying to France and would be staying there for a couple of concerts, then on to England, then back home. We had April off, and our North American concert schedule started in May.

I gulped down the rest of my drink, my hydrated brain finally kicking into gear.

For sure, I'd be texting Regan about this new rule. The break-in was a while ago, and I hadn't even been home at the time. It was nothing. And I didn't want Dawson camped out in my house all night. He'd been with us all day, and now this? A twenty-four-hour shift? And what about his son back home?

And why did that last concern pop into my head at all? Maybe I needed tequila instead of water…

"You can't go twenty-four hours without sleep. That's ridiculous and totally unnecessary."

Dawson shrugged and stared at me. "I've done it before."

"Forget it. I'll just meet Frankie in my dressing room and be done with it," I snapped.

"Wow, so enthusiastic." Dawson smirked.

"Well, I was until five minutes ago."

"Five minutes ago, you couldn't remember his name."

I was about to bite back when I caught Brodie motioning for me from across the room.

Good thing, too, because for some strange reason, this exchange between me and Dawson was making my blood race.

In fact, my cock was finally awake again.

Oh, fuck no.

My hands were so sweaty that I nearly dropped my bottle. Shaking my head, I placed it on the table and made my way over to Brodie.

"What's up?"

"What's going on with you and Dawson? Lately, there's more arguing than flirting."

I scoffed. "He's up my ass about everything. And get this, if I want to bring home that guy I met earlier, Ricki—"

"Frankie."

"That's what I said. Dawson has to stay on site all night. Like, what the fuck, Dee?"

"It's the break-in. It rattled everyone. Regan is just trying to keep us safe."

"It's too much."

"It's temporary."

"It's annoying. And easy for you to say. Your personal life isn't affected."

I began to pace.

"What else is going on? And don't fucking start that 'nothing' bullshit. It's me, yeah?" Brodie stared at me, and I finally gave in.

"I've been getting weird text messages."

Brodie's expression fell. "From who? What do they say?"

"I don't know who! That's why it's weird. The messages are from unknown numbers with texts like 'I keep waiting for you' and 'I'm the only one who loves you.' I block them, but new ones appear. It's been going on all month."

Brodie ran a hand through his dark curls. "Have you told Regan or Dawson?"

"No. And I don't want to. As soon as they find out, they're gonna take my phone away and put me in lockdown. And then I'll really go out of my mind."

"Sorry, Iain, but you're my brother. I don't care what kind of security measures they put in place; you need to tell them. Now."

Fuck, I didn't want to.

"Please."

Brodie never uttered the P-word, and the worrying look in his hazel eyes told me to relent.

"I'll tell them this week."

"Iain," Brodie warned.

Once he got something in his head, Brodie wouldn't let go.

"This week. I promise. I swear on my favorite Martin acoustic."

Brodie nodded and took a final chug from his bottle.

"Good. Now let's get back out there and give the crowd their money's worth."

I felt lighter than I did a few hours ago. Telling Brodie was a load off my mind.

As I glanced around the room, my eyes inevitably found Dawson's.

Telling *him*, however, was a whole other story.

One that I'd prefer to skip.

I told Brodie I would do it this week. That didn't have to mean tonight.

Ace gave us the signal to get our asses back in gear, and we made our way to the stage. I picked up my 1984 Konicki electric and stood in my spot, ready to rock.

I could hear the MC on the other side of the curtain, making jokes and getting the audience ramped up again.

"You guys want to go out when we're done here?" I asked.

Faise rolled his shoulders behind his drum kit. "I don't know—"

"Come on, we haven't gone out for ages. Let's hit a club and go dancing," I urged.

Faise looked at Ronin, and Ronin turned to me. "Why the fuck not? We've been cooped up recording all month."

"Yes!" I pumped my fist. "Dee?"

"Sure, as long as Van—"

"Duh, you and Van are a package deal now. Tied at the hip. And ass. And dick," I quipped.

Brodie gave me the finger. "Oh, it's on, Holls. Let's see if you can keep up with me."

"Please, I've got more energy than the three of you combined."

"Don't forget your VIP guy," Ronin added.

"He can tag along."

"What's his name again?" Brodie asked me with a smirk.

And fuck, I blanked. Again.

They all started laughing the longer I stood silent, and I gave them two very special fingers.

"Remember *his* name?" Brodie asked and pointed to the wings.

And stupid me, I turned around.

Like I could ever forget about Dawson.

CHAPTER 5

DAWSON

ain had been acting weird all week.

He never hooked up with that Frankie guy the night of the concert. Iain didn't hook up with anyone, even when the band went out clubbing afterward.

In fact, he hadn't snuck out or hooked up all week. And I had to wonder if he was feeling ill or something. Or maybe I was reading too much into his strange behavior.

With each passing day, however, he got more agitated, and so did I.

And now we were flying to France. Maybe that was it; he had travel nerves?

Tour buses were more Iain's thing. You could stop and get out every couple of hours if needed and walk around. But a nine-hour flight was different. Even on a private jet.

Instead of worrying about my primary, I browsed the emails that Regan had sent me last night.

All the hotels and venues in Paris had been security approved. I reviewed the layouts of the buildings and prepared our entry and exit plans while the cabin crew was moving about, getting the plane ready for departure.

My team—Lennie, Petyr, Xavier, Valen, Geoff, Will, and Quinn—sat in the back of the plane with me, trading notes for the upcoming trip.

Iain and Brodie were sitting two rows ahead of me, side by side, with Ronin and Faise across the aisle. Van was facing Brodie and beside him sat the band's new manager, Harlow Hines. All the guys were talking, so I guessed everything was all right. Even though Harlow looked stressed, bouncing his knee and tapping the arm of his seat.

I'd be nervous in his position, too.

Brodie had been vocal about the fact that he was unhappy with their current music label, Bandit. The CEO of the label, Greg Haddley, had outed Van when his relationship with Brodie started back in the fall. I'd been witness to many of the arguments after that, and I knew it was only a matter of time until Wayward Lane would be cutting ties. Their contract was up in May.

It made me think about the future of my team. We were hired by Bandit, so I assumed that once Wayward left, we would be assigned to a new band.

I'd probably never see Iain again.

A painful knot formed in my stomach.

Which was hilariously ironic. Iain had pushed me to my limit, yet when he wasn't around everything seemed dull in comparison.

Fuck.

I kept replaying Bibi's advice in my head, but I stubbornly refused to listen to it. I'd heard and seen other bodyguards cross that professional line, and it did not end well. Once you lost objectivity, you were fucked. And out of work.

And I couldn't afford to do that.

Just before take-off, I video-called my son.

My mom was looking after him, as she usually did whenever I had to travel with the band. I also had a nanny, Paige, who helped her out while I was on the road. Back when I shared custody, I got to see Jaxon twice a month, mostly on weekends. But now that it was just me, the long days and longer nights of my schedule were starting to wear. Jaxon saw his grandmother more than me.

"Hey, Jax."

"Dad! Guess what!"

"What?" I asked as I stared at his earnest little face.

Jaxon was my spitting image, except he had blue eyes instead of green. Oh, and he was good-natured—a sunny chatterbox to my grumpy silence. Despite the grief of losing his mom two years ago, he was doing well in school. So much that he'd skipped a grade and was now in class with nine- and ten-year-olds. I worried it might be difficult for him to navigate, but not Jaxon. He was his mother's son, making friends wherever he was.

I smiled when I saw he had on his favorite PJs—the ones with stars and planets on them—and was sitting up in bed with my mom.

"I'm reading a story to Nana!" Jaxon yelled out, and I lowered the volume when everyone on the plane turned to stare at me.

Oops.

"You sound just a little bit excited, bud," I teased him as I finally felt my tension ease.

"The boy in this book is like me. He loves music and cats, and goes on adventures!"

"Cats, huh?"

He'd been begging me for a cat for months, and my willpower was weakening. His ninth birthday was coming up in April, and I knew I'd be making a trip to the local animal shelter.

"That sounds awesome." I leaned forward. "We can read it together when I get back from my trip."

"How long again?"

"A few weeks."

"I miss you already, Dad."

"I miss you too, bud. You be good for Nana, okay? And Paige."

"I will. Where's Holls? Can I meet him?" he shouted.

Oh jeez. My son was eight going on eighteen.

Jaxon loved all kinds of music and when I explained to him that I worked for a band, for Wayward Lane, he was beyond excited. He asked to meet all the guys in the band, but Iain in particular. And yes, I only let him listen to the PG songs, which weren't too many.

Jaxon was learning to play the piano and was now hounding me for guitar lessons. Guitar lessons and a cat. We were going to have one noisy house in short order.

I held off on introducing Jaxon to the band, though, since I didn't want to use my position to hold a family tour.

Keeping that line in place.

But Jaxon was persistent. He got that from me.

"Uh, he's talking to his friends right now, Jax."

"No, I'm not."

Iain plopped down on the empty seat next to me and waved at my phone. "Hey, Jaxon! Nice to finally meet you."

"Nana, look, it's Iain Holloway! He's my favorite musician!"

My face began to heat, and I caught Iain's amused expression.

"Really? Well, you gotta drop by the studio next time. We can give you a tour and jam. Do you play any instruments?"

What was happening right now? My heart began to pound so hard and fast that I was lightheaded. My mouth was dry, too.

Damn circulated air.

"Piano, but I want to learn the guitar next," Jax explained.

Iain nodded. "Cool. I started out playing piano, too."

"Dad, when you get back home, can you take me to the studio?"

"We'll talk about it. Now it's time for you to finish your story with Nana and go to sleep."

"It was nice to meet you, Jaxon," Iain replied with a wave.

"You too. I'm gonna tell all my friends at school tomorrow!" Jaxon shouted, and despite the lower volume, his voice carried.

The chuckles of my colleagues seated nearby echoed in the cabin.

All it took was one phone call and my personal-professional boundary was gone.

"Good night, bud. I love you."

"Love you too, Dad."

"Put Nana on, please."

The screen went blank until my mom came into view. Her red hair was now white but just as long and thick as it was when she was young.

"Hey."

"He's never going to sleep now," she teased me.

"That's my fault," Iain added, leaning against my shoulder, pointing to himself.

His hair tickled my jaw. My breath caught, and I struggled not to fidget.

Why the hell was he still sitting beside me? And why the fuck did he always smell so good? Like leather and citrus.

I'd been in training all day, so I probably smelled like stale sweat.

I turned and glared at him, but he just laughed and shook his head.

"Kathryn Everly," my mom announced. "It's nice to meet you, Mr. Holloway."

"Iain, please."

What? He never told strangers to call him by his first

name, but now my family was the exception? I'd entered some kind of twilight zone.

"So nice to put a face to the name. Dawson talks about you all the time," she added.

"Does he?"

"Do you mind?" I turned to him, my cheeks hot. "I'm having a personal conversation."

"Then why do you have it on speaker?"

I had no reply to that.

"Not to be rude, but your son is kind of a grump," Iain said and pointed to my face.

"He doesn't get that from me," she fired back.

"Anyway," I interrupted. "Mom, are you sure you're gonna be okay for the next few weeks?"

"I will be fine."

"I'll call you tomorrow then. Love you."

"You too. Be safe."

I tapped *end* and turned to Iain.

"What the fuck was that?" I demanded.

"That was me saying hi to your mom. And your son. Who, by the way, is your twin. Only, he's into music, so he's way cooler. And he's nicer."

"That's 'cause he's never had to work with you."

"He's eight. He shouldn't be working at all."

"Smart ass."

Iain smiled at first, and then, just as quickly, a look of sudden panic crossed his face.

"I'm getting strange text messages from unknown numbers," he blurted out.

"What?"

He nervously licked his lips, and my eyes locked on his mouth.

I quickly glanced up, and that wasn't any better. His deep brown eyes were so serious and framed by long blond eyelashes. This close, I finally noticed the dark circles under his eyes, and that unsettled feeling I had all week was confirmed.

"Here." Iain tapped on his phone and shoved it at me. "Look."

I took hold of his cell and glanced at the text messages.

> Unknown number: I miss you

> I saw you today, but you didn't wave to me

> Your last concert was so good. I was standing right in front of you. But you ignored me.

> Why are you with so many men? Am I not enough for you?

I kept scrolling. There must have been twenty or so messages. Fear and anger slammed into me, and all my protective instincts went into overdrive.

"How long has this been going on?" I calmly asked, even though I felt anything but.

My hand gripped his phone so hard I was in danger of cracking it in two.

"Just over a month."

"Around the break-in?"

Iain nodded.

"Brodie knew something was bothering me last week at the concert. I promised him I would tell you."

"And you thought, what? 'I've got some stalker after me, so I'll wait another few days to tell my security lead?'"

Every word that came out of my mouth was louder than the next. Heads turned, but I ignored everyone but the man sitting beside me.

"We don't know for sure it's a stalker. And I knew what

would happen, all right? I need my phone. You can't cut me off from the world entirely."

"This needs to be investigated. We'll get you a new phone as soon as we land in France. Of course, it would have been easier if you'd told me before we were on a plane headed overseas," I bit out. "I'll let you keep this one until we get your replacement. But don't erase any messages. I want to keep tracking them."

"I deleted and blocked the first few that came in. But not in the past two weeks."

"Could it be an ex?"

"I don't date. No romantic relationships."

"Never?"

Iain shook his head.

"Someone you rejected?"

Iain rolled his eyes. "That's a long list."

Yeah, and that was a dumb question. There were probably hundreds of men he'd had to turn away. There were only so many hours in a day.

I picked up my phone and typed an urgent message to Regan. We'd need to revise our security protocols.

"I'm sure it's just some weirdo who will stop once they realize I'm not responding," Iain reasoned.

I glanced over and sighed. "Regan and I will be the judge of that."

"What does all this mean? Because if you put any more restrictions on me, I'm not kidding, Daws, I'm gonna lose it."

"There will likely be additional security measures in place, yes. Round the clock. And we'll have to vet your partners with twenty-four hours' notice."

He shook his head. "Jesus, I might as well write 'out of business' on my ass."

I pulled out a pen and handed it to him.

Iain was not amused.

CHAPTER 6

IAIN

"I ain, wake up. You're going to miss breakfast."

The deep rumble of a familiar voice teased my ear.

I blinked and found myself face-to-face with Dawson. Or rather, my cheek was squished against his massive shoulder. His green eyes were amused for a change. I liked it when he got that wicked glint in his eye. It was rare, but it changed his entire face.

And turned a handsome man into something so stunning my breath caught.

Fuck, no, it's Dawson. Stop thinking about him that way.

Breakfast. And then I realized that I fell asleep on him—all night.

Why did that feel so fucking good?

Probably because he ran hot, and the air in this plane was freezing cold.

Instead of leaning away like I should have, I burrowed my face back into him and closed my eyes again. God, his smell—man sweat and the hint of a spicy soap—was amazing. He never wore cologne, and I was a fan.

Dawson grunted, but I couldn't tell if it was a good one or a bad one. Knowing him, knowing me, probably the latter.

"Iain, we're landing in an hour. Do you want coffee?"

Reluctantly, I opened my eyes again and eased myself from his person.

"Oh, yeah."

Dawson motioned for the cabin steward. I mumbled my breakfast order, a latte with lots of brown sugar and an omelet, and shook my head, trying to wake up.

I looked around and noticed everyone else was already eating and talking. And not paying us any particular attention.

I shivered and grabbed the fleece blanket that the steward had placed over me and pulled it tighter around my body.

The last thing I remember from last night was Dawson reaming me out for not telling him sooner about those stupid messages. Then we bickered, and I closed my eyes for a moment… I guess I fell asleep. Strange, since I rarely slept on airplanes.

Even at home, I was restless.

Maybe it was the relief of finally telling him about those texts. Or maybe it was something else…

Memories of last night floated through my mind. Dawson had been talking to his son, and I overheard my name. The next thing I knew, I'd sat beside him and introduced myself to his family. My nosy brain just wouldn't let up.

There was something about glimpsing a part of Dawson I'd never seen before that had me finally spilling my guts. The guy rarely smiled or laughed, and I admit, watching him talk to his son, the look of unmistakable happiness on his face, it made my stomach swoop.

Or maybe I was just reacting to air turbulence.

Whatever the case, the next thing I knew, I was blurting out my secret.

I thought for sure it would've taken me another week.

"Now that you're done drooling on me, let's go over the plan for our arrival. Regan is going to—"

I held my hand up.

"Wait. I need caffeine and carbs before any serious conversation can take place."

"Sorry, I forgot how testy you are first thing in the morning."

"I'm not testy," I groused, then sighed when I heard his snort of laughter. "Okay, maybe a bit until I have caffeine. And you're one to talk."

"I'm not always grumpy. In fact, I'm a morning person. Always have been. I love being up early." He grinned and then sipped on his coffee.

Dawson was smiling. At me.

"Who are you right now? And who enjoys getting up early?" I grumbled.

"Do you know that you talk in your sleep?"

I shook my head. "No way."

"Yes, way."

The steward returned with my latte, and after thanking them, I took a grateful sip. Hot and perfectly sweet, I let out a porn-worthy groan and noticed Dawson shifting in his seat.

"I don't talk in my sleep," I muttered.

"You do. It's cute."

Cute? Dawson was calling *me* cute? I'd been called a lot of things but never that. I stupidly wanted to hear more, and at the same time, I knew he was just bugging me. If I were a cat, I'd be hissing at him by now.

I didn't like this role reversal at all. I was the teaser, not the one who got teased.

"Can we go back to talking about my stalker, please?"

"Technically, we shouldn't be calling them a stalker yet. They're a person of concern."

Instead of grinding my teeth, I took another sip of coffee.

"And the plan?" I bit out.

Dawson set aside his cup of coffee and sighed. "Like I said last night, we're getting you a new phone. Regan will have it at the hotel. I'll monitor this one, so if there's anything you don't want me to see, you better delete it now. You'll have one of the team with you at all times. And I've contacted the hotel we're staying at to ensure you and I have connected rooms."

"That's overkill."

"It's already done."

"Fuck!"

I was gonna talk to Regan about all this. Connected rooms?

"But if I'm getting a new phone as soon as we get to the hotel, I don't need this one. As much as it irks me to have you rifling through my personal business, I have nothing to hide."

"Let's get one thing straight." Dawson leaned in closer. "I'm only looking through your phone to find clues about who might be targeting you. That's all."

"People store everything on their phone, their whole life. How would you feel if the situation were reversed?" I bit back.

Dawson shook his head but said nothing.

Then he pulled out his phone, pressed his thumb on the home button, and offered it to me. "Go on."

"What?"

"I unlocked it. Take it."

"I'm not gonna look through your phone!"

"It's only fair. You feel, and rightly so, that your privacy is about to be violated. So, this is the best I can do."

I was about to snap at him again when the steward returned with my breakfast.

"Eat first," Dawson commanded. "It's going to be a long day."

"Yes, sir."

"Iain," he warned.

Finally, I had the upper hand again.

I tucked into my breakfast and ignored Dawson and his phone even though my curiosity was dying for me to learn more about the man. The bits and pieces I'd already discovered in the past twelve hours were more than I had gathered in the several years we'd worked together.

But my inquisitiveness would have to wait.

Brodie sauntered down the aisle and stopped by my seat. I knew by that shit-eating grin on his face that I was about to get razzed.

"Is Dawson as snuggly as he looks?"

"Better," I quipped and gave my best friend a choice finger.

"He took good care of you. Even tucked you in with a blanket."

"You did *what*?" I turned to Dawson.

His cheeks pinked up, making the freckles on his face stand out.

"You looked cold! What was I supposed to do?"

"I don't need taking care of."

"Anyone sitting beside you would have done the same thing," Dawson snapped. "If the steward offered you a blanket, would that be okay?"

"Yes, but that's their job."

"So, I should have just let you sit there and shiver? I'm in the wrong?"

"I didn't say you're in the wrong—"

"Uh, guys," Brodie interrupted.

"Yeah?" I looked up.

Brodie shook his head. "I'm gonna give you the same advice you once gave me. Just fuck already and give the rest of us some peace and quiet."

Brodie turned around and headed back to his seat.

Dawson cleared his throat and then pulled out his laptop.

I stood up, set the blanket down, and walked down the aisle to reclaim my original seat.

Distance was what I needed. Away from *him*. from the reminder that my life would be out of my hands for the next while.

Grabbing my headphones, I blasted the loudest, angriest rock music I had in my downloads and drowned out any more thoughts of Dawson or our discussion.

An hour later, we descended into Charles de Gaulle airport.

Dawson and the rest of our security team moved us through the terminal quickly, but fans spotted us when we went through customs.

As soon as we cleared, we were bombarded with requests for autographs and selfies.

"Keep moving," Dawson bit out.

"No."

I stood my ground and glanced at Brodie, and he nodded.

"A few photos, and we're done," Brodie declared.

Dawson's hand gripped my bicep, and I looked up at him. "Dawson?"

He had his sunglasses on, so I couldn't see his eyes, but he gave a curt nod.

One woman began to talk, first in broken English and then French, proclaiming how excited she and her friends were to meet us.

This was the type of thing I loved. That I lived for.

When a total stranger from the other side of the world connects with the music you created, when it brings them joy, it makes all the other shit in this business worthwhile.

We signed the T-shirts they were wearing, someone's bag, and, in one case, a guy's arm. He said he was going to have the signatures tattooed. Now that was a superfan.

More people stepped forward and asked for selfies.

We posed for photos, but I noticed that the crowd around us was swelling.

Flashes went off.

Someone yelled out Brodie's name. Another voice screamed for Ronin and Faise. Cheers and yells echoed in the arrivals area as more and more people began to push around us.

Then I heard my name being chanted. Everything got louder, and I got jostled. A tendril of fear sparked, and my ears started to ring. Fucking hell, not here, not now.

God damn those messages for fucking with my head.

"Okay, that's enough. Too many people," Dawson barked as he and Lennie took hold of me.

I felt immediate relief at Dawson's words and his quick action. And for the first time in a long time, I was grateful to have him at my side. I forgot how fast these situations could spiral.

Our fleet of security ushered us away, cutting through the mass of people. We filed out of the terminal to the pick-up location.

More flashes went off as we passed the final doors and exited to our SUVs.

"Holloway, I love you!!" someone screamed, and I turned my head, but I couldn't see who was yelling.

"Arretez! Stop," Dawson yelled out and turned to Lennie. "Get him in the vehicle."

Lennie opened the back door of the first SUV, pushing me, then Brodie and Van, inside.

Ronin and Faise were usually in the second car, with the rest of our group in car number three.

The doors slammed shut, but then I heard someone pounding on the window. The glass was tinted, so all I could see were vague shapes.

Then Lennie's earpiece crackled.

"Step away from the vehicle!" Dawson yelled out.

The door opened, and Dawson jumped into the passenger seat.

"Go!" Dawson ordered our driver.

We peeled out of the airport and headed for the highway.

"Everyone okay?" Dawson asked.

"We're good," Brodie replied. "Man, that escalated so fucking fast. Not sure why, but that kind of thing still surprises me."

The ringing in my ears had ceased, but my heart was still pounding away. I reached inside my denim jacket with a shaky hand to grab my cigarettes, then realized that smoking probably wasn't the best idea since Brodie was in the car with me. No smoking around our lead vocalist, or he would justifiably take my head off.

"Holls?" Dawson asked and turned around.

"Fine. I'm fine," I answered with a quick smile.

I wasn't. I hadn't had a panic attack in years. Make that fifteen. Fuck.

"Next time, let security decide whether it's a good idea to stay and sign autographs."

Dawson's comment had me snapping out of my headspace, and I finally made eye contact with him.

His gaze didn't waver from mine. He knew. He goddamn knew how shaken up I was.

Why could I fool everyone but him?

Surprisingly, Dawson reached back and gripped my knee.

The reassuring touch didn't help my racing heart in the least.

CHAPTER 7

DAWSON

was always calm in a crisis, but that mob at the airport had fucked with my steadfast control.

My heart, too.

An hour later, even after we'd checked into the hotel, it was still beating hard and fast.

I'd been in worse situations, so why the freak out?

Iain.

I sure as fuck noticed Iain's sudden panic when the band drew more attention, the crowd swelled, and a few fans became aggressive.

My only thought had been to get him out of there as fast as possible. Get all the boys in the band out of there, but, yeah, Iain was my priority.

I trusted the rest of my team to do the same.

Everything turned out all right, thank fuck.

Regan was waiting for us at the hotel, and I gave her the rundown. She wasn't happy at how I'd given in to Brodie and Iain's demand. I knew better, and yet, I felt bad because I knew that the fans meant so much to them. They weren't like other asshole rockstars I'd worked with before. The boys of

Wayward Lane were always approachable. Or as approachable as we'd let them be.

The luggage arrived, and the boys settled into their suites. The band's creative team, including stylists for hair and makeup, had arrived prior to us. Harlow was acting PR on the trip, so he was already on his phone, preparing for the days ahead.

Everyone had a couple of hours to nap, eat, and then change.

The band and all security were situated on the penthouse level, with Iain and I at the end of the hallway, near the stairwell and the elevators. Brodie and Van were next to me, and Ronin and Faise were at the other end of the floor, with my team sharing the surrounding rooms.

By five that evening, rested and recharged, we were on our way into the heart of the city for a TV interview at a major French news station.

But Iain still looked pale and quieter than his usual self.

Instead of sitting up front, I switched with Lennie and sat beside Iain.

It was only a ten-minute car ride to our first stop.

I pulled a brand-new phone out of my jacket pocket and offered it to Iain.

"Your new cell. We've already programmed the numbers for our entourage and transferred data and photos. Don't give this number out to anyone outside of our group. No one unless I vet them first. Understood?"

"Yup."

Iain's terse reply and lack of eye contact chafed, but I ignored it.

He was unhappy with our connecting rooms, but there was nothing to be done.

Regan agreed with my plan, and we'd started investigating those text messages. How this unknown person got Iain's number, I had no idea. I could only assume it was either someone in his inner circle, which was highly disturbing, or a past lover. So far, there were no direct threats against Iain—or anyone close to him—so it was pointless to go to the police.

We'd need his full cooperation to review everyone in his life, and I couldn't see that conversation going well either.

He could sulk all he wanted. What did I care? I had a job to do.

I wasn't here as his friend.

And that painful knot in my stomach was back.

Truthfully, even though Iain drove me nuts, there was something about him that I was drawn to. I was sure that Iain felt more deeply than even his friends realized.

And people with sensitive hearts were the ones I wanted to protect the most.

Iain slowly took the phone from me and placed it in the pocket of his black leather jacket. He had on dark baggy jeans that rode low on his hips. Black patent cowboy booties and a ripped T-shirt completed the look, along with several silver bracelets and earrings. His hair was loose, but the band's stylist had done something different to it. The waves were bigger, tousled, you know, kinda messy. Sexy as hell is what he was. Like he'd just rolled out of bed after a long night of fucking…

I had to stop that line of thinking right now.

Iain sighed. "You're staring."

"You're hot."

Every conversation in the vehicle came to a sudden silence.

"I mean, it's hot. In here. It's hot in here," I stammered.

Thank God I wore black because I was starting to sweat through my T-shirt and jacket.

Jesus, Daws. Get a hold of yourself.

"Len, turn the heat down," I barked.

"It's not on," Lennie replied with barely restrained laughter in his voice.

I was never gonna live this down.

Iain leaned in and whispered in my ear, his warm breath making me shiver. "Thanks for the compliment."

I refused to look at him or anyone else in the vehicle for the rest of the ride. Even though I caught Lennie's eyebrow raise in the rearview mirror. I shook my head in response and then ignored him.

Ignored everything except the gorgeous man sitting next to me. Iain had the man spread going on, one of his denim-covered thighs touching mine. I had Brodie on my other side, and I had no legroom to move, well, anywhere.

One of Iain's hands was resting on his upper thigh. Slowly, that hand moved north, until he rested it on his hip, his fingers almost touching his covered dick.

And me thinking about Iain's beautiful cock was so goddamn dangerous right now.

How much longer was this trip going to take?

My phone pinged. *Thank you, work.*

I tapped on the message from the TV program's head of security.

"Change of plans. Pull into the parking garage," I instructed Lennie. "First left after the light."

Word of the interviews was out, and the sidewalk outside the building was filling with interested fans.

Once we found our way inside the parking garage, we headed for the service elevator.

A short while later, we found ourselves on the tenth floor of UniqueTV, the biggest entertainment news program in the country. We were whisked down a long hallway to a green room, the pre-show space.

The guys were mic'd up, prepped again by the makeup crew, and guided to the set.

Lennie and I stood in the wings, as usual, surveying. Once the guys were seated and the producer did the intros, they were ready to go live.

Then I noticed that Harlow was missing.

"Where's Harlow?" I asked Lennie.

"He was on his phone in the green room."

"He should be out here; they're about to go live. Van was always on watch during these things."

"I'll text him." Lennie pulled out his phone and tapped on it.

A minute later, and still no sign of the band's manager.

The TV presenter, a handsome guy with slick hair, a designer suit, and a dentist-worthy smile, sat down.

They were a go in three, two, one…

"I'm Jean-Luc Giroux, and welcome to another edition of Célébrité Ce Soir. I'm here today with a band that has recently become one of the best-selling groups in rock 'n' roll history. With a unique blend of electric anthems, intense performance style, and full-on glamour, I'm talking about none other than Wayward Lane. Merci, thank you guys for being here tonight."

"Thank you for having us," Brodie stated, and each guy in their turn said hello.

"You're in Paris for the next week for three sold-out shows, February thirteenth to the fifteenth. Tell us why you chose our city to start your European tour this year."

Brodie looked at the guys and then leaned forward. "Originally, we were gonna play Europe in the fall, but personal plans meant shifting things around. And one of the concerts is on Valentine's Day, so where else would we perform but right here in the city of love?"

Jean-Luc smiled. "Well, we're only too happy that you chose us. What are your plans in town when you're not rehearsing or performing?"

Faise leaned forward. "Lots of restaurants, no question."

"Art galleries," Ronin offered.

Iain nodded and offered Jean-Luc a flirty smile. "Clubs.

We're gonna hit the clubs hard. Paris has the sexiest men, am I right?"

The announcer flushed and pulled on his tie.

I held back an eye roll.

"Brodie," Jean-Luc cleared his throat, "the last time you were interviewed, you had just eloped with your manager, Ivan Cross, in Las Vegas. How's married life?"

Brodie let out a dirty chuckle while the rest of the guys groaned.

"I think you can tell by the smile on my face that it's amazing. I've never been happier."

"So, is this the start of a trend? Are the rest of you guys looking for love?"

Iain, Faise, and Ronin all shook their heads vehemently, and I had to stifle a chuckle.

"I'm happy for Brodie and Van, but I'm enjoying the single life," Ronin replied as he waved at the camera. "Et je suis tellement heureux d'etre ici, en Paris."

"And Ronin speaks French, mesdames et messieurs," the announcer gushed.

Faise rolled his eyes. "Barely. He was practicing with Van for days. You didn't hear him butcher those words the first ten thousand times like I had to."

Ronin playfully swatted his best friend on the arm.

"Faisel, your personal life has been under intense pressure lately. You were last seen in California, where your brother is in rehab. How's he doing?"

Faise's smile faded, and he turned to Ronin and then looked over at us in the wings.

All the guys visibly stiffened.

Judging by Faise's reaction, I guessed the question was not vetted beforehand.

And I looked around and noticed Harlow was still missing.

"He's still in treatment," Faise finally replied. "And that's all I'm going to say on the matter."

Jean-Luc turned to Iain. "Iain—"

"Holloway," Iain returned.

Uh oh. I recognized the intense glint in Iain's eyes. He did not like his friend in the hot seat. This interview was going to turn south real fast if Jean-Luc wasn't careful.

"Je m'excuse, Holloway. What about your personal life? You're known as the most mischievous playboy of the band. Are you happy with the single life or are you looking for love?"

How about asking them about their next album? Why all the personal questions?

I texted Harlow with a more direct message.

> Get out here now. This interview is starting to nosedive.

"I'm pretty sure the term is fuckboy not playboy. And I'm happy and looking for a good time. Nothing serious, just fun."

"Well, according to the tabloids, you have a lot of it."

Iain cocked his head. "I do. I enjoy my life, and I don't need to justify it to anyone."

Jean-Luc nodded. "You guys have known each other since you were in high school, correct?"

"That's where all four of us met," Brodie answered. "But I've known Holls since we were six."

"Holloway, your mom was a talented pianist who died tragically at a young age. Is she the reason you got into music?"

Fucking hell.

No one, and I mean no one, asked Iain questions about his family. He could talk about his sex life, no problem, but his childhood? Everyone knew that was a no-go zone.

Everyone except this reporter. And the band's manager, who was still MIA. And not responding to my messages either.

I turned to Lennie. "Find Harlow."

I typed another furious message, getting more pissed off by the minute.

Where are you? We need you here now.

Iain clasped his hands together tightly. "I've been passionate about music all my life. Next question."

"You're working on a new album. Any hints on what we can expect?"

My tension eased a bit.

Brodie glanced at the guys, and they nodded in return. "It's going to be a bit different from our previous albums. This time, all the songs are ones that my husband and I have co-written, so the album feels more personal. But of course, fans can still expect gritty lyrics and memorable hooks."

"I can't wait until it drops. Are you going to be performing Sideline? Has that been recorded yet?"

Brodie shook his head, his dark curls bouncing. "Unfortunately, not at this time."

"Why not? The song went viral at your now infamous New Orleans concert in October, and fans are clamoring for it."

"The fans will have to wait for a bit. But it will be released eventually."

Jean-Luc nodded. "Is it because you're cutting ties with your label? There have been rumors about your unhappiness with Bandit Music since your marriage became public. Van wasn't out prior to your relationship, isn't that right?"

Brodie's expression darkened. I just knew that whatever was going to come out of his mouth next was going to be front-page news.

"There's a rumor that you're fucking the owner of this news station. Care to comment, Jean-Luc?"

The presenter turned purple and nearly fell out of his chair.

"And that's all the time we have for this evening," Jean-Luc announced with a nervous smile to the camera. "I'll be back shortly with more news from the entertainment world."

Someone yelled, "We're out."

All hell broke loose.

CHAPTER 8

IAIN

I vaulted up out of my chair and got into Jean-Luc's face.

So did all my brothers.

The show's crew crowded around us, and everyone started yelling at the same time. Jean-Luc was screaming at Brodie, but Brodie gave it right back. He never backed down from any fight.

Van stepped up to us, along with Dawson and Lennie. Van took hold of Brodie's arm and said something quietly to Brodie, calming him down—a bit.

I started in for Jean-Luc, but Dawson put his body between me and my target.

"Who cleared those questions?" I demanded over the din. "And where the fuck is Harlow?"

"I'm right here."

Harlow finally appeared beside Brodie.

"What the hell, guys?" Harlow scoffed. "Can't you even do one interview without it becoming a scandalous headline?"

"Us?" Brodie snapped and pointed at Jean-Luc. "He was the one asking invasive questions that we were not prepared to answer. I thought we made it clear back in December that kind of shit isn't tolerated."

"Did you vet the questions?" I asked Harlow point blank.

He glared at me. "It's the highest-rated and most-viewed entertainment program in France. There was no need."

"Sorry, but I beg to differ," Van bit out. "Your job is to protect the band, not let some reporter ambush them like that."

"Oh, yeah? Well, you're not in charge anymore, Van, so keep your opinions to yourself!"

"Don't you dare fucking talk to him like that!" Brodie charged at Harlow.

Lennie stepped in front of him, barring any further escalation.

"Lennie!" Dawson yelled out. "Everyone to the green room, now!"

Suddenly, we were all ushered away from the stage to the pre-show guest room.

Me and the guys were fucking furious—swearing and pacing back and forth. Well, they were.

I was more shocked than angry at this point.

Van took Brodie in his arms and started whispering in his ear, and I watched as my friend finally nodded and visibly calmed.

Dawson had taken hold of my arm and hadn't let go. And for once, I appreciated his protection. I admit, I leaned into him and appreciated his warmth. I was freezing. So fucking cold that I was trembling.

"Are you okay?" Dawson whispered.

"No. And before you ask, I don't want to talk about it."

The question about my mom had rattled me. Badly. I was lightheaded, and my hands were shaking.

"I'm sorry."

"For what? This isn't your fault," I replied and pointed at

Harlow. "He's the one who should apologize. He's too busy on his phone kissing Greg Haddley's ass to do his job."

Greg was our boss and a cagey asshole. Long story short, Greg had outed Van to the media at the onset of his relationship with Brodie, and we were having none of it. Once our contract was done, so were we.

Still, we stuck to our agreement and didn't publicly comment on the feud.

"Don't start, Holloway," Harlow snapped. "I work my ass off. Unlike some people who spend more time fucking around than playing actual music."

My shock turned to anger, and I lunged forward. "You asshole—"

I made self-deprecating remarks about my fuckboy reputation, and my band brothers teased me, but that was it. They never questioned my ability or my dedication to our music.

Dawson quickly swiveled, stepping in front of me, still not letting go. Gripping both of my arms, he glanced down at me with concern in his eyes. My stomach flipped over, just like it did before I took to the stage. I could feel the heat of his hands burning through my leather jacket, and foolishly, I wanted to step closer to him. Instead, I nodded and said, "I'm okay," and he looked over his shoulder.

"Not one more word, Harlow. I fucking mean it," Dawson boomed. "I will not hesitate to report you to Regan and Greg. Xavier, take him to the elevator and bring him back to the hotel. We're gonna stay here and cool down for a while before we head out."

Xavier motioned to the door and stepped beside Harlow.

"Don't touch me," Harlow growled. "I'm going."

Once Harlow was gone, I finally breathed a sigh of relief.

Dawson gave me a reassuring squeeze and let go.

I wanted to say "don't". No matter how crazy I drove him, and vice versa, I always knew he was looking out for me. The question about my mom had emotions I didn't want to deal with rising to the surface, and I suddenly longed for comfort.

From Dawson, of all people.

"What the fuck was that?" I asked out loud, stunned by my reaction.

I wasn't just referring to what had happened in that interview…

"That was our manager selling us out," Brodie scoffed.

"I don't know that I'd go that far," Van added. "But he did drop the ball. Several balls."

"That's 'cause he has none himself," Faise snapped. "I told him, no questions about my brother. That's a hard no. Not to mention Iain's mom. Jesus Christ!"

There was a knock at the door, and a woman with a severe brunette bob and a sharp suit stepped forward.

"I'm Lilianne Germain, the producer of the show. I just want to clarify something and make sure everyone is okay."

Brodie was about to rip into her, but Van stepped forward. "The guys were not prepared for some of those questions, Ms. Germain."

"Mr. Hines was asked, in advance, if there were any topics Jean-Luc should avoid, any hard limits. We sent him the list of questions by email, and he said there were no issues."

Van shook his head. "And that didn't surprise you?"

The woman's cool façade cracked for a split second. "As I said, he confirmed that we were good to go. That's all we needed. I'm sorry if everyone in the band was unprepared, but that's not our fault. Also, the comment made by Mr. James about Jean-Luc was totally inappropriate."

"Thanks for the clarification, but don't expect any apology. I don't give them," Brodie snapped.

"Given your reputation, Mr. James, I'm not at all surprised," she remarked. "We hope you enjoy the rest of your stay in Paris."

We grumbled out "sure," "yeah," and "yup." She didn't look impressed and quickly turned and left the room.

"What's next on our agenda?" Faise asked. "And please tell me it includes booze."

"You have a private table booked at a nearby restaurant, and then the rest of the night is open," Dawson replied as he checked his phone.

"I don't know about you guys, but I'm beat from traveling and we have rehearsal tomorrow," Ronin commented. "Let's go have a nice meal, some wine, and chill. We can hit a club another night."

"I have a suggestion—" I started.

"The strip club can wait." Brodie smirked.

"Haha. I was going to say I'd like our security team to join us for dinner. A thank you for intervening in that situation."

Often, Dawson and his team would sit at a nearby table, keeping an eye. Sometimes, on the road, they'd join us for meals but usually watching over us, not as part of the group.

"That's a great idea," Faise encouraged. "Holls is right. You guys saved us from taking that situation from bad to worse. It's the least we can do."

"Uh, I'll run it by Regan, but it should be fine. Thanks," Dawson replied, his face flushed.

The big guy was all kinds of adorable when he was flustered. Just like on the ride over here.

And why my mind was now thinking that was just plain stupid.

Brodie walked up to me and pulled me into a hug, then Faise, and Ronin.

"Are you guys okay?" Brodie asked.

He might be the snarkiest of all of us, but he also had a big heart. And we all looked out for each other.

I nodded. "I'm good."

"Me too." Faise smiled.

"Then let's get the fuck out of here," Ronin announced.

"What about Harlow?" I asked. "We still gotta talk to him about what happened. And reaffirm some guidelines."

"Tomorrow. Give everyone a night to calm down and regroup," Van suggested and smiled at Brodie.

Brodie stepped away from us, took his husband's hand, and pulled it up to his mouth. Gently kissing Van's knuckles, Brodie never lost eye contact with his husband. I didn't understand the whole "crazy in love" thing myself (and monogamy even less), but even I couldn't deny the palpable electricity between them. Hell, if the Eiffel Tower wasn't lit up tonight, these two could substitute.

Only Van could calm the intense hurricane that was our lead singer and my best friend. And as for Van, well, I'd never seen him laugh so much as he did these past few months. If this was love, it looked damn good on them.

"Let's go," Dawson announced and nodded at Lennie, who led us out of the room and over to the elevator.

Ronin gripped Faise's neck, bringing him in close and kissing the top of his head with a loud smack.

"Ew, gross! I don't want your fucking germs," Faise grumbled and pushed Ronin away.

The two of them began to tussle as we waited for the elevator.

"I just want to make sure my boo is okay," Ronin replied and puckered his lips again.

"You're ridiculous." Faise laughed and swatted his face.

Watching my band brothers goof around made my tension ease. I wanted to get back to normal.

"What a fucking start to our trip," I muttered, as the doors opened and Dawson and Lennie ushered us inside.

We all managed to fit in one go.

"Wait for the headlines. Jean-Luc is probably going to sue." Faise chuckled.

Brodie scoffed. "Fuck him."

Dawson got in last and stood in front of me, but there

were so many of us in the small space that I was nearly rubbing against his ass. Well, rubbing against all of him.

My dick liked what was happening way too much, but my brain was a firm no-go.

Why him? Why now?

"I'm all for tight spaces, but this is ridiculous," I commented as I pushed at Dawson's broad back.

"There's plenty of room," Dawson muttered, not moving an inch.

"Not with you taking up most of it. Do you have to stand so close?"

Dawson shook his head. "I'm not sure why this is suddenly an issue. It's my job to protect you, so I'll stand as close as I damned well need to. Stop fidgeting. Enjoy the ride."

Dawson's cheeky statement and bossy tone made my cock throb. Oh, this was *so* fucking bad.

"Enjoy the ride?" I mouthed to Brodie, standing next to me.

Brodie snorted. "Hey, Daws, I've wanted to ask this question for ages… are you this bossy in the bedroom?"

Dawson glanced over his shoulder, but instead of looking at Brodie, his green eyes caught mine.

"Wouldn't you like to know?"

Yeah.

Yeah, I think I would.

CHAPTER 9

DAWSON

Why did I let Brodie get me into trouble?

I should know by now to ignore his taunts and keep my mouth shut.

And, to make things worse, I had to look at Iain when I responded.

I wanted to give the guitarist a taste of his own medicine. He'd flirted with me for ages, and most of the time, I ignored it. But man, I was reaching the end of my patience.

And hell, yes, I was bossy in bed, but he didn't need to know that.

God, just thinking about bed and Iain at the same time was not helping matters.

Thank fuck Regan wasn't around, or she'd have yanked me from Iain's detail as soon as the words left my mouth.

Iain wasn't in the wrong when he suggested the elevator was crowded. But honestly? There was nothing I could do about it. And being close to him was the only place I wanted to be.

Okay, that line of thinking was not professional, but hey, I'm still human. And put me next to a gorgeous man like Iain, and yeah, I'm gonna notice.

By the time we got out of the elevator and back into the SUVs, my calm demeanor was back in place. I sat up front this time, giving myself some much-needed distance from Iain. I texted Regan with details about the dinner, then called the restaurant to ensure they added four more seats to the table.

Fifteen minutes later, we entered L'Escalier, an upscale bistro in the eleventh arrondissement. With dim lighting, red velvet booths, and sexy music, the place was designed for romance, as evidenced by the many couples occupying most of the space. It was kind of funny to watch our motley crew of rockstars and bodyguards in a room full of elegantly dressed Parisians and their intimate tables for two.

Our host greeted us warmly and we were guided to the back of the restaurant, where the bar was located. A few heads turned to stare at us, but no one got up and made a fuss. They kept to their own business, and I was confident that we'd be good here.

It didn't take long for the staff to lead us to a large table that was private but not completely cut off from the rest of the room. It was near a rear exit, which was perfect. I picked the spots where my team would sit, facing outward, but let the band get settled in first.

"Len," I leaned over to my colleague. "I'll sit on the far end with Ronin and Faise, you okay with Iain and Brodie?"

"Of course. And probably a good idea after that elevator ride."

I nodded. "Yeah, I know better than to let Brodie goad me."

"Just be careful, yeah? I know the way Iain flirts with you. And the way you look at him."

"I'm just doing my job. And Iain's just being Iain. He doesn't mean it."

I don't know who I was trying to convince, myself or

Lennie. I wasn't special to Iain, just a thorn in his side that he wanted to get rid of.

"If you say so," Lennie murmured.

I walked over to the table and sat down. I'd grabbed a sandwich this afternoon, but it was nearing nine, and my stomach was seriously displeased.

Of course, I horrified the server when I said I wasn't ordering wine. None of the security staff were. We got sparkling water while the boys ordered a couple of bottles of ridiculously expensive cabernet sauvignon.

Once our dinner orders were taken—steak frites all around—the guys got into a heated discussion about rehearsals and which club they wanted to hit tomorrow night. Lennie suggested a few spots, and the guys began arguing about which would be best.

Since I wasn't into the party scene, I kept out of the conversation and studied the room.

I studied Iain.

Okay, my gaze inevitably strayed to him more than once. He looked relaxed now, but I wanted to be sure he was okay.

Then my phone buzzed.

Incoming call: Regan.

I signaled to Lennie that I was leaving. Standing up, I answered the phone, stepping away from the noise at the table and into the narrow hallway near the kitchen.

"Yes, boss?"

"Sorry to interrupt your dinner, but I wanted you to know that Holloway's old phone keeps getting messages. The tone is escalating. Whoever it is, they're very angry he left the country. I'm forwarding these for your info."

The nerves in my belly took flight. "Okay, I'll have a look."

Regan sighed. "What about the new number?"

"Nothing so far."

"Any other odd happenings?"

I thought back and remembered the night of the charity event. "It's probably nothing, but I got a call the week before we left. Unknown number, and no one said anything when I answered. I didn't think anything of it at the time, but now—"

"You think it might be the same person?"

"The timing is interesting. And I don't really believe in coincidences."

"Me neither. I hate to say it, but it's got to be someone close to him. How else would they have access to your number as well as his?"

My stomach tightened, and it had nothing to do with hunger.

"We're talking about a small list then. Their manager, assistants, security staff… fuck Regan, I don't even want to think about any of our team being behind this."

"I don't either. But the suspect list is wider than that. We should consider anyone associated with Bandit Music. Someone who, even if they don't have direct access to Holloway's number or yours, could gain it by accessing company information. Also, this person doesn't know about the new phone, so I have a feeling it's not someone in your group in France but back here at home."

She was right, and that gave me some sense of relief.

"Should we contact the police?" I asked.

"The messages are creepy, but there's no direct threat. In the meantime, I'm going to call my contact in the Nashville PD and get her take. For now, we conduct our own investigation into Bandit."

"How do we do that without alerting employees? What about HR? What about Greg?"

"I have to inform him first and get his okay."

"We can't just start investigating everyone."

"Internally, no. But we *can* hire an independent private investigator."

"Bandit has what? Two, maybe three thousand employees?"

"One hundred and twenty-six in the Nashville region. That's where we're going to focus."

"Because of the comment about the last concert?"

"That and the fact that this person is still messaging his old number. This person is local." Regan paused. "Did you notice anything else unusual at their last show? Any audience member who stood out?"

"No. Nothing."

"I'm confident you're safe overseas, but don't let your guard down and don't tell Holloway. We don't want him to think he's got nothing to worry about."

"You got it, boss. Oh, by the way, the incident tonight at their interview—"

"I saw your text."

"We should keep a close eye on Harlow. He threw the band under the bus tonight. Now, I don't know if that was on Greg's orders or his own decision, but the guys were upset, and rightly so. It nearly came to blows. Do you think he could have anything to do with this? I mean, on Greg's orders, as some kind of payback for their contract feud?"

"Off the record, I wouldn't put anything past Greg, and he always has someone else do his dirty work. But I think it's unlikely. Still, let's have the team keep an extra close eye on Harlow, just in case."

"Done." I sighed, running an agitated hand through my hair. "I know we're employed by Bandit, but if the company is doing anything to fuck with Iain—"

"Holloway is in good hands. Go with your instinct. I'll back you up."

"Thanks, Regan."

"Enjoy your dinner. We'll talk tomorrow at the rehearsal."

By the time I got back to the table, the steaks had arrived, and everyone was enjoying their meal. I sat down and dug in, ignoring Iain's inquisitive stare that I could feel from all the way across the room.

I'd barely started to eat when the chef himself, a man named Didier Laurent, appeared in his white uniform. He talked to the band, asking how they were enjoying the meal and, of course, gushed over them like a true fan.

Didier was a good-looking guy with dark hair, loads of tattoos down both arms, and a wicked grin. As he made his way down the table, he stopped beside me and pointed at my plate.

"You don't enjoy the steak?" Didier asked.

"I just sat down a few minutes ago, so—"

His grin was wide and welcoming. "Ah, thank God! I was starting to worry I'd lost my touch."

"I've only had four bites, but every single one is amazing."

"So happy to hear. And you are?"

I reached out my hand. "Dawson Everly, I'm the security lead. Nice to meet you."

"The pleasure is entirely mine," he replied with a flirty grin as he gripped my hand tightly.

"Didier, join us for a drink!" Brodie called out.

"Absolument, but I only have time for one glass. I don't trust my sous chef entirely. If your dessert soufflé is half risen, don't blame it on me."

The server brought another chair and placed it between me and Ronin.

I finished my steak frites while Didier conversed with Ronin and the rest of the guys. The chef was a big music fan and world traveler, so they had much in common, chatting about concerts and the best places to visit around town.

One glass of wine became two, as Didier and the band members became fast friends.

I had just finished clearing my plate when Didier turned

to me. "No drinking on the job for you, eh? That's unfortunate."

"I'm used to it. Gotta stay sharp and fit."

Didier gave me a long once-over. "You are that. Very handsome indeed."

I smiled in return but felt… nothing.

As much as I was flattered, the timing was all wrong.

Come to think of it, the timing had been wrong for a while. I hadn't had sex in, fuck, close to a year. If I wasn't busy with work, I was with my son, which meant little to no time for my personal life. Not that I was complaining, but hooking up had taken a backseat to everything else. Maybe when this trip was over, I'd take a night off and have some adults-only fun.

"Do you get any time off while you're here?" Didier asked me, leaning closer.

"Unfortunately, no."

It wasn't a complete lie. But getting laid was not at the top of my mind on this trip.

All my attention was on the blond musician sitting at the other end of the table. I looked over to find Iain giving me the stink eye again.

What was it now?

Without thinking, I placed my napkin on the table and stood up. "Excuse me, Didier."

Glancing at Lennie, I made the gesture to switch places. I rounded the end of the table and made my way to the other end, sitting opposite Iain.

"What's wrong?" I whispered.

"Nothing. I'm finally enjoying myself now that I'm not being suffocated by you," he replied, refusing to make eye contact.

Iain reminded me of a beautiful, temperamental cat. He was all hisses and bites, but I never let that stop me.

A lock of his long hair slid over his cheek, and I forced

myself not to lean over to brush it back behind his ear. I could imagine his reaction to that. He'd probably bite my finger off…

"What is it?" I asked again.

Finally, Iain sighed and looked at me. "I'm getting a headache. I want to go back to the hotel."

"All you have to do is say," I replied and turned to Van. "We're gonna head out; Iain needs to rest."

"Tonight's on me," Van replied and motioned for the server.

"Oh no, dinner is on me," Didier announced as he stood up and held up a hand. "I insist. You are my guests, and it was a pleasure to host you this evening."

"But—" Brodie started.

"But," Didier interrupted. "You are welcome to leave a tip for my hard-working staff. They will appreciate it."

"That we can definitely do," Van replied with a smile.

Didier said goodnight to everyone but stopped when he got to me. He handed me his business card.

"If you find yourself in need of a tour guide while you're in town, give me a call."

"I, uh, thanks," I replied and pocketed his card. What could I do? If I didn't take it, I'd only make the guy feel bad.

Iain abruptly stood up, the table rattling.

Didier glanced at Iain, then turned back to me. "You're welcome."

CHAPTER 10
IAIN

couldn't wait until this day was over.

First, that fuck-up of an interview, and now this? Like I needed to watch some hot French dude come on to Dawson?

And the fact that Dawson took his goddamn card?

So, my hookups had to endure the third degree while he's free to fuck whoever, whenever?

And would he? Was he attracted to Didier? And why the hell did I give a shit?

Fuck this.

"I'm out of here."

I stepped away from the table before anyone could stop me.

Dawson called my name, but I shook my head and moved like my ass was literally on fire. I ran down the hallway to the exit, slapped the restaurant door open, and felt the damp winter air wash over me. It wasn't raining, but it was misty, and fog had started to roll in, making everything around me hazy.

I turned the corner and leaned against the brick wall of the building.

Reaching inside my jacket, I yanked out my packet of cigarettes and lit one, taking a long drag.

I'd had three, no four, glasses of wine, and I was still tense as fuck.

"Iain!" Dawson called out.

"Don't! Don't lecture me."

"Iain." Dawson walked over to stand in front of me. "Please don't run off like that. It's not safe."

"According to you, breathing isn't safe."

"Not with those cigarettes," he muttered.

I threw the cig on the ground and glared at him.

"Easy for you to say. You can do whatever the hell you want. Go out when you want and fuck who you want, like master chef back there."

Dawson shook his head. "I took his card to be polite. I have no interest—"

God, I was so relieved and infuriated at the same time.

"I don't care!" I yelled. "That's not my point. Don't you get it? You have freedom. You can walk out on the street and just... fucking... be!"

Dawson stepped closer, forcing my gaze up. My heart was racing like a getaway car, faster and faster.

"What do you want me to say, Iain? You signed up for this life. And you know what? You're not the only one who's stressed out. I spend each goddamn day monitoring everything that moves around you, assessing threats, and never letting my guard down. And when I'm not at work, I'm trying to help my son, who, despite his incredibly sunny disposition, is still grieving the loss of his mom. He's not even nine, and he barely complains. And I can't afford to just up and quit my job because I'm frustrated or because you're always a pain in my ass!"

The mention of Jaxon and his mom reminded me of my own, and I blinked back the unwelcome tears that suddenly threatened. It also deflated any remaining anger in my system, making me feel like a whiny fool.

"I'm sorry," I whispered. "I know. I know that everything you do is to protect me. And that this is the life I signed up for. And I know that I'm not the easiest person to work for—"

Dawson snorted, and the sound had me stifling a chuckle.

"I just… that reporter tonight set me off. Mentioning my mom, and I can't… I don't want to go there. I'm terrified that it will be all over the news when I wake up tomorrow. And the last thing I need is more scrutiny."

And I was also worried that something worse was going on with me. That maybe my mom's battle with mental illness wasn't unique to her. When I was performing, I felt high and bright, but then, afterward, coming home to an empty house and not being able to do anything without gaining media attention was getting to me.

Or maybe I was just going through an early mid-life crisis.

My sex drive was also unsettling. When I did get it up, I wasn't exactly enthusiastic. And every hot, available man I met recently didn't do much for me.

Well, except for…

Dawson placed his hands on my shoulders, and I gripped his forearms, not thinking, just acting on instinct. He was so strong, and I could feel his pulse jumping as fast as mine under his heated skin.

"I'll reach out to Zoe," Dawson offered.

"But Harlow is supposed to—"

"She's the head of PR, not Harlow. Between you and me, I want you to be very careful around him. That whole thing tonight has left me with a bad feeling. And don't look at social media for the next while."

"Easier said than done."

"Is it just that, or is anything else bothering you?"

I stared up into those deep pools of green. "Well, I—"

"Holls, are you okay?"

I turned at Brodie's voice to find him and everyone in our party standing on the sidewalk staring at us.

Dawson jolted and pulled away from me.

"I'm fine. Sorry I ran out like that. That question about my mom tonight fucked me up."

Brodie, Ronin, and Faise walked over and surrounded me. "It's gonna be okay."

"It will be, thanks," I squeezed Brodie's arm. "I don't know about you guys, but I need sleep."

"Pot, then sleep."

"Ronin, pot ain't legal here," Faise warned.

"Okay, a nightcap, then sleep."

We all agreed with that.

———

The next morning

Someone was banging on my door, but I turned my face into my pillow.

"Iain! Wake up!"

Dawson's voice was so clear it sounded like he was in my room. I jolted, rolling over so fast that I nearly fell out of my bed.

Half asleep, I reached for my phone and tapped it. It was just after ten.

"No!" I yelled back, unwilling to get out of my warm cocoon.

Not only did I not feel like getting out of bed, but this interruption was depriving me of my morning wank session. And I didn't want to think about the fact that Dawson's deep voice made me shiver and made my semi turn into a raging hard-on I couldn't ignore.

"Get up and get your workout clothes on. We're going to the gym," Dawson announced.

Exercise? My boner deflated just like that.

"No!" I yelled back.

"I'm giving you ten minutes to get changed, or I'm opening this door."

Fuck. This. Man.

I threw off the duvet and walked over to the door, wrenched it open, and stood there, stark naked.

Dawson was already in shorts and a T-shirt, his red hair a spiky mess. He hadn't shaved, and I was a fan. His eyes ran over me, and I caught the pink flush that ran up his neck and cheeks.

"Get dressed," he demanded, then reached down into a duffle bag and threw a jockstrap at me. "We're going to work out some of your frustration."

"I was about to do that on my own." I waggled my free hand.

He rolled his eyes.

"And I have much sexier jockstraps than this," I replied as I glanced at the plain white garment and noticed something different. "Why the cup?"

Dawson smiled. "You. Me. Jiujitsu lesson. Get dressed."

Then he slammed the door in my face.

Oh, it was on.

I stalked to my bathroom and quickly washed up. After pulling my hair into a bun, I headed back to my bedroom and searched my closet for workout clothes. I slipped on the jockstrap, then a pair of black shorts, a matching tank top, and my running shoes. Normally, I preferred a run on the treadmill or, even better, a run outside, but for now, kicking Dawson's ass would have to do.

I snorted at the thought of me taking down my bodyguard.

It was never going to happen, but hey, I was gonna do as he said and relieve some frustration.

I walked back over to the connecting door and knocked on it.

As soon as Dawson opened the door, I pushed my way into his room.

"Just so you know, I'm gonna kick your ass for waking me up."

"You can try." Dawson chuckled and crossed his arms over his chest. "Please, make yourself at home."

"I'm just curious to know if you actually sleep."

I made the mistake of glancing at his bed and the messy sheets. I thought for sure Dawson would be a total neat freak, and his bed would already be made by now, but nope.

Then I pictured him lying on those very same white sheets, his sculpted body laid out like an erotic piece of art.

No, no, no. Don't go there.

"I do. But I usually only get five or six hours at most. And you know, I kept waking up, what with you talking in your sleep and all."

"Fuck off, I do not. And you can't hear through that door."

"Uh, yeah, I can," Dawson nodded, a shit-eating grin on his face. "I also heard you singing in the bathroom five minutes ago."

Now, it was my turn to blush. I didn't even realize I was singing, but I guess I was always in my own musical world.

"Let's go. The longer we talk, the harder I want to kick your ass," I snapped.

Dawson chuckled and grabbed his phone from the nightstand. Then he placed a gentle hand on my lower back, guiding me to the suite's main door.

A short elevator ride later, we found ourselves in the gym on the twentieth floor. The place was almost empty, with a few people on the treadmills. Dawson guided me to a private workout room.

"Today, we're going to practice grappling."

"Sounds painful. What is it?"

Dawson stood in front of me and placed his hands on his hips. "Grappling is sort of like wrestling. It enables a smaller fighter to take on a more aggressive opponent. And combined with striking, it's very useful in self-defense."

I was going to wrestle? With Dawson? My brain told me this was not a good idea.

My dick, on the other hand, was all in.

"Ah, that explains the cup. But still, I much prefer to do my wrestling naked. In bed."

The corner of Dawson's mouth kicked up as he stepped up close to me.

"Are you ready?"

"That's a loaded question."

"Iain," Dawson warned.

"Go ahead and manhandle me," I teased. "I'm up for it."

CHAPTER 11
IAIN

A half-hour later, I had all new material for my spank bank.

I was sweaty and sore but surprisingly energized.

Who knew grappling was so much fun? Not that I was going to tell Dawson.

He was already annoyingly smug when he was in fight mode. And I could see why. It was sexy as hell to listen to him explain every move and to feel his powerful body move against mine with such control.

Too bad about the clothes between us and the fact that Dawson kept barking at me when I didn't pay attention to what he was saying.

Can you blame me?

Halfway through our session, he'd taken his shirt off. And that's when I knew I was done for.

"Okay, next move," Dawson panted as he wiped his brow. "This is called the bow and arrow choke."

"Sounds kinky."

"Pay attention," Dawson playfully swatted my back. "Sit down."

I sat on the mat, and Dawson slid behind me, his crotch snug against my ass, his taut legs wrapping around my waist.

Fucking hell. Was jiujitsu supposed to be sexy, or was it just me?

"We can try this standing up, but sitting down in this position is how I learned."

"Me too. Reverse cowboy is an art form."

"Stop it." Dawson sighed. "Now I'm going to reach around with my arm. I place my hand near or over your neck—"

I cackled. "This is like the start of my favorite porn scene."

"Iain," Dawson growled.

God, I loved it when he said my name like that. No one else said it that way. Like I'd worked him up so much he couldn't take anymore.

He squeezed his legs tighter around me, and that didn't help my racing heart or my hardening dick at all. "I'm trying to teach you something that might save your life."

"I know, and I appreciate it, but I'm kinda distracted."

Between the combined smell of our sweat, the heat of the room, and the way his larger body enveloped mine…fuck, I was so turned on I wanted to roll over and rub myself all over him, then ride him until we achieved a different kind of endgame.

"Imagine I've just smashed your favorite guitar into a million pieces."

I grabbed Dawson's arm. Hard.

"That's it; grab my forearm with your left hand and my tricep with your right," Dawson instructed. "Remember to pull me forward. Do not let my elbow get behind your shoulder, or I've got all the leverage I need to take control."

I pulled at Dawson's arm, but he was so strong. "I don't think I can do this."

"Try your best," he murmured gruffly in my ear. "I'm not

going to do anything to hurt you, your hands and arms least of all. Trust me."

I did. I was safe in Dawson's arms.

I could let go, and I knew he would catch me.

And that right there scared the fuck out of me. A man who could make me feel that way was damned dangerous.

Dawson's legs tightened around my waist as he tried to roll us over. I pulled on his arm as instructed, and I managed to keep him from taking me back.

"Good, that's very good," Dawson whispered as he suddenly let go and shuffled away from me. "We're done for the day."

Then he scrambled off the mat and stood up, offering his hand.

I took it and noticed he was trembling. "Are you okay?"

"Yeah, just, uh, I need water. I'm dehydrated."

"How about breakfast?" I smiled as I got up on my own shaky legs. "I'll order room service."

"I can order it when we get back," Dawson turned away from me.

I grabbed a couple of towels from the nearby stack and threw one at him, covering his entire head and shoulders.

While I was doubling over with laughter, Dawson yanked the towel off and turned around. And, oh shit, judging by the fire in those green eyes of his, I was in for it now.

He stalked toward me in purposeful strides until loud voices interrupted, and the door swung open.

"Oh, hey, sorry. We didn't know the room was occupied."

Two fit-looking guys in their twenties appeared. From their accents, it sounded like they were American, too, but from the south. With shaved heads and wide smiles, I could hardly tell them apart. Then I noticed the shorter one had tattoos on his arms.

"We're just leaving," Dawson replied, motioning for me to follow him.

"Thanks," the tattooed one replied and cocked his head when I walked past. "Wait a minute, I know you."

"I've got one of those faces," I replied and walked beside Dawson.

"You're Iain Holloway! Wayward Lane!" the other guy yelled out.

Busted.

I nodded. "I am. Nice to meet you."

The taller one held out his hand. "I'm Hawk, and this is Lewis. I can't believe this is happening! The lead guitarist from Wayward Lane, this is so fucking cool!"

I reached out and shook his hand, smiling in return. It was always nice to meet an enthusiastic fan.

Lewis smacked his forehead. "Fuck, what a time for me to forget my phone!"

"We have to get going anyway," Dawson reminded me, placing a hand on my lower back.

"We'll be at your concert on Valentine's Day," Hawk announced.

"Really? Well, give Dawson your name and number and we can invite you backstage."

"Are you kidding?" Lewis blurted out.

I heard Dawson's growl and looked over to see him shaking his head.

"Enter your details; we'll have to do a security check first and get in touch with you," Dawson explained as he passed over his phone.

"Yeah, of course."

Once the guys finished entering their information on Dawson's phone, we said our goodbyes and made our way back to our rooms.

"What do you want to eat?" Dawson asked as he unlocked the door.

"An omelet with ham, cheese, and veggies. Croissants with jam. And lots of coffee."

"I'll place the order and knock when it arrives."

Dawson headed for his room and slammed the door. What got his jockstrap in a knot?

Shaking my head, I retreated to my bathroom.

A hot shower was desperately needed.

Once I'd stripped down and stood underneath the heated spray, I replayed the morning in my head. Every time Dawson's hands touched my body, or anytime he so much as brushed against me, every nerve ending came alive.

It felt like I'd been edged for hours.

I grabbed my body wash and soaped up my throbbing dick. A sexy vision of Dawson covering my body with his, taking my cock in hand, and giving me orders in that husky voice of his had my balls tightening.

I'd barely gotten two strokes off when my phone began to ring.

"Fuck!"

I quickly rinsed off and stepped out of the shower, reaching for my phone on the counter.

It was Harlow. I tapped *accept* and *speaker*.

"What?" I snarled as I yanked a towel off the shelf and wrapped it around my waist.

"Good morning to you, too. Or afternoon since it's almost noon."

"What do you want?"

"Pre-rehearsal meeting in Brodie's suite at one."

"I'll be there."

I tapped *end* and looked at myself in the mirror. I untied my hair and left it down. It was messy, but I didn't care. And I didn't bother shaving, either. After throwing on a pair of worn jeans and a T-shirt, I knocked on the connecting door and waited until Dawson answered.

"Breakfast isn't here yet," he said when he opened the door.

He was fresh out of the shower, too, in black jeans and a T-shirt that showed off his incredible body—a body that was distracting me at an alarming rate.

"That's fine. I thought we could talk anyway. Harlow just called. We have a meeting at one. I want you to be there."

"Me? Can't I just wait outside in the hallway?"

"No. You'll be the peacekeeper in case things get out of control."

Dawson nodded and waved me inside. I walked over to the sofa in the corner of the room and sat down.

"Thanks for dragging my ass outta bed this morning. I do feel better."

Dawson nodded and bit his lower lip. Was he nervous?

"Are you alright? You seemed jumpy at the end of our workout."

Dawson stared at me and swallowed hard. "I'm fine. I was thirsty. I mean, I was dehydrated. I forgot to drink water when I woke up."

He finally walked over and sat beside me, tapping on his phone. "I texted Zoe. It appears that question about your mom last night has created interest from the media. She's already fielding calls and emails. She's going to talk to you later today, but it's fair to say there will probably be more news items about it."

I let my head fall back against the sofa cushion. "Christ."

"I'm sorry."

Without thinking, I reached out and touched Dawson's forearm. "Don't apologize for something you didn't do. This is all on Harlow. And maybe part of it is my fault, too."

"Why you?"

"My mom—" I paused, a lump forming in my throat.

I looked at Dawson. Was I really going to tell him?

"You probably know this already from my bio, but my mom died when I was ten—an accidental drowning. But afterward, there was a lot of speculation around town that maybe it wasn't an accident. She had mental health problems.

Depression. I tried to ignore the gossip, but the older I got, the more I couldn't handle it. And my dad, well, he'd checked out of my life since her death. As soon as I finished high school, the guys and I left town to start gigging." I paused. "I don't talk about her or what happened. So I think that probably makes people more curious."

Dawson squeezed my hand. "You don't owe the media, or anyone, any explanation. Your feelings and your past are your own."

"They can write about my sex life all they want. But this family stuff? It just cuts too deep. And I don't like to talk about it with anyone, not even the guys."

"I can only imagine. I mean, Jaxon has gone through a lot these past two years, but at least he's got me and my mom. And my sisters, even if they live far away. And a great therapist he can talk to."

"He's a lucky kid."

"Iain, it's not my place, but—"

Dawson was interrupted by a knock at the door that startled both of us.

"Oh, it's room service," Dawson murmured and got up to answer the door.

I stared at his back as he walked away, and I studied him. Not just his body but the way he carried himself and the way he interacted with the concierge, Georges. I recognized him from our visit last year and waved. Georges smiled and waved in return, but he kept talking to Dawson. I heard Dawson ask about his family and then the mention of Jaxon. Dawson was smiling and talking in an animated way that was rare.

Who was this man? I mean, besides being my badass bodyguard.

And why was I suddenly intent on knowing everything?

CHAPTER 12

DAWSON

ain and I shared brunch and spent a whole hour without arguing.

I should've been happy, relieved. Had our relationship turned a corner? Was I finally seeing the man behind the rockstar image?

Yes. Or maybe that was the problem.

I was seeing him, and I liked what I saw—a lot.

And it wasn't all physical. Although, grappling in the gym earlier sure proved that, yeah, I wanted to get as close as possible to the sexiest man I'd ever met. Which wasn't smart at all. Then again, my rulebook tended to fly out of the window whenever I was with Iain.

But there was still something he wasn't telling me. And I wasn't about to go one step forward and two steps back.

Patience. Watch and listen.

Like now.

The band had gathered in Brodie's suite for a meeting with Harlow. Before their manager arrived, the four guys had their own private conversation while Van and I chatted on the sideline.

And now that Harlow was here, things were not going well. To say the least.

"What's *he* doing here?" Harlow asked, motioning at me.

"*He* has a name. And I asked Dawson to be here. Not that I owe you any explanation since he's my bodyguard."

"He doesn't need to protect you here."

"I don't know about that," Iain mumbled.

"What happened last night, Harlow?" Brodie snapped. "I want an explanation before I contact Greg directly."

"Go ahead." Harlow shook his head and adjusted his suit jacket. "Look, I admit that I should have done a better job at preparing you for those questions—"

"Are you kidding me?" Faise bit out.

"But, in all fairness," Harlow continued, "the questions they asked are all based on public knowledge. There's nothing threatening or nefarious going on. Faise's brother *is* in rehab; it's not a secret. And Holloway's mother—"

"Don't!" Iain yelled and stood up to pace. "Do not go there."

I looked at Van, and his concern mirrored mine. Both of us moved closer to Iain.

"Everything is fair game when it comes to the media," Harlow countered. "That's celebrity life. Or did you all forget?"

"Whose side are you on?" Ronin asked.

"The label's, of course. You know, the one that pays for your mansions, cars, and every other luxury you have."

"You've got that the wrong way around." Brodie leaned forward. "We bring in the money. The label was damn lucky to sign us."

I didn't miss his use of the past tense.

"So, the more attention you guys get, the more money you'll make. Fans want to know all about your life, including your family and anything to do with you. You might as well give them what they want to know instead of refusing to answer these questions. Now, you can dislike me all you want, but this comes from the top. No more evasive answers."

"This isn't about money. And what does Zoe have to say about all this?" Brodie asked.

Harlow scoffed. "She's not in charge on this trip; I am."

"I looked at the press clippings today," Van interjected. "There are reporters camped outside Rae's rehab facility, and there are now several articles about Iain's mom."

"You know what? I'm done. I'm not doing promos or interviews while we're here." Iain pointed at Harlow and sat back down.

"I'm with Holls." Brodie nodded. "We do the concerts, and we're done."

"I agree," Faise replied.

Ronin nodded. "I'm with you guys."

"That's a violation of the terms of your contract," Harlow reminded them.

"What's Greg gonna do? Cancel the sold-out concerts?" Brodie sneered. "No fucking way. And we may be public figures, but that doesn't mean everything is fair game. Get Greg on the phone. Now."

Harlow pulled out his phone and tapped it. Then he placed it on the table in front of him. After a few rings, the voice of Greg Haddley answered.

"What is it now, Hines?"

Harlow leaned forward. "I've got the guys on speakerphone."

"We're done with PR on this trip, Greg," Brodie snapped. "No more interviews. Last night was bullshit."

"Stop being oversensitive, Brodie, and get on with your job."

"In case you didn't hear me, I said we are not doing any

interviews for the next two months. Unless, of course, Harlow can assure us that he will let us review the questions in advance."

Silence on the other end of the line was followed by a loud sigh.

"Fine. Hines, do as Brodie requested."

I was shocked. And confused. Greg was known to be the type never to back down.

"You got it, boss," Harlow answered, a surprised look on his face.

"Anything else?" Greg asked.

Brodie tapped on the phone to end the call.

"We done now?" Brodie asked as he walked over to the door and opened it. "We've got a rehearsal to get to."

"I'll meet you guys over there."

"No need. Not today."

Harlow grabbed his phone, stood up, and left the suite without saying another word.

Brodie slammed the door behind him.

"I can't wait until May," Brodie stated.

"Just a few more months, mon coeur," Van replied, pulling his husband into his arms.

"Don't look at your socials," I added. "And I didn't want to say while Harlow was here, but I did message Zoe. She's fielding a lot of inquiries back home, mostly about Iain's mom."

"Are you okay, Holls?" Ronin asked.

"I will be. Like I told Dawson earlier, I don't care about speculation when it comes to my sex life, but my childhood is off-limits. If, and that's a huge if, I ever want to talk about it, it should be my choice to initiate the conversation."

Everyone agreed.

"Enough of this shit, let's go play some music. It's my form of therapy," Iain quipped.

An hour later, we arrived at the Palais D'Or, a smaller

venue in the fourteenth arrondissement. Regan met us at the rear entrance with her usual brisk nod and perfect timing.

While Xavier did the rounds of the building, I got the guys settled in with Ace and the rest of the stage crew.

Regan pulled me aside. "I just got off the phone with Greg. I gather the guys let him have it?"

"They got Harlow to agree to pre-screen the upcoming interviews, but I have my doubts. Greg's playing a game. He knows they're going to walk soon."

Regan nodded. "By the way, Greg confirmed we can hire a PI to look into these text messages."

"That's good."

"It's a start. I don't think Holloway's in any danger as of now, but we can't take any chances. Has he been okay so far, or is he still trying to slip out from under you?"

Out from under me? That brought to mind a very different kind of cat-and-mouse game—one that involved Iain's gorgeous, naked body under mine. And fuck, I shouldn't even be thinking like that while standing in front of my boss.

"I think I'm finally getting through to him," I replied.

Then I glanced over and caught Iain sticking his tongue out at me. I shook my head, but I couldn't help but smile.

"Or maybe not. We had a self-defense practice this morning, and then we talked over breakfast in my room."

Regan's eyebrows nearly shot up to her hairline. "Really?"

"Also, something happened on the plane ride here—" I started.

"That better not mean what I think it does."

"No, not that," I quickly replied.

I was such a fucking liar. I couldn't stop thinking about Iain and not in my security capacity. But nothing had happened. Okay, maybe grappling with him this morning had awakened more lusty fantasies. Now, all I could picture was wrapping my naked body around his…

"Dawson?"

"Sorry. I was calling my son, and suddenly, Iain popped into the seat next to me and started talking to him. And to my mom. After that, he told me about the text messages."

Regan cocked her head and studied me. I hoped to hell she couldn't read minds because she would not be happy with the direction of my thoughts about Iain.

"Maybe he finally realizes that his security isn't a game and that we're looking out for his best interests," Regan replied. "We're our own kind of family, and we look out for each other."

The sudden blast of a guitar riff jolted me. I watched Iain and Brodie playing together.

"I hope so. But I'm not letting my guard down. When Iain gets stressed, that's when he acts out. If we can keep an eye on him without being too overbearing, he's less likely to want to break out."

"What's the plan for tonight?"

"The guys are headed to Nuit Eternelle, a nightclub not far from the venue."

"Remember New Orleans," Regan reminded me. "I want four of you everywhere they go—the dance floor, the bathrooms, you name it."

I nodded. I was not going to let some drunken asshole assault Iain ever again.

"Don't worry, boss; I won't let him out of my sight."

"Them."

"What?"

"You said 'him.' I'm talking about all the guys."

"Of course."

Regan's gaze sharpened, and I coughed into my fist.

"Wow. Is it dry in here, or is it me?"

"It's you," she responded quickly. "I'm taking a flight to London this evening to review the next leg on the schedule. Contact me day or night if anything comes up. I'll be back the morning of the fourteenth."

"I got it under control, boss."

"I hope so."

I had a feeling she was not talking about work.

CHAPTER 13

IAIN

Thank fuck for rehearsal.

It wasn't as energizing as a live performance, but I still got excited whenever we hit a stage. It helped me get out of my head. Which was kind of funny since most people didn't use work as a distraction; they needed distraction from work.

Then again, was this really working? It never felt that way to me. Yeah, we played hard, and there were late nights and travel, but my career was my passion, one and the same. Take away the money, and I'd still be playing.

But, upon entering the venue, we noticed right away that our instruments and the general state of the theatre were chaotic. Two of my guitars were still in their cases, which meant they hadn't been tuned yet, which was surprising. Everything should've been ready to go by the time we got here.

Ace and Tommy were bickering back and forth as they worked on Faise's drum set.

I picked up my favorite Konicki, the only guitar that had been set up, and strummed a few chords. It sounded good.

"Hey Ace, what's happening?" Brodie asked.

"Sorry for the delay, guys, but Faise's drum kit was damaged in transit. We've spent the better part of the day fixing it, and I had to source a new kickstand. I texted Harlow. Didn't he tell you?"

I glanced at Brodie, and he just shook his head. "Nope. And from here on out, text us directly. We're having a bit of a communication problem with him."

"You got it."

"My babies," Faise exclaimed as he stepped up behind the kit.

"It's all fixed," Tommy reassured him with a nod. "Let's test it out."

"Check the rest of Iain's guitars and then the mics," Ace directed.

The guys and I reviewed the set list and decided which songs we wanted to practice.

Once our instruments were tuned and ready to go, so were we.

Then I noticed Dawson and Regan talking in the wings. It looked like something big was going on until Regan nodded and made for the exit.

"Holls, are you playing or what?" Ronin yelled out.

"Yeah, of course."

"Stop staring at your hot as fuck bodyguard and start strumming," Brodie teased.

"Shut up."

Brodie chuckled. "I'm surprised you invited him to our meeting with Harlow. I thought you wanted to get away from Dawson?"

I held the neck of my guitar in one hand and gave him the middle finger with the other.

"No thanks, I prefer Van's fingers," Brodie quipped.

Instead of replying, I started playing the intro chord to Filthy Pain.

I closed my eyes and forgot all about that meeting, the interview last night, and the past month.

When I finally opened them, there was Dawson on center stage, staring at me.

Same as always, except the look he was giving me now was less hard-ass and more "I want your ass." Or maybe that was my wishful thinking?

So, I did what I usually did when faced with something I wasn't prepared to deal with. I ignored it and stuck my tongue out.

He rolled his eyes at me, and just like that, we were back to normal again.

I was glad we weren't fighting, but that didn't mean everything was fine. I wasn't comfortable with this growing awareness between us. As much as Dawson turned me on, there were less complicated men I could screw.

Ones I didn't have to deal with the next day.

Guys who didn't make me feel anything more than simple lust.

———

Three hours later, we were done with rehearsal. We ventured back to our hotel to change and head out for the night.

There were a few messages from Harlow about a promo photo shoot tomorrow but no further interviews until concert day.

Good.

All I needed tonight was a sexy man to get rid of any lingering tension.

Part of me wondered what kind of reaction Dawson would have. Not that I cared, but he was extra protective lately when it came to strangers. And given our adjoining suites, he'd probably be waiting on the other side of the door just in case he needed to break it down and come to my rescue.

I snorted at that thought.

Would he listen the whole time? Would the sounds of me fucking someone else drive him nuts?

And why did I suddenly care? I'd had lots of security witnesses when I was fucking around with a guy. My bandmates went through the same thing. I never thought to question it until now.

I picked out my favorite pair of leather pants, a linen button-down, and my leather jacket. I kept it simple, avoiding any jewelry tonight and leaving my hair in its messy state. I didn't care about shaving, either.

Once I finished getting ready, I texted Dawson and waited by the door.

When he opened it, I was surprised to see him dressed in slim black trousers and a matching button-down with the sleeves rolled up. Those taut, veiny forearms of his were the stuff of my dirtiest dreams.

"Are you done staring?" he asked me, a smirk on his face.

"I wasn't staring. I was just shocked that you own something other than jeans and a T-shirt."

"Look who's talking. You wear that leather jacket every single day."

"It's soft and fits me perfectly. Why mess with a beautiful thing?"

"Exactly," Dawson replied and placed his hand on my lower back, guiding me out of the suite.

He was doing that a lot lately, touching me more than usual. But I don't think he realized it. And there was something about his firm touch, the way he took control, that made me want to lean into him.

Don't go there.

"You got the NDAs ready?" I asked.

I noticed Dawson's jaw clench and the way his eyes iced over.

"All set. But I really would prefer twenty-four hours notice to—"

"Come on, Daws," I interrupted. "I just want to fuck and send the guy on his way. I'm not letting this person into my home, just my hotel room. And you're next door, so I'm secure. Relax."

Dawson stalked down the hallway and slapped the elevator button. Hard.

"What crawled up your ass?" I bit out.

"Nothing."

"If I sneak off without telling you, you're pissed. If I tell you I'm going to bring a guy back here to the hotel, you're pissed. What the hell do you want from me?!" I shouted.

"Keep your voice down," Dawson snapped as he stood with his hands on his hips, his posture rigid. "I'm just doing my job."

"I appreciate that, but I'm as secure as I can get. And in case you haven't realized by now, I'm an adult. I've been on my own since I was a teenager, and despite my celebrity, I can and do take care of myself."

"Oh yeah, I forgot, you don't need anyone." He scoffed.

"Excuse me?"

Dawson didn't look at me but instead stared at the elevator doors.

"Nothing."

"Yeah, nothing. That's why we're fighting to begin with." I sighed. "Look, I don't know how this stupid argument got started, but I'm finishing it. Just have the NDA ready, so I can actually enjoy myself tonight."

Dawson inhaled sharply and then let out a long exhale. "I'm sorry. I was way out of line."

I felt my own irritation deflate. "I just don't understand why you got so angry."

Dawson finally looked at me, and the intensity of his green gaze had me taking a step forward. He swallowed hard and stepped back.

Wasn't that always the way with us?

"It doesn't matter," Dawson replied in a clipped tone. "You've made your intentions clear, and I will do everything to ensure tonight is as seamless as possible."

The doors opened, and he motioned for me to get in.

I stepped inside and crossed my arms.

Now I really needed a drink and a fuck.

The ride down was silent and awkward. Dawson appeared calm but I noticed how fast his chest moved in and out, like he was out of breath. His face was flushed, and his hands were balled up into fists. I swore I could hear his heart beating as loudly as mine.

I had the insane urge to reach out and touch him and, at the same time, run as far and as fast as I could.

What the hell was going on here?

We finally arrived at the parking garage and headed for the SUV. Will and Quinn were waiting by the cars and waved us over.

Dawson opened the door for me, per usual, and I could tell by his cold glare that there was no more conversation to be had. Fine with me. He wanted to act like an ass; he could go for it. I had a party to enjoy.

I got in beside Brodie and Van. Once I was seated, Dawson slammed the door. With so much force, the SUV rocked.

Brodie elbowed me. "Fuck, what's wrong with him?"

The front passenger door opened, and Dawson slid in, nodding at Lennie in the driver's seat.

"Nothing," I repeated, echoing Dawson's earlier response. "Nothing is wrong, isn't that right Daws?"

Dawson nodded but stayed silent.

Smart man.

Brodie and Van exchanged a look, and I sighed. "What?"

"We know who he's mad at, if not why," Van whispered. "He's just trying to look out for your safety."

"Why do you automatically assume I did something wrong?"

Van and Brodie both started laughing.

I ran a hand over my hair, tugging at the ends. "Dawson and I are never going to see eye to eye because he enjoys telling me what to do, and I don't like to hear it."

"I'm sure you'd enjoy taking his orders in the bedroom," Brodie quipped.

"Jesus Christ," Dawson grumbled from the front seat, shaking his head.

Thankfully, he didn't turn around.

"Dee," I warned, my face hot.

"What? I can tell that Dawson is a total power top." Brodie cackled. "And you're a sassy bottom who likes—"

"Enough," Dawson demanded.

For once, I agreed with him. I slapped my hand over Brodie's mouth to shut him up.

"Can't you make him stop?" I asked Van.

Van shook his head. "You know I have no control over what comes out of his mouth."

Brodie pulled my hand away and grinned. "Yeah, only what goes in it."

Everyone in the car groaned.

Brodie leaned into me and whispered. "You're welcome."

I rubbed my middle finger against my nose and glared at him. "For what?"

Brodie just shook his head and laughed.

CHAPTER 14

DAWSON

I couldn't look anyone in the eye.

Which was kind of fucked up, given what I did for a living.

Still, after that argument with Iain and then Brodie's comments in the car, I was sure that my expression would give me away. In more ways than one.

Of course, I hadn't told Iain what was really bothering me because I didn't want to face what I was feeling.

I hated the idea of him fucking anyone but me.

There, I finally admitted it.

Christ, I was a walking stereotype. The bodyguard falling for his client. Ugh.

I had no business being possessive over him. He was my detail, not my lover.

And Brodie hadn't been wrong either. I was a total power top. But his comment about Iain made me wonder. As argumentative as Iain was, all I could do now was picture him as a sassy bottom.

Talk about shit timing.

"Boss?" Lennie called out.

"Yeah?"

I turned to my colleague as we reached the club's VIP room. The guys headed for the bar, and Lennie and I stood on the periphery.

"Everything okay?"

I nodded. "Of course."

Lennie stared at me like Regan had earlier. Did my poker face need work?

"Brodie really got you good."

"He's a troublemaker. Him and Iain. But I'm used to the teasing."

I waved it off, but inside, I was a fucking mess.

I watched Iain as the boys ordered their shots. The bartender leaned forward and gave Iain a smile I knew all too well. Iain was looking to get laid tonight, and suddenly, I couldn't imagine remaining unaffected.

What didn't bother me a year ago was suddenly a problem I didn't know how to solve.

Iain and I were a disaster at the best of times, never mind if we crossed the professional line. I had control; fuck, I loved being in control. But this heat that was now flashing between us... I hadn't counted on that. And I didn't know if I should try to put out the flames or fan them higher.

I'd never met anyone who challenged me the way Iain did. It was heady, exhilarating, and scary as fuck.

"Is it just teasing?" Lennie asked.

"Of course. Nothing is going on."

"Well, you're looking at that bartender like you're going to eviscerate him. And not in the usual bodyguard way."

"After that incident in New Orleans—"

"The guy's just talking to him."

The bartender was flirting. And I wondered if he would end up as Iain's fuck buddy for the night. Just the thought made my stomach clench painfully.

I tore my glance away from my detail and looked at my colleague and friend.

"Daws, it's me. I know you, and I know him. Something's changed. What's going on?"

I bit my lip, unsure if I should say anything at all.

"I'm telling you this as a friend, in confidence," I started, and Lennie nodded. "Ever since the break-in, when I got put back on Iain's detail last month, well, our arguments are still passionate, but different. More intense."

"Oh, fuck."

"Nothing has happened. Or will happen. I'm sure this is just me needing to go out and get laid. It's been a while."

"We've all witnessed how he flirts, but I just thought it was his way of trying to distract you."

"It is. Or it was," I paused. "I don't think I'm the only one who's feeling the shift between us."

"Best to tell Regan to switch you back to Brodie."

"For what reason?"

Lennie grimaced.

"Exactly. She'll want to know why. If I say anything at all, I'm done. Maybe kicked off the team for good."

"She wouldn't do that."

"If my… feelings become an issue, I'll tell her. And who knows, maybe it's time for me to do something different. I can't work this job forever."

I turned my attention back to the boys.

Ronin dragged Faise off his barstool and pointed to the dance floor. After a brief back and forth, Ronin swatted Faise's ass, and Faise ran after him. Xavier followed them. Brodie and Van stayed behind, lost in each other as usual.

And Iain? He was pouring back the shots, one after another. He put on a good rockstar show, but the man could not handle his liquor. At least, not the hard stuff. He was gonna be sick as fuck if he wasn't careful. And drinking that much made me worry about things like the ability to consent.

Before I knew it—before Lennie could warn me—I was stalking off toward the bar and slid in beside Iain.

"Slow it down. It's tequila, not water."

Iain paused but refused to face me.

"You really are the biggest pain in my ass, you know that?" he snapped and threw back the shot.

"I wish."

Iain choked on his drink and spewed it all over the bar top.

The bartender, the cute guy with a perfect smile and big blue eyes, looked surprised and slightly horrified. I nearly rolled my eyes. I'm sure he'd witnessed much worse.

Iain grabbed a napkin and wiped his mouth. "Funny."

If only he knew I wasn't joking.

Then he stood up and turned to me. "This truce we had going this morning? It's over. I'm going to join my friends on the dance floor. Do your job and follow me, but if you so much as try to interrupt when I'm having a good time, I will insist that you be reassigned."

I stared down at his big brown eyes and knew that if I said anything else, I would push him away for good. Iain's defense mechanism was back up again.

Biting my tongue, I nodded.

He walked over to Brodie and motioned for him and Van to head down to the dance floor. Lennie and I followed them, pushing through the crowded room.

We moved through the mass of writhing bodies, the smell of sweat and cologne overwhelming. I stood on the periphery and watched the band as more and more people crowded around them. My nerves were running high and hot, but that wasn't unusual in this type of situation. We had to be prepared to act in a split second if things got out of hand. There were a shit ton of bouncers in this place wandering about so that gave me some measure of comfort. Professionally speaking.

Personally?

I was irrationally jealous of every man who sidled up to

Iain. One man was more stunning than the next, and it hit me how foolish I'd been to think my reaction to him could be reciprocated.

He could have any man he wanted. And he did.

Soon, two guys were dancing with him, one at his back and one at his front, and fuck me, this was torture.

I watched as the guy in front of him ran his hands up Iain's chest and neck. Their heads leaned closer, and the man cupped Iain's face.

And Iain? He wasn't pulling away.

I tapped my earpiece. "Xavier, Quinn, one of you get down here ASAP and sub for me. Lennie's in charge."

Lennie gave me the okay signal, but his expression was concerned.

Once I spotted my colleagues headed toward me, I made a beeline for the stairs and the VIP room.

I couldn't watch Iain anymore. I just couldn't.

Then I berated myself for reacting at all. I'd seen Iain make out with his fuck buddies before, and it never bothered me.

"Stupid. Get yourself under control," I whispered to myself as I headed for the bathroom.

I splashed water on my face and took a few deep breaths. I could do this.

Iain was a job, just a job.

Despite repeating that mantra over and over, I couldn't bring myself to walk out of that fucking bathroom.

Iain

I was going out of my mind.

But not for the reason you might think.

I had not one, but two sexy guys rubbing themselves all over me.

What more could I ask for, right?

How about a decent hard-on? My cock was barely interested, and I was so freaking angry at myself that I wanted to scream. A half hour ago, I was hard as a rock while arguing with Dawson, and now this.

Fuck that man for screwing with my head.

Both of them.

The guy in front of me grabbed my face and leaned in to kiss me, but I turned at the last second, and he licked my neck instead. Not that I was paying attention, since my eyes were on Dawson. He looked like he was about to tear through the crowd and throw me over his shoulder. A part of me hoped he would do exactly that.

Then he was leaving the dance floor, leaving me, and my brain snapped into gear.

He never left his post and not in crowded places like a club.

Something must be wrong. Really wrong.

"I gotta go," I yelled, pushing away from the twosome surrounding me.

Quinn passed Dawson and took his place on the dance floor.

I was about to bypass Lennie to head upstairs when he grasped my arm. "Don't. Leave him be."

"What?" I yelled out.

Lennie shook his head. "Don't start something with Dawson that you have no intention of finishing."

"What the hell are you talking about?"

"I see the way Dawson looks at you, Holls. And the way you look at him. Something is going on between you two."

I shook my head, unwilling to believe him. Or myself. It couldn't happen.

Even though I was already thinking about Dawson more than any other man who had come into my life, and we weren't even lovers.

"He never leaves his post," I blurted out. "He never leaves me."

Lennie nodded. "And that right there should tell you everything you need to know."

Was Dawson jealous of the guys I was dancing with? Is that why he left? And why did that thought make my blood run hot and my dick throb? I'd never been one to be turned on by possessive behavior before. No one staked a claim on me. I didn't belong to anyone but myself.

But the way my heart was now racing out of control, it seemed my body more than liked the idea of belonging to Dawson.

"I need to talk to him."

"Don't fuck him over, Holls. He doesn't deserve it."

Lennie had a point. Even if I did feel something for Dawson and him for me, it would go nowhere. He had a job to consider. And fucking around with my bodyguard was just asking for trouble neither of us needed.

"Take me back up to the bar," I said to Lennie. "And get an NDA ready."

CHAPTER 15

IAIN

L ennie escorted me back to the VIP room, where I proceeded to down more shots of tequila and made eye contact with the cute bartender again. Marc? Michel? I was fucking horrible with names at the best of times.

What did it matter anyway? He had a taut body and sexy lips. What more did I need?

"When are you done here?" I asked the bartender, giving him an appreciative smile.

"I'm clocking out in a half hour."

"Come back to my hotel?"

"Love to," he replied with a wink.

Lennie was sitting nearby, and I nodded to the bartender. "You'll need to fill out an NDA first."

"No problem."

Exactly. I had no problems. I was buzzed, I had a fuck friend for the night, and Dawson was still out of my sight. I should be ecstatic.

I was anything but.

Still, I vowed that by the time we got back to my hotel room, I'd be relaxed and ready to fuck. Just like I always was.

I wouldn't let a sexy bodyguard with incredible eyes mess with my life. And these fierce feelings rattling around inside me for Dawson were temporary. They didn't mean anything.

After Lennie got the bartender's signature—his name was Michel—he sat down beside me with his club soda.

Michel gave me a nod, then walked over to talk to one of his colleagues.

Lennie tapped on his earpiece. "What's up?"

I could hear bits of his conversation and guessed he was talking to Dawson.

"Okay. I got it."

"Where is he?" I asked.

"He's on his way back to the hotel. Except, there's a change in plans."

My stomach tightened. "And that is?"

"I'll be staying in your adjoining suite from here on out. Daws is taking my room down the hall. He's gonna ask Regan to put me on as your primary."

I nodded and took another shot of tequila, swallowing past the lump in my throat.

"Why so glum, Holls?" Brodie yelled out.

I looked over to find Brodie and Van walking up to the bar. Ronin and Faise were also back, along with a couple of guys I presumed were their fuck friends for the night.

"I'm not. I'm fine."

"Where's Dawson?" Van asked.

"Back at the hotel. I'm on Holloway's detail from here on out," Lennie announced.

Van sat down beside Lennie and ordered a beer.

Brodie placed a hand on my shoulder. "Come sit with me."

Michel opened a bottle of champagne and placed it on the bar top. I grabbed it and followed my friend over to the big couch in the corner of the room.

"What happened?" Brodie asked as we sat down.

"Nothing happened," I snapped, taking a swig from the bottle. "The bartender is coming back to the hotel with me, and Dawson is off my back. Everything is fucking perfect."

Brodie leaned forward. "Is it possible that—"

"Don't, Dee. Don't go there. This is not you and Van, all right? Dawson and I are… this isn't a love story. We're just… I mean, I've got these feelings, but nothing good can come of it. It's temporary."

"He looked pretty upset when he saw you dancing with those guys."

"You noticed?"

Brodie nodded. "Never seen him look at you like that before."

I swore and downed another mouthful of champagne. "That's not my problem."

"Then why do you look and sound miserable?"

"Because I—" I paused and looked around. "If you dare breathe a word of this to anyone, I swear I will personally remove your balls."

"Ouch, pinky swear it is."

"I'm serious."

"Go on," he urged me.

"Lately, I'm having a hard time, well, getting hard. For anyone except *he who shall remain nameless*."

Brodie stared at me with his mouth wide open.

"Dee?"

Brodie shook his head and ran a hand over his face. "Sorry, I think I'm in shock."

"You're not the only one," I mumbled.

"And yet, you're bringing that bartender back to the hotel?"

"I figure now that Dawson's out of my sight, and if I can relax enough, everything will be fine."

"You know I went through something similar before Van."

"I remember. You were extra snarky because you hadn't gotten laid in months."

He nodded. "Other guys just weren't doing it for me. My heart knew it wanted Van, and only Van, and my body finally caught up."

"There's no heart involved here. Just lust. And that's easily dealt with," I replied, taking another swig from the bottle.

"You know, it's okay to like a guy."

I coughed and shook my head. "What are we? Back in high school?"

"You never want to let anyone get close to you, Iain. As social as you are, you only have a handful of friends and no romantic relationships, just hookups."

"Well, I am a rockstar fuckboy," I quipped. "I have a reputation to live up to."

Brodie smacked my shoulder. "I mean, you guard your heart. Because you're a sensitive guy, and you've dealt with a lot of pain and loss. You're running from Dawson 'cause you're afraid to let him get close."

Brodie always knew how to hit a note with accuracy. Not that I was going to admit to anything.

"Jesus, Dee, falling in love has short-circuited your brain."

Brodie laughed. "No fucking way. It just made me see things much clearer. And I know you, Iain. We've been friends for far too long."

I bit my lip. "No matter what I might feel, Daws works for us. I can't go there."

"Hello? I fell in love with our manager."

"That's different."

"Why?"

I didn't have an answer. "It just is."

"I think he could be good for you."

"That might be true, but the reverse isn't."

"What?"

"I'm not a good bet for anyone, Dee, let alone a man who has his shit together. Fuck's sake, he's a father."

"So? You think I was a good bet for Van?" Brodie shook his head. "You're just scared because you've never been in a relationship before."

Before I could say anything else, Michel appeared in front of us. "Hey, I hope I'm not interrupting?"

I looked up at him. "Not at all."

"I'm done with my shift. Are you ready to go back to the hotel?"

"Give me five minutes?"

"I'll wait with your bodyguard." He smiled at me, then Brodie, and walked away.

I turned back to my friend, who was giving me the stink eye. "What?"

"That has disaster written all over it."

"Nah." I stood up. "I'm sure it'll be fine. I think. Yes, fine. I can do this."

"If you have to give yourself a pep talk for sex, it's not going to be good," Brodie snarked as he got to his feet.

"Shut up."

"Have fun. Don't think about Dawson while you're fucking."

"Dee—"

Brodie suddenly pulled me into a crushing hug and whispered in my ear. "Go with your gut, Iain. It never steers you wrong."

I pulled back but didn't say anything. I knew Brodie was right, but the fear was still there.

Instead of following his advice, I walked over to Michel, who was in conversation with Lennie.

"You ready?" Lennie asked.

"I am."

I said it with confidence.

And I was so full of shit.

That lingering unease followed me out of the club, into the SUV, and back to the hotel.

So much so that by the time we were in the elevator heading upstairs, I was full-on fidgeting, tapping my feet, and biting my fingernails. I was pretty sure I was having a major panic attack—another one.

When the elevator doors opened to the thirtieth floor, and all three of us stepped out into the carpeted hallway, my lungs seized up. I couldn't breathe.

"Are you alright?" Michel murmured, touching my arm.

"N-not really. I don't feel so good."

Lennie coughed into his fist.

Michel chuckled. "That's what happens when you mix tequila and champagne."

Yeah, that was it.

"Raincheck? Maybe tomorrow night?"

Michel studied me with a wry smile.

"Maybe," he replied and stepped back into the elevator.

"Sorry."

He shrugged. "Ç'est rien. This hotel has a fabulous bar, so I might as well have a drink before I leave. Au revoir, Holloway."

He gave one last wave, and the doors closed.

My relief was palpable. Pretty sure I let out the inhale I'd been holding onto since I'd left the club.

"I never thought I would live to see this day," Lennie muttered as he ushered me down the hallway.

"I said I don't feel good. And he was right; I shouldn't have mixed that alcohol."

"Sure, that's why you look so relieved now, and you're actually breathing again."

"You know, sometimes your observation skills are really annoying. And what just happened stays between us."

"My bodyguard lips are sealed," Lennie made a zipping motion over his mouth.

When we got to my suite, Lennie opened the door, did a room check, and then motioned for me to enter.

"I'm going to check out my room and go grab my stuff," he said to me as he walked to the connecting door.

I turned from the entryway and headed for the bathroom.

Until I heard a door open.

"Oh, I thought you were already gone," Lennie announced.

I stopped short and listened in.

"No, it's fine," Dawson replied in a quiet tone. "I'm sorry about earlier. Just forget I said anything, okay? It's all under control. I'm not going to have Regan take me off Iain's detail."

"You know, Iain has—"

"I don't care what Iain has. Or who. You've vetted his guest or guests, so all's good. I'm calling it a night."

I heard the door slam, and I quietly wandered back out to the bedroom.

"Well, it looks like things are back to normal. Dawson is still on your guard duty. Have a good night, Holls."

"You too, Lennie. And thanks."

He paused as he was leaving like he wanted to say something. Then he shook his head and left.

I stared at the connecting door, wondering what I should do.

Do I knock on it and face Dawson? Face this desperate need for him that kept building inside of me?

Or should I leave it be? Let him think I was with someone else. Cut off this reckless desire before it took hold of me.

Before it changed everything.

CHAPTER 16

DAWSON

I leaned against the connecting door, my heart still pumping hard and fast, my stomach roiling.

Knowing that Iain was right next to me, so fucking close, and yet, with someone else…

No.

I wouldn't allow my emotions to get the better of me. I never let personal feelings get in the way of my job. I could do this.

Strange thing was, I didn't hear anything next door except the sound of running water and then total silence. That was odd. I knew for a fact Iain was very vocal when he was with a partner.

And fuck, I had to stop that line of thinking. Pushing away from the door, I made my way over to my bed.

Instead of ruminating on what Iain was doing—or who he was doing—I picked up my phone and video-called my mom.

"Hi Dawson, how's France?"

"Beautiful, but cold. How's things back home?"

"Great. Jaxon and I are just finishing up dinner."

She positioned her phone so I could see my son, who was

scarfing down what looked like a bowl of pasta. He had tomato sauce over half his face, and it made me smile. Fuck, just seeing my family made the ache near my heart a little less painful.

"Dad!" Jaxon dropped his fork and reached for the phone.

"Hey, bud, I miss you. How was your day?"

"I got a hundred on my math test!"

"Wow, that's incredible!"

"And then Nana took me for my piano lesson. I told Allison that I met Iain Holloway."

Jeez, he was never going to let that go.

"Well, I talked to him; I didn't meet him in person. Not yet," Jaxon continued. "And Allison said I'm ready to start learning guitar. When you come home, can we book lessons?"

I was proud as hell of my son, but his keen interest in music had me a bit worried. Then, I realized I was getting ahead of myself. Just because Jaxon wanted to play several instruments didn't mean he wanted to be a future rock-star...did it? He was only eight, soon to be nine. He probably wanted to be a number of things, a musician least of all.

"I'll talk to her when I get back, okay?"

"Yes!" Jaxon exclaimed. "Did you see Iain today?"

"I saw all the band members at rehearsal."

"Can you send me a video from one of their concerts?"

"I'll be working, but I tell you what: when I come home, I'll find some clips to share with you."

Ones that PR could edit for PG purposes.

"Okay. I miss you lots, Dad."

"I miss you more, bud."

"Nana, can I be excused now?" Jaxon asked as he turned away from the phone.

"Of course. Go wash that sauce off your face and then find a show for us to watch, all right?" my mom replied in the background.

"Bye, Jaxon. I love you." I blew him kisses, and he handed the phone back to my mom.

"Hey, Mom."

"What's wrong?"

"Nothing, I'm just tired. It's two-thirty in the morning here."

My mom raised one eyebrow at me, and I sighed. I could never fool her about anything.

"It's personal."

"Is it Iain?" she asked.

I stared at her, unable to speak.

"I hear the way you talk about him. And I know you. You like him."

"The man drives me nuts."

"Exactly. You love a challenge."

"Mom—"

"But there's the fact that you work for him. And he's a rockstar with quite the reputation. Not that I read the gossip sites that much, but Iain certainly does get a lot of attention."

Ugh, talking about this with my mom was giving me a headache. "Can we please change the subject?"

"I saw the way he looked at you on that video call. It's not just you."

"I'm hanging up now."

"Dawson, what have I always taught you?"

I sighed. "To fight for the people I love."

"And?"

"Mom, I never said anything about...that."

"You also know better than most how short life is. You can't be an island forever."

Knock, knock.

I was never so thankful for an interruption in my life.

"Someone's at the door, I gotta go."

"Love you."

"You too."

I tapped *end* and set my phone on the nightstand. There was another knock. But it wasn't coming from the exit door; it was the connecting one.

What did Iain want? Did he run out of condoms and lube?

I got up and walked over, mentally bracing myself, and wrenched open the door.

"What?"

Iain stood there, still dressed in those sexy leather pants and his linen shirt, half unbuttoned. And in his bare feet. He always walked around like that at home. And sometimes the studio. Couldn't stand socks or footwear in general, which, for some strange reason, I found cute as fuck.

Listen to yourself.

Iain Holloway was gorgeous any time of the day, but I liked him like this, disheveled and relaxed. Then I noted the half-empty liquor bottle in his hand and remembered the guys he was dancing with at the club. They were probably in his bed right this moment.

I shook my head at my stupid thoughts. "What do you want, Iain? It's almost three in the morning."

"I can't sleep," he muttered.

"Go snuggle up to your fuck friends," I snapped and slammed the door in his face.

I turned on my heel, but Iain banged on the door again. But this time, harder and louder.

"Keep it down; we're in a hotel with other people around," I hissed as I threw open the door again.

"For your information, I didn't c-come back here with anyone," Iain declared, waving the bottle in the air. "Well, I did but I told him to leave."

"What?"

"But I f-fucking should have let him stay. But of course, I c-couldn't. And it's all your fault!"

"What are you talking about, and what's the point of this conversation?"

"You! I'm talking about y-you. Always you. Messing with my goddamn head," he bellowed and pushed his way past me into my room. "And I don't... I don't know what to do."

"Just come on in for starters."

Iain ignored my sarcasm and began to pace, unsteady on his feet.

"I d-don't know what I'm doing," he confessed.

"Iain—"

"I'm so fucking frustrated, I could—"

"Stop," I demanded.

Iain did as I requested but ran an agitated hand through his blond waves.

"What's going on?" I asked calmly, even though I felt anything but.

"This," he pointed between us. "*This* is what's going on. D-don't tell me I'm the only one here."

Given how fast my heart was beating and how quickly my dick was filling, no, he wasn't the only one.

"Just go to bed. You've been drinking. We'll talk in the morning, okay?"

I was too worked up tonight, and I needed him gone. He was standing so close, and then I realized he was looking at me with hunger in his eyes and then at my bed like he was imagining the two of us...Fuck, no.

My ironclad control was so close to breaking.

"I need to t-talk now. I can't sleep."

"Iain," I warned.

"Now," he repeated and stalked up to me, pushing his finger into my chest.

"Fucking brat," I whispered.

Before I realized what I was doing, I spun Iain around and pinned him against the nearest wall, my larger frame enveloping his from head to toe. His body trembled beneath mine, and he dropped the bottle on the carpeted floor.

Then I cursed myself for letting him get to me. I started to pull away, but he reached back and gripped my hip, holding me in place.

"Please," he moaned and shoved his ass back, rubbing it over my denim-covered cock.

"Fuck, Iain."

"Yes, f-fuck me."

Grabbing a handful of his silky hair, I pushed it aside and leaned in to whisper in his ear. "It doesn't work like that. Not with me."

Iain moaned and swiveled his hips, torturing my throbbing dick.

"Why didn't you bring those guys back to the hotel?" I gasped, sliding one hand down to cup Iain's hip, stilling him.

He needed to stop moving right fucking now. This wasn't the time or place for this to happen. Hell, it shouldn't be happening at all.

Yeah, and that's why you pinned him to the wall, right? And why you want to reach down and stroke that sexy cock of his?

Don't think about his perfect ass or his pretty cock…

But I gave in to temptation and looked down at the bulge in his pants. I'd seen his cock so many times, but I never imagined I'd finally get the chance to touch and taste it myself. Just the thought of jerking him or sucking him off had my balls drawing up tight.

"I c-couldn't… I can't…" he moaned. "They didn't turn me on."

I swear my heart stuttered, and my hand tightened on his hip.

"And it's n-not just tonight," Iain continued, his breathing choppy. "It's been like that for a while. No one. I don't want anyone. Well, only you."

Me? I was the one he wanted?

Fucking hell.

A rush of exhilaration swept over me.

Then I remembered how much he'd been drinking.

Calling on every ounce of control I had, I pulled back, far away from the heat of his long, lithe body.

"Daws."

He groaned my name like a plea, and I... I could never deny Iain.

"Lie down."

"What?"

My body was shaking as hard as his, but I was not going to fuck this up. He needed to sleep off his drink, and we needed to talk in the clear light of day.

"Lie down on the bed. Go to sleep. I'll be right here." I pointed to the nearby couch.

"Lie with me. I don't want to b-be alone."

"Iain."

"Please," he whispered.

Fuck, this man. Why couldn't I say no?

I nodded and walked away to close the connecting door and ensure everything was locked up tight. After I secured the room, I checked my phone on the nightstand and turned off the lamp. The curtains in my room blocked out most of the glittering city lights, but not all of them, casting the far end of the suite in a pale glow.

Behind me, I heard Iain getting undressed. As much as I longed to turn around and watch him, I didn't.

Once I heard the rustle of sheets, I pivoted and reached for the duvet. I left my jeans and tank top on and slowly slid under the covers.

As soon as my body hit the mattress, Iain rolled over and snuggled into me like he was made to fit in my arms. Like we'd been doing this for ages. Instinctively, I wrapped one arm around him and pulled him tighter.

He was still trembling, and without thinking, I ran a soothing hand down his bare back. Fuck, his smooth skin felt better than good. Everything about him—his heady smell, his possessive grip on me, his sudden vulnerability—it all hit me like a punch to the gut.

Neither of us said a word, and slowly, eventually, I felt his body calm, his limbs warm and heavy against mine.

"Did we w-wake you when we came in?" he asked, his voice hoarse with fatigue and drink.

"No, I was wide awake."

"Because of me?"

I didn't see any point in lying.

"Yes."

"I heard you t-talking to someone. Heard it through the door."

"I was on the phone with Jaxon."

I felt his smile against my shoulder and shivered.

"How is he?"

"He got a hundred percent on his math test today. And, of course, now he's bugging me for guitar lessons."

Iain chuckled, and his warm breath kissed my skin. "Smart kid."

"Smarter than me, that's for sure."

Iain tensed, and I realized I was still rubbing his back. So much for self-control.

"Why does this feel so fucking good?" he whispered.

I was so overwhelmed by the surge of intense emotions that I couldn't answer him.

Was Iain really here in my arms? It was unexpected, unreal. Would I wake up tomorrow to realize I'd dreamt it all?

"Go to sleep, Iain."

He gave a long sigh, and a few minutes later, I heard a soft snore.

I wondered if I would hear him talk in his sleep again.

That thought brought a smile to my face, and surprisingly, a short while later, I drifted off and joined him.

CHAPTER 17

IAIN

always slept in fits and starts, so I wasn't surprised when I woke up to a darkened bedroom. I'd probably only been out for three or four hours.

What was shocking?

I was in bed with my bodyguard.

And I hated sharing a bed with anyone—especially the guy who had ruined my libido for anyone else.

To top it all off, I wasn't just lying beside him, but I was wrapped around his body, holding on to him like he was one of my prized guitars. I was a possessive motherfucker when it came to the rare things I loved.

Not that I loved Dawson.

That would be reckless on a level I'd yet to achieve.

Lifting my head off his chest, I stared up at his face, and memories of the night before began to flicker in my mind.

I remembered the club. And drinking a lot of tequila and champagne, and fuck, I reeked of both. I'd been dancing with a few guys, and then Dawson had walked off. I'd tried following him, but Lennie stopped me. Then, I headed back to the hotel with the cute bartender, but I ended up alone. Knocking on Dawson's door, we had another argument. He pinned me to the wall and, fuck, I liked that memory a lot, as evidenced by my now fully erect cock.

Then I admitted to Dawson that he was fucking with my head. Did I tell him he was the only one I wanted?

Shit. *Way to make things awkward, Iain.*

I should roll away, get up, and go back to my room. Forget last night ever happened.

But I didn't.

Because a part of me deep inside that had been cold for so long was now a fucking inferno.

And no one could be more shocked than me.

Like my band brothers, I liked to fuck and hit the road, so to speak.

Well, Brodie used to. Now, he was magnetized to Van.

But me? I didn't enjoy sleepovers.

I'd had enough of that early on in our career when the guys and I had to share crowded buses and shitty motels.

Now, I liked my space. I was a restless sleeper anyway.

So why, then, didn't I get up? Walk away.

Why did I want to lie here and stay? With Dawson?

"Stop angsting and go back to sleep."

The sudden interruption of Dawson's deep voice had goosebumps popping up all over my skin.

Normally, him telling me what to do would result in me telling him to fuck off, or some variation, and then doing the opposite.

So why did I get a primal thrill when he did it here and now?

Being in his bed made me realize there might be some orders I wouldn't mind taking. Preferably when the two of us were naked.

I placed my head back on his chest and listened to the soothing sound of his steady breathing, matching my own.

Since I was used to being independent, it was strange for me to take comfort in anyone else.

I closed my eyes again, and the next time I opened them, it was bright in the room.

But I was alone.

Well, not quite. I pushed the heavy curtain of my hair out of my face and looked around, spotting Dawson sitting on the nearby couch, his phone plastered to his ear. In his usual black jeans and T-shirt, his red hair wet, he was barking orders into the phone.

"Did you run that security check? Make it a priority. They're not getting any backstage passes until they pass the screening, and they keep texting me."

Pulling the sheet up around me, I inhaled Dawson's spicy scent, and fucking hell, my morning wood was so hard, it was damn near painful.

I sat up in bed and rubbed the sleep from my eyes, then grabbed Dawson's pillow and placed it over my lap, willing my cock to calm down.

"I gotta go," Dawson declared as our eyes met.

He placed his phone on the table in front of him.

Then he stood up and stalked over to me, his eyes running down my covered body in a gaze so heated I'm surprised the sheets didn't ignite.

"How are you feeling?" he asked as he sat on the edge of the bed near my feet. "There's water and meds on the table."

"I'm fine," I replied, my voice hoarse with sleep. "A bit dehydrated, but surprisingly, no headache."

Suddenly, I was nervous and awkward like I never was.

What do I say to the man I couldn't stop thinking about, the one who held me all night long but didn't make a move?

What in the ever-loving hell was going on?

"I ordered room service, and it should be arriving shortly. Same order as last time; I hope that's okay?"

I nodded and reached for the glass of water, sipping it slowly to ease the enormous lump in my throat.

"So, are we going to make stilted morning chit-chat or talk about what happened last night?" I finally asked.

Dawson chuckled and shook his head. "I figured I'd let you shower and eat first. You need something to wear off that alcohol."

"I didn't have that much. I was still able to talk. And walk. Without falling down, I might add. I can tolerate a lot more than most people."

"We'll agree to disagree. It smells like a distillery in here."

"That's because I'm pretty sure I dropped a bottle. Somewhere."

"You did, but luckily, it was almost empty, so there was hardly any spillage."

"That's too bad; I enjoy making a mess."

"Iain—"

God, I loved to tease him.

"Go shower." Dawson stood up. "I've left a pair of my sweats and a T-shirt in the bathroom. We can talk when breakfast arrives. I think we both need caffeine for this conversation."

"Ouch. You know, I could just slip back into my room, and we could pretend last night never happened."

Dawson stilled and looked down at me. "Is that what you want?"

I licked my lips and shook my head. "No."

Did I really just say that?

"Because it's not too late. And nothing happened."

"That's not entirely true."

I threw the sheet aside, swung my legs over the edge of the bed, and stood up, clad only in my tight black briefs.

Dawson stepped back, hands in his pockets, but not before I heard his sharp inhale.

There was no hiding my hard-on, and yeah, my body

liked being in Dawson's bed. More than liked it. Being anywhere near Dawson was starting to become addictive.

Was this a smart idea? Not in the fucking least.

Did I need to feel his body against mine again?

Oh yes. But more than last night. I wanted to touch and taste and discover every single thing about him. A heated kiss or a quick fuck just wouldn't do.

I walked around him, but not before trailing my hand over his bare forearm.

Like strumming that first note, one simple touch with Dawson was electric.

"Iain."

I fucking loved the way he moaned my name. I wanted to hear him say it again; I wanted him to scream my name so loud that everyone around us could hear.

But I kept walking, heading for the bathroom and shutting the door behind me.

I turned on the shower and stripped off my damp briefs. Fuck, we hadn't even kissed yet, and I was leaking pre-cum like crazy.

Stepping into the glass enclosure, I let the heat of the spray wash over me. As much as I wanted to jerk off, I didn't. I was gonna hold off as long as I could. Until I had Dawson's big hand wrapped around my dick.

Ignoring my raging boner and aching balls was no easy feat. Grabbing Dawson's shampoo, I lathered up and quickly rinsed off, then picked up his bar of soap and finished washing.

When I stepped out of the shower a few minutes later and reached for a towel, I heard voices on the other side of the door and the familiar rattle of the room service trolley.

An unwrapped toothbrush, mouthwash, and a new razor were on the counter. After gratefully brushing my teeth, I drank another glass of water and then slipped into Dawson's green sweatpants. With a "Proudly Philly" logo down the side, they were huge, but I tied the drawstring as tight as I could and rolled up the bottoms.

Then I lathered up my face and shaved off my scruff.

Finally, with a smooth jaw and minty breath, I pulled on the white T-shirt he'd left for me. It was also big, but I liked it. Everything smelled like Dawson. Never in my wildest dreams did I imagine that wearing another man's clothes would be something I'd ever want.

God, listen to me.

Whatever was going on here went far beyond my experience. So much so that I didn't know whether to laugh or freak out again.

Getting naked and getting off with the object of my desire was always my end goal, not this. Cuddling in bed, wearing each other's clothes, eating together, talking. Talking? I only had experience with the dirty kind, so what the fuck was I gonna say?

A loud knock on the bathroom door startled me out of my headspace.

"Stop freaking out and get your sexy ass moving. Your breakfast is getting cold."

I yanked on the sliding door to find Dawson standing there, with one hand on the door frame, an easy smile on his full lips. Unlike me, he hadn't shaved, and the red scruff suited him. He was like a hot mountain man, the bodyguard version.

"Sexy ass?"

Dawson gave me a blatant once-over. "Sexy, gorgeous, delectable. You and your ass. Now hurry up."

"What's with the flirting and then bossing me around in the same sentence?"

"Are you complaining?"

I struggled not to smile. "I don't know. It's hot when you do it, but if anyone else talked to me like that, in any other situation—"

"Aw, are you saying you have a crush on me?"

"If anyone has a crush, it's you," I countered. "You let me use you as a body pillow last night."

"But I didn't cop a feel."

"That's because I'd been drinking, and you're a gentleman."

"You know that word?"

I gently shoved his chest, but he was a solid wall, immovable. His smile faded as we stared at each other.

He bent forward, so close that I just knew he was going to kiss me. A rush of adrenaline coursed through my body, and all my senses heightened. My lips tingled, and he hadn't even touched me yet.

"You look hot as hell in my clothes," he whispered against my lips, teasing me.

"Too bad there was no underwear."

"Oops."

"Are you going to stand here and just breathe heavy on me or actually kiss me?"

He raised one eyebrow. "What did I say about giving orders?"

"I can't...remember."

Dawson smiled, and I held my breath.

"Food first," he announced and slapped my ass.

Then he walked away.

I stood there in shock until my temper unleashed. He'd flipped the table on me again.

"Did you seriously just turn down a kiss from me for food?"

"Your rockstar ego is showing. Sit. Eat. Kissing will come later."

"Kissing will not be happening at all! Ever!" I snapped.

Dawson laughed and poured two cups of coffee. He added brown sugar and cream to one, then held it out to me.

"And I can fix my own damned coffee," I growled as I walked over to grab it.

"I know. But I enjoy taking care of you."

My hand shook when he passed me the cup, and I nearly spilled the entire thing.

He enjoyed taking care of me?

My racing heart told me I didn't mind it so much, either. The fuck?

He stood up again and guided me over to the sofa. "Sit down and relax, sweetheart."

I flushed hot, sweat breaking out all over my body.

"That's it." I slammed the cup down on the table, the coffee sloshing over the rim. "What the hell, Dawson? I'm not your sweetheart."

"Not yet."

The confidence in his voice had me shivering. "Are you drunk?"

He shook his head and sipped his coffee, calm as can be. "Nope."

"Am I?"

"Not anymore."

CHAPTER 18
DAWSON

f Iain thought we were gonna fuck and forget, he was sadly mistaken. I was not putting my career in jeopardy for a casual screw.

I didn't know any more than he did about what the future held, but I sure as hell knew this wouldn't be a hookup.

And I admit I fucking loved teasing him and turning his game around. Gone was his cool rockstar persona. Instead, Iain was flushed and flustered, and he was so incredibly attractive like this. So much so that it had taken all of my willpower not to lean down and taste those sensuous lips of his.

I just knew that once I had my mouth on him, I was never going to stop.

That should've scared the shit out of me. This was Iain, who was allergic to anything that resembled a relationship (outside of his friendships). Why, then, did I ignore the warnings in my head and keep pushing forward?

Why did my heart keep pulling me toward him?

I didn't know the full answer yet, but here I was.

Once I stopped teasing him, he sat beside me on the sofa, and I passed him his plate.

We ate in silence for a few minutes until Iain pointed to the sweatpants I'd loaned him.

"You're from Philly? How did I not know that?"

"Born and raised. And you never asked. And I don't talk much about my personal life."

"I guess we have one thing in common," he replied in between bites of croissant. "How did you end up in Nashville?"

"I got a job referral from a celebrity client. Someone I used to train one on one."

Iain cocked his head. "Train?"

I nodded. "Martial arts, mainly judo and jiujitsu."

"Have you always been into that?"

"I started learning when I was twelve. I desperately needed an outlet. My dad left us, no contact, the year before, and Mom had to work two jobs to pay the bills." I paused and took a sip of my coffee. "Let's just say I had a lot of unresolved anger to deal with. Anyway, one of my teachers offered judo lessons at a nearby dojo. I didn't want to go at first because of the expense. But Mom insisted on it, along with therapy. She was right."

"I'm sorry about your dad."

"I made peace with it a long time ago." I shrugged. "But I suppose part of me will always wonder why. When Jaxon was born, my whole world shifted. He's my everything. And I couldn't understand, still don't, how my dad just left us like that. But I've done my work on it. I have a wonderful family, and I'm grateful."

Iain's big brown eyes surveyed me intently, and then he hesitantly reached over and touched my hand. I wanted so badly to reach over and kiss him, but I was also happy to finally have a real conversation with him. No yelling, no flirting. The real deal.

Then, as quickly as he'd touched me, he pulled his hand back.

"Anyway, my mom's been a rock," I continued. "My sisters and I turned out all right and it's all because of her."

"What did you do after high school?"

"I started working full time."

"You didn't go to college? I'm so glad I'm not the only one."

"Couldn't afford to. In my final year of high school, Mom was diagnosed with lymphoma. So, after graduating, I became the sole breadwinner for two years. By that time, I'd gone from being the dojo student to the teacher. Then I started taking on private students on the side."

"And the bodyguard work?"

"One of my clients was a singer who was relocating to Nashville. He'd just signed a big record deal and mentioned the security company assigned to him was looking for people. The pay was double what I was earning. I applied, did their three-month training program, and have been working in security ever since."

"Was that Bandit?"

"No, Stellar Recordings. Bandit bought them out four years ago. Thankfully, I retained my job."

"And you like what you do? Well, except for working with me."

His left knee began to bounce, and I placed my hand on it, giving him a reassuring squeeze.

"I do. Especially working with you. You might drive me crazy sometimes—"

Iain snorted.

"—okay, most times. But I wouldn't trade it for anything. Still, I won't be in this job forever."

"Are you thinking of leaving?"

I didn't miss the tentative way he asked.

"It's getting harder for me to leave Jaxon behind for weeks at a time. Before, when I had shared custody, it worked out. But now, I'm the only parent he has. And he needs me. I just haven't had time to figure out what the next step is."

"I'm sure you'll work it out," Iain replied, and suddenly stood up. "Well, thanks for breakfast, but I have to get dressed. We've got soundcheck at noon."

What just happened?

"Iain?"

He walked over to the connecting door and unlocked it. "What?"

"You didn't finish eating."

"I'm not hungry anymore." He paused as he reached for the door handle. "And thank you."

"For what?"

"It's a good thing we didn't kiss, yeah? I mean, that would've been a big mistake. Right?"

"Would it?"

Without saying another word, Iain left the room.

Iain

I stumbled into my bedroom and ripped off Dawson's clothes as fast as I could.

Dawson's admission that he might leave his post sent me into an unexpected tailspin. Suddenly, I didn't want to smell him or be surrounded by him. Things were moving in a direction I hadn't anticipated, and I didn't know what the fuck I was doing. Or what Dawson was doing with me.

You're frustrated. Easily fixed.

Well, not so easily. Dawson was the only guy I wanted, and yet, this attraction went far beyond sex. And I had no idea how to stop it.

A buzzing sound reminded me I'd left my phone on the nightstand. I picked it up and glanced at my messages, reading Brodie's first.

Brodie: How was the rest of your night?

Iain: I ended up alone. Sort of.

Brodie: What does that mean?

I didn't sleep with the bartender. I freaked out, and he left. I banged on Dawson's door, we argued, then we slept together. Well, there was no fucking involved. Just sleeping.

Brodie: Are you serious?

I told him I didn't want to be alone. It was just the alcohol talking. It's been a long month.

I noticed three dots appearing…then disappearing.

Brodie: Bullshit! The truth finally came out. You like him. Maybe more than like?

Fuck off. I'm frustrated. That's all. I don't like his teasing.

Brodie: ?

He flirts and bosses me around—telling me to get my sexy ass out of the bathroom, and then orders me to eat! Me! Then he almost kisses me, but doesn't, slaps my ass, and calls me sweetheart. The fuck is that? And still, no sex. My cock is confused, and my head hurts.

Brodie: Including Ro and Faise. Yo, bitches, intense shit is going down with Iain and Dawson.

NOTHING HAPPENED.

Faise: Slap my ass and call me sweetheart? LMFAO

Ronin: Haven't you been fucking each other all this time? Why is this news?

No, we haven't, and we won't.

Brodie: What about last night?

We slept in the same bed, but that was it.

Faise: Sounds like someone's got it bad for the smoking hot bodyguard

I had a moment of weakness, and it's over. BTW did you know Dawson is from Philly?

Faise: Total change of subject, but yeah, of course.

I just found out.

Brodie: ?

His sweatpants

Ronin: Explain

He loaned me some of his clothes.

Brodie: Did you enjoy wearing them?

Iain: No comment

Faise: His "Proudly Philly" sweatpants?

You've seen them?

Faise: Sure, sometimes we train together.

Doing what?

It better not be jiujitsu. I didn't want Dawson wrapping his body around anyone but me.

And that line of thought was scarier than this group thread.

Faise: Judo. He's a great teacher.

Ronin: Agreed

Wait, he trains both of you?

Brodie: Me too. Van likes to watch.

WTF? How did I not know this?

Faise: After you got assaulted in NOLA, I thought it would be a good idea to learn self-defense. He's awesome.

He's not grappling with you, is he?

Ronin: No, boo. There's no naked wrestling involved. That's just you.

There's nothing going on!

Brodie: Yeah, just flirting, sleeping together, and calling you sweetheart. Nothing, haha.

> He had the chance to kiss me, and he didn't take it.

> Faise: Maybe he's waiting for you to make the first move. I mean, given your reputation and his job, he's risking a lot.

> So, who's excited for the first show tonight?

> Brodie: Don't change the subject.

> See you guys in an hour

I placed my phone aside and shook off that whole alarming convo.

Shoving that discussion far, far away, I changed into my usual outfit of jeans, a T-shirt, and my leather jacket, but added a scarf and my sunglasses. Throwing on my favorite cowboy boots, I was ready to go. I grabbed my wallet and phone and texted Dawson to let him know I was set.

Then, I carefully folded Dawson's clothes.

I should've knocked on the door and handed them back to him.

Simple. Easy. Last night—and this morning—never happened.

But I didn't do that.

Instead, I left the clothes on my bed. Seeing them there gave me a sense of comfort I couldn't explain. But there it was.

And this time, no easy joke came to mind.

I couldn't even fool myself.

CHAPTER 19

IAIN

We always did our soundcheck five hours in advance of showtime.

Well, showtime for our band meant the VIP meet and greet before the actual performance, which started at seven. So that meant soundcheck was from twelve until two. Then we chilled out for a few hours, Brodie rested his voice, we got our clothes and makeup done, then it was VIP & promo, and then showtime.

And everything was on track for another successful concert run.

If only I could concentrate on what I was supposed to be doing—playing guitar—and not the person I wanted to do.

Dawson had been nothing but his usual stern self when he escorted me to the venue: no talking, no touching, no heated glances. The sunglasses helped, too. Both of us were wearing them, which was telling.

But I didn't like this back and forth. Dawson and I were both acting like one person in public and another behind closed doors.

And I was getting whiplash.

Yeah, I know. I couldn't make up my mind. I was off-kilter

when he teased me and stupidly hurt when he went back to his uber-professional mode. Not that I had any reason to feel that way.

There were more pressing problems than my sex life. Or lack of.

First, our manager had yet to show up. In the past, on concert days, Van was always the first one on scene, but Harlow was MIA.

"Anyone heard from our manager? That is if we still have one?" I asked as we stood on the stage.

Brodie shook his head as he stood before his mic, testing out his guitar.

I turned to Faise and Ronin.

"Nope," Ronin replied with an eye roll.

"Me neither," Faise added.

I turned to Regan and Dawson, who were standing in the wings, talking to Van.

"Regan, can you get hold of Harlow? None of us have seen or heard from him since yesterday."

"I'm on it," she replied, pulling out her phone.

"As far as I'm concerned, Harlow can stay away," Brodie muttered.

"I don't like him any more than you do, but his no-show is unsettling. I'd rather keep an eye on him, if you know what I mean."

I set aside my Konicki and picked up my Gibson. Testing out the opening riff of "Nine Gone Wrong," the sound was off. Once I'd played around with the tuning, I tried it again.

"Sounds good, almost there," Tommy called out, and I nodded in agreement.

I started again, this time with Brodie doing the vocals and me on backup. I leaned into the mic and sang the first chorus, but the feedback pinged loudly.

"Shit, that sounds awful. Ace?"

I looked over, but he was busy typing away on his phone.

"Yeah?" Ace looked up, his face flushed. "Sorry, I got side-lined. Hold on."

He put his phone in his back pocket and walked over to fiddle with the mic. Then I noticed that he'd cut his long hair by several inches, and it now barely touched his shoulders. It suited him. We often joked together about who could grow their hair the longest.

It appeared I was now winning.

"Damn feedback issue with these mics lately," Ace grumbled. "I'm gonna look into replacing them for the next round in May."

"What's with the haircut?" I asked.

"Just cleaning it up a bit. Don't worry, I ain't chopping it all off. Colm would not be happy if I did that."

Our sound engineer had hit it off with one of Brodie's PR dates back in October. Colm was a twenty-something model and actor, and no one had been more surprised than Ace when they sparked.

"Should I assume your haircut means Colm is headed here?"

Ace nodded, a huge grin on his face. "He's flying in tomorrow for a photoshoot. I haven't seen him in over five weeks."

"Will he be at the show?"

"I wish. His flight doesn't get in until nine."

"Come party with us afterward."

"Well," Ace flushed again. "Given that it's been over a month since we've seen each other—"

"I get the picture. Enjoy your reunion," I teased.

"Oh, we will."

Jesus, I was surrounded by ridiculous couples in love. And, of course, as soon as I had that thought, I looked up and met Dawson's intense stare. Like he could read my fucking mind, he gave me a slow smile that had my cock jerking.

Thank God for the cover of my guitar.

I shook my head and started playing the riff to "Wanton Destruction". Dawson started to laugh.

That song was us, all right.

Then Regan tapped him on the shoulder, and he looked away.

Breaking out of my trance, I turned back to the guys.

They were all staring at me with stupid grins on their faces.

"Get back to work!" I yelled out.

After a couple more rounds of adjustments on the rest of our equipment, we tested out "Filthy Pain."

Everything sounded great, and we were ready for a break. We had lunch together, and then Brodie and Van headed to one of the dressing rooms. Ronin, Faise, and I chatted with the stage crew.

Finally, Harlow showed up. No explanation was given, and none of us cared enough to ask.

Harlow accompanied us to Brodie's room, where the hair and styling crew waited.

"You've got five interviews post-show," Harlow explained. "I've pre-screened the questions and will be on site. Let's try and give them appealing sound-bites and hints at the upcoming album and tour. Van, I'd like you to join us. The press loves your relationship with Brodie, so let's play up that angle. Give them more of what they want. Insights into your life with one of the hottest singers on the planet."

"One of?" Brodie replied, and the rest of us chuckled.

There was a knock at the door, and Bibi stuck her head around. "Holls, do you have a moment?"

"Sure," I replied. "I'll be right back."

I followed her out into the hallway.

"What's up?"

"That came for you." She pointed to a box on the floor just outside the second dressing room. In it sat a large bouquet of white roses with red tips.

"It's probably from the label or something. Or some fan. You can put them anywhere."

Suddenly, Dawson was walking down the hallway and nodded at Bibi.

"Regan told me Holls received a gift. Did you see the delivery person?"

Bibi shook her head. "The flowers were there when I arrived. I just spotted Iain's name on the envelope."

Dawson crouched down to grab the small card clipped to the flowers.

Dawson opened the card. "Fuck."

"What? Who is it from?" Bibi looked at me.

He stood up and showed us the card.

Iain,

This is a reminder that I'm thinking of you, no matter how far apart we are.

Don't keep ignoring my messages. I love you, but my patience is running out.

Dawson tapped on his earpiece. "Regan, please head downstairs to the dressing room. We have a problem."

"What's this about?" Bibi asked.

"Keep this between us," Dawson warned. "But someone's been sending Iain disturbing text messages over the past month. Ever since the break-in."

Bibi's face fell. "A stalker?"

"It sounds like it, but there's been no direct threat so far."

"If only I'd been here earlier," Bibi started. "Maybe I would've—"

"Chances are the delivery person has no idea what this is about. They're just the messenger."

Regan hurried down the hallway, and when she stepped up beside us, she glanced down at the flowers. Dawson held up the note. She read it and sighed.

"Okay, I'm going to find out where this delivery came

from. Let's see if we can trace the payment. Did anyone sign for the arrival?"

"I told Dawson the flowers were here when I arrived," Bibi explained.

"Daws, take pictures of this and then dispose of the flowers. I'll get all our team on stage for a briefing. I'm calling Greg to give him an update, and we go from there."

"What about the rest of the band?" Dawson asked. "I think we should inform them about what's going on."

"Brodie knows," I blurted out, finally finding my voice. "I mean, about the messages."

Regan nodded. "The band, Van, Harlow, and Ace. That's all for now. Bibi, why don't you join me for the briefing."

"Of course," Bibi replied and followed Regan down the hallway.

Leaving me alone with Dawson.

He pulled out his phone and took pictures of the flowers and the card, then pocketed the note.

"You okay?" he asked me.

"Would you be?" I snapped.

"No."

Dawson threw the flowers in the trash, then steered me into the second dressing room and closed the door.

"We're going to do everything we can to figure out who's behind this. I promise."

I nodded, my body shaking, my mouth suddenly unable to move.

"I'm not going to let anyone hurt you, Iain."

"Can I just go back to getting ready for the show? I need my routine, now more than ever."

"As long as you promise not to sneak off."

"There's no one for me to sneak off with," I scoffed and began to pace. "I can't smoke a joint because pot's illegal here. The only thing I can do is drink or smoke a cigarette. Oddly enough, I'm not in the mood for booze, and I forgot my smokes back at the hotel—"

"Iain—"

"And now, thanks to that fucking asshole stalker, I'll have you guys on my ass every second. It's only going to get worse from here."

"Sweetheart."

"Don't call me that!" I hissed and placed my hand over his mouth. "Are you crazy? What if someone hears you?"

He pulled my hand away. "Like who?"

"Like your boss. Bibi. Harlow—"

"Iain—"

"What if this thing escalates, and I have to go into hiding? What then? I think I'm gonna—"

"Iain!" Dawson shouted.

"What?"

Dawson backed me up against the door and cupped my face in his hands.

Fuck, why did nothing feel as good as his touch?

"Look at me," he demanded. "Look at me."

I finally did as he asked and watched his eyes darken.

"Breathe, okay?" he murmured softly. "We'll deal with this situation one step at a time. Just breathe."

"Breathing's overrated."

Then I did what I'd been longing to do for what seemed like forever and closed the distance between us, reaching up and taking his lips in a fierce kiss that couldn't wait any longer.

And I forgot everything but the feel of his mouth and the heat of our bodies as we strained closer to each other.

There was no tentative exploration.

His hot tongue tangled with mine, aggressive, full-on fucking my mouth, and I could not get enough.

He delved his hands into my hair, tugging gently, angling my head for a deeper kiss. I slid my hands around his hips and back over his round ass, and he groaned so loudly I swear the door behind us rattled.

God, the way his beard brushed over my sensitive lips, it was the most delicious burn, and I didn't care how red and swollen my lips would get; I needed more.

More kisses, more Dawson.

He gently bit my lower lip and soothed it with a teasing flick of his tongue. I was punch-drunk, lust flooding my veins, the need for him so intense that my legs nearly went out from under me.

Until someone knocked on the door, interrupting the best goddamn kiss of my life.

"Dawson, you in there? Where's Iain?"

Fucking Harlow.

"Shit," Dawson panted as he reluctantly pulled back and cleared his throat. "Yeah, we're in here. We'll be back in Brodie's room in five minutes, okay?"

Harlow didn't reply, and I didn't give a shit.

All I could do was stare at Dawson. I wasn't the only one with red lips and flushed skin. Just when I thought he couldn't get any sexier.

"Jesus Christ, I need to calm myself down," Dawson growled and adjusted himself. "Your lips are lethal, sweetheart."

A shiver ran through my body when he called me sweetheart. The way he said it, so low and full of desire. I liked it far too much to admit.

With my back against the door, I was sweating and panting for air, like I did at the end of a show.

Dawson ran a hand down over his cropped beard and licked his lips. "Don't run away from me. We're gonna finish what we started."

"After the show," I promised.

"God, four hours seems like forever."

Oh, fuck yeah. If one frantic kiss rattled me like that, I

could just imagine what was gonna happen when we finally got naked. We'd probably set that hotel room on fire.

And that line of thinking was not helping to deflate my hard-on in the least.

"Let's go talk to the guys," Dawson whispered.

I looked at his fucked out expression and imagined I looked the same.

"I need another minute."

We were never going to hear the end of it.

CHAPTER 20

DAWSON

A half-hour after that incredible kiss, my lips were still burning.

My lips, my face, my entire body, fuck, even my mind was on fire.

I don't know how I'd managed to speak afterward, but Iain and I eventually calmed ourselves down and headed back to Brodie's dressing room, where we told the guys what was going on.

Not with me and Iain, but with his stalker.

One bit of shocking news at a time, please.

My protective instincts launched into overdrive as I became aware of Iain in a way I'd never imagined. I wanted to wrap him up in my arms and reassure him that everything would be okay. But reassurance—and more—would have to wait.

"I want extra security for Iain at all times. And I want a PI to look into this," Brodie announced as he sat beside Iain. "I don't give a fuck if Greg doesn't agree, we'll pay for it."

"Hell, yes." Ronin nodded, and Faise agreed.

"Security is well in hand," I replied and then flushed

when I thought about where my hands were recently. "And Regan's already hired an investigator. We will do everything we can to figure out who's behind this. We think it's someone back home, so the threat to him here is minimal."

"We need to make a statement," Harlow interjected, his phone buzzing repeatedly.

He'd been busy typing away the whole time I was talking and finally looked up.

"What do you mean?" Iain asked.

"This kind of thing will send the fans into a frenzy. It's gold."

"Are you suggesting Iain use this stalker as a publicity tool?" Van asked.

"Yes. I'll talk to Zoe and give her a heads-up. The more spotlight we put on the stalker, the more likely it is that he, she, or they, will be revealed."

"Or you'll piss off the stalker, and the situation will escalate," I added. "After all, attention motivates that type of obsessive behavior."

Harlow rolled his eyes. "The fans will rally around the band in their time of need. It's a great story."

"It's my life!" Iain snapped. "How would you feel?"

Harlow started chuckling. "Stop being oversensitive, Holls. Nothing's gonna happen to you. It's probably just some weirdo who will move on to someone else once he gets bored. But we might as well take the situation and turn it in our favor. Greg just texted me, and he agrees."

"Get out," Brodie said quietly.

It was close to showtime, after all, so he didn't raise his voice, but the angry glint in his eyes could not be denied.

Harlow sighed and stood up. "I'll go. But it's already a done deal. I'll prepare a statement for the interviews after the concert."

Then Harlow sauntered out of the room.

Van looked at me with worried eyes, and I understood his concerns. "I'll talk to Regan. I don't know how much sway she'll have over Greg, but it's worth a shot."

"Do you really think making this news public might fuel the stalker?" Van asked.

"I don't have a ton of experience with this, but yeah, I do. If Iain publicly acknowledges what's going on, the stalker might see that as a sign that their 'relationship' is real."

"Can we stop talking about this for a bit?" Iain asked as he looked at me. "I want to finish getting ready."

I stepped outside the dressing room and waved the stylists and Lennie back inside.

The guys were subdued until Iain finally asked Van to get them a round of drinks. I couldn't blame them one bit. It had been another stress-filled meeting with Harlow, and I wasn't sure how much more the boys could take. I'd been witness to several music managers, and Harlow was pretty standard, but so unlike their experience with Van.

They all knew the media game by now, but that didn't make it any easier. If anything, four years ago, they were barely a blip on people's radars, and now, every time they blinked, someone was posting about it on social media. The tabloids were going to latch on to this stalker story and milk it for all it was worth, which left me with a very bad feeling.

All my focus was on figuring out who was trying to get to Iain.

I worked on my laptop while the guys had their makeup and hair done. Regan and I messaged back and forth with the PI back in Nashville. Regan's contact in the Nashville PD had agreed to look at the phone messages and unofficially start a file. That was the best they could do. It wasn't much, but it was a start.

Regan was busy tracking down the flower delivery while I made a list of anyone who had met with Iain back in Nashville during the past six months. I went through security log sheets and sent requests for as much video footage as I could —from the rehearsal studio to Bandit's head office to the clubs the guys frequented. The studio or office wasn't a problem, but the clubs, well, it was unlikely they would cooperate without police warrants.

Bibi returned to the dressing room and offered everyone more drinks and snacks. I took a bottle of water and a bag of pretzels and munched on them while watching Iain getting his hair done. The stylist, a twenty-something guy named Payton, was gushing over Iain's hair. Just remembering how those soft strands felt in my hands had my body heating and my cock twitching. I honestly could not blame Payton in the least.

Until Payton's flirting with Iain kept going, and my jealousy began to mount. I kept shoving in pretzels, determined to keep my possessive streak under wraps. I'd probably break a tooth from all the grinding going on, never mind the crunchy snacks.

"So, Holls, who gave you the beard burn?" Brodie asked.

I choked on a pretzel and began to cough violently.

"You all right there, Daws?" Ronin asked with a shit-eating grin on his face.

Reaching for my water, I took a long sip and managed to clear my throat. "Fine. Good."

"No comment," Iain replied.

"Come on, it's not like you to kiss and *not* tell." Faise chuckled.

"I'll make you a deal," Iain returned. "You and Ronin finally admit that you've been in love with each other since high school, and I'll tell you about the beard burn."

"Ooh," Brodie clapped his hands together. "This is getting good."

"Fuck off," Faise grumbled.

Ronin's face was bright red. "As if."

I felt Lennie's stare on me, but I kept typing away. Best to ignore the shitstorm that would soon pass.

"It was me," Payton announced.

I whipped my head up so fast that my neck cracked.

"But you don't have a beard," Ronin countered.

"Baby, these lips are aggressive."

"Really?" Ronin gave Payton the once over. "What are you doing after the show?"

"You, if you're lucky." The stylist winked at the mirror, and Ronin fanned himself. "Or maybe you back there, the handsome Viking with the red hair?"

I felt my face heat, and I realized I was staring—at Iain, not Payton—and shook my head. "Thanks, but I'm on the clock."

"I've never let that stop me," Payton quipped as he sprayed Iain's hair. "Some of the best sex of my life has happened on the job. Or, in the chair to be specific."

"Storytime, Payton, tell us more," Ronin encouraged.

"You couldn't handle it, baby."

"Please, we're rockstars. We've seen and done it all. And that's not just a saying," Brodie bragged. "Like there was this one time, in Spain, at this house party, a group of—"

Van groaned and got up. "And I'm going upstairs now."

"Honey, come on, no one compares to you," Brodie purred.

"I love you too, but unless you want me to go caveman and haul you out of here over my shoulder, it's best I don't hear any of your stories."

"You lucky bitch." Payton pointed his hairbrush at Brodie.

"I am." Brodie waggled his eyebrows at Van.

Van pulled Brodie up off his chair and into his arms, giving him a thorough kiss.

"At least someone is getting their pre-show rocks off," Iain muttered.

For once, I understood Iain's frustration.

Van gave Brodie one last kiss. "No more talking; rest your voice."

"Yes, *Daddy*," Payton piped up.

"And with that, I'm leaving," Van replied, his face flushed as he headed for the door.

Payton finished spraying Iain's hair, "You're done, beautiful. Next."

He motioned for Faise to sit down for his turn.

Payton took a step back, and his heel caught on the cord of the blow dryer. Thankfully, Lennie was nearby and grabbed hold of Payton before he tumbled to the ground.

"Thank you," Payton gasped as Lennie righted him again.

"No problem."

Payton stared up at him. "I need my arms back so I can work."

"Oh, sorry," Lennie replied, and dropped Payton's arms, stepping back.

"No complaints here." Payton smiled at him. "I didn't catch your name."

"Len, it's nice to meet you."

"You too. If you ever need my services," Payton pulled out a business card and handed it over.

"Thanks, but I just clip it myself."

Payton gasped and pulled his card back. "Well, we can't be friends then."

Lennie's confused expression at Payton's joke made me want to laugh. Len was great at picking out a threat in a crowd, but he couldn't read a flirtation at all.

"Uh," Lennie glanced around, looking panicked.

"I'm teasing you," Payton replied and put the card in Lennie's jacket pocket.

"Hey, I thought you were flirting with *me*," Ronin called out.

"You're sweet, honey, but not my type." Payton winked. "Besides, I don't think Faisel would like that."

Ronin got up. "Now wait—"

"We're not together," Faise scoffed.

Payton pointed to Faise and then back at Ronin. "Really? I thought for sure that you two—"

"No!" Faise and Ronin yelled out at the same time.

CHAPTER 21

IAIN

stood in my spot on the stage and waited for the countdown.

Unlike the rest of the guys, who looked relaxed and ready to rock, I was a seething mass of nerves. Was it the fact I had some weirdo sending me creepy messages, or that Dawson and I all but outed ourselves to the band? Probably both. I mean, let's face it, the guys already knew what was up with Daws and me, but knowing and seeing it happen in real-time were two different things.

But my personal life would have to wait. The show, as you know, must go on.

I checked my earpiece one last time and nodded at Brodie.

To distract myself, I replayed that kiss with Dawson in the dressing room. I was still shaken up, and fuck me, for a guy who'd done a shitload of kissing, that was saying something.

I glanced over and spotted Dawson in his usual place. But the look he was giving me was not about protection. It was pure sex. Instead of yelling at him, I shook my head. He mouthed, "What?" all innocent-like, and I rolled my eyes. Like he didn't know he was eye-fucking me. But the last thing I wanted was for his boss to take notice. Then Dawson would be gone, and just the thought of losing him made me break out in a cold sweat.

And we hadn't started performing yet.

The lights dimmed, and I turned my attention to the audience as the curtains raised.

I strummed the first chords of "Never Look Back" and felt the surge of energy from the crowd as they screamed our names and started singing the opening verse.

Man, I fucking needed this tonight. That was the power of music and live performance. It fed something inside of me and brought me out of my head.

I lived purely in the moment, and there was nothing better.

I sauntered up and down the stage, calling out to the crowd while Brodie sang about leaving home and forging a new path. As usual, our frontman was a fan favorite, and I could hear his name chanted over the din.

Without question, and knowing that Dawson was watching me, I put a little extra oomph in my strut tonight.

Thirty minutes in and four songs later, my fingertips burned, and sweat poured down my body.

"Thank you! Merci!" Brodie yelled out as we paused between songs. He leaned on the mic stand and waved at the crowd. "It's so great to be back in Paris. We love this beautiful, magical city."

Fans screamed so loud in response that it startled even Brodie.

"Whoa, we have rabid fans tonight," he stated with a smirk. "Just the kind I like. So how about a big round of applause, please, for my band brothers, Holloway, Faise, and Ronin!"

We all took a bow and waved.

"Now, besides me, who here wants to hear Holls sing tonight?"

The fan screamed and clapped, and I shook my head.

"Come on over, Holls! I promise I won't bite," Brodie teased me. "Not too hard."

I stalked up to him and leaned into the mic. "I thought you didn't like to share."

"My husband, no fucking way. But a song? Anytime."

Hoots and hollers rang out around us.

"Let's sing 'Broken Doors,'" I suggested.

It was one of our slower songs. Not quite a ballad, but like Sideline, a song that Van had written for Brodie.

Faise started in on the drumbeat first, and the rest of us joined in.

I wasn't the best vocalist, but I had my moments. As long as there were no high notes to hit, I was good.

Brodie and I had been taking the stage together for years, but this incredible feeling of creating music together never got old. No matter how many concerts or tours, every time felt like the first.

He led on the vocals, and I harmonized, back and forth, until we reached the chorus, and Ronin and Faise joined in. When our combined voices hit just right, it gave me goosebumps.

At the end of the song, Brodie playfully kissed me on the cheek.

"Let's hear it for my friend, Iain Holloway!" Brodie shouted and squeezed my shoulder. "And now, folks, back to our regularly scheduled programming. I think it's time we all enjoyed a little… 'Filthy Pain!'"

I laid into the opening riff of our most popular song and walked back to my spot on the stage. Halfway through the number, Brodie threw his shirt out to the audience and kneeled in front of them in nothing but his black leather kilt.

Fans at the front of the stage were losing their fucking minds, screaming and reaching out to touch him. Brodie threw his head back and moaned out those filthy lyrics like he was having sex right there on stage. The atmosphere intensified, and I felt the heavy pulse of the room—the smell of sweat, the heat of the lights, the writhing mass of bodies. Like a mass orgy, the fans went fucking nuts and threw shirts, underwear, you name it, on stage.

Brodie pumped his hips and leaned back, his dark curls now wet and plastered to his face, sweat rolling down his chest and his tattooed arms.

I glanced over at Ronin, who'd joined in and was standing in just his jeans and bare feet, his long, dark hair swaying around his face as he closed his eyes.

Not to be outdone, when the song ended, I threw off my T-shirt and ran up to the edge of the stage to launch it into the audience. Then I walked along the edge, touching hands and feeding off the excitement of the crowd.

By the time we reached our break, we were all out of breath and took a quick bow before the curtains closed.

Brodie finally got back up on his feet and shook his head, sweat droplets flying everywhere. "Fuck, you guys are on fire tonight!"

As we walked off stage, I spotted Dawson with his arms crossed, his gaze giving me a possessive once over that had all the hair on my body standing on end.

"Ooh, someone's ready to fuck," Brodie whispered in my ear, one sweaty arm slung around my slick shoulder.

"Shut it, Dee," I hissed. "If Regan overhears—"

"Sorry, Holls. I don't want to deprive you of the dick."

"Hey, he's not just that," I snapped back.

Brodie grinned at me. Clever motherfucker.

I watched as Brodie walked off and into the arms of his husband.

I grabbed a towel from Tommy and went to stand beside Dawson.

"So, what's the verdict on the show so far?" I asked him.

I was still out of breath. From performing or from being in Dawson's presence, I didn't know.

"It's one of the best I've ever seen. You're fucking amazing."

I waved his compliment off. "Brodie's the real star."

"Don't downplay your talent. You have a gift, and everyone can see and hear it. Fuck, the way you pull those sounds of that guitar, it is something else, sweetheart."

"Daws," I warned and looked around. Thankfully, no one seemed to be paying us any particular attention. "Stop with the, you know—"

"Sweetheart?"

"Jesus Christ," I grumbled, wiping my face to hide my reaction.

Secretly, I lit up inside when he said it. Which was so fucked up. Cutesy nicknames or endearments usually made me gag. Hell, listening to Van and Brodie was bad enough.

"See, they'll think I'm calling you that to tick you off," Dawson reasoned. "Bickering is how we roll. Stop worrying."

"Stop worrying?" I turned to face him. "You're standing here eye-fucking me the whole time I'm on stage. Don't tell me no one's going to notice *that*."

"It's not just when you're on stage," he smiled down at me, his green eyes riveted to mine.

"Stop it."

I reached for a bottle of water and gulped half of it down.

"You make drinking water look sexy," Dawson whispered. "I am in so much fucking trouble."

I wiped off my neck and chest, then threw the towel aside. "You? I'm the one in danger of popping a boner before I head back on stage."

"If we had time and privacy, I'd take care of that for you. I know how much you enjoy getting head."

I squeezed the bottle so tight that the rest of the liquid erupted like a geyser all over my hand and the floor at my feet.

"Shit."

Dawson chuckled, grabbed another towel from the nearby table, and gently wiped my hand and then the floor.

"I'm gonna go stand with the guys, where it's safer. For both of us," I added.

Dawson nodded and looked around, assuming his usual stern pose. But I didn't miss the way his lips curled like he was trying not to smile.

Dawson did what no one else ever could.

He rattled me so badly that I was now fleeing to the other end of the wings.

CHAPTER 22

DAWSON

After two more sets, the guys took their final bow and headed off stage to rehydrate, get touched up, and get dressed for their interviews.

Harlow, of course, was on Iain right away. And I heard the whole conversation, but the longer Harlow talked, the paler Iain got, and the more my temper sparked.

I pulled Regan aside. "Harlow is going ahead with this plan to make Iain comment about the stalker. Did he clear that with you?"

Regan nodded. "It comes from Greg. Unfortunately, it's out of my hands. But trust me, I don't like this idea any more than you do. This is going to send the media, and likely the stalker, into a frenzy."

"Any word on the source of the flowers?" I asked.

"Tommy recalled seeing a van with a delivery logo in the alleyway around noon. We traced it to an online floral service, so the order could have come from anywhere in the world. But they can't tell me who placed it."

"But maybe we can find someone who can, you know, dig around and find out?"

"I know of a couple of people who could do some snooping."

"And they would be?"

"The less you know, the better." Regan smiled. "So, what's the plan for tonight?"

My face flushed. "Ah, the guys have been invited to Xtra. It's a gay club not far from the hotel. Quinn checked it out earlier. But we'll see how the interviews go. Iain may prefer to head back to the hotel afterward."

I was really hoping that was the plan. I just wanted to be alone with him again, to finish what that kiss started. But Iain loved being social, so maybe my dick would have to wait. I realized that where Iain was concerned, I was okay with it. He was worth waiting for.

"You guys haven't been as volatile as you usually are," Regan commented.

I shifted from one foot to the other, then realized I was fidgeting.

"He still doesn't like being under constant guard, but Iain also knows I only have his best interests at heart."

Regan nodded and stared at me. "You do what you have to keep him secure."

I nodded. "I'll tie him to my bed if I have to."

Regan raised one eyebrow, and I felt a blush creep up my cheeks.

"You know what I mean," I added.

"Is there anything you need to tell me?"

"No, boss."

She sighed and shook her head. "It happens a lot, you know."

"What?"

"Bodyguards falling for their clients. The whole protector thing creates a certain bond. But it rarely works out. And we both know why."

Iain was a world-famous rockstar, and I was, well, me—a

single, ordinary, thirty-one-year-old dad with bills and a sad track record when it came to relationships.

Regan's comment put a damper on my earlier confidence. All I could think about was making Iain mine, but what would happen tomorrow morning? Would he brush me off the way he did every other lover?

I knew that for me, my heart was already involved, and one night would never be enough, but Iain… Iain was Iain. He didn't trust deeper emotions, and that right there should've been enough to send me running.

Then I looked over at Iain sitting there, and I noticed his hands were shaking. Harlow just kept on talking, either oblivious or callous to Iain's mood. Either way, it pissed me off.

I nodded at Regan. "Excuse me."

I walked over to stand beside Iain, placing my hand on his shoulder. "Is everything okay?"

"No," Iain replied at the same time Harlow said "yes."

"What we're discussing is none of your business," Harlow snapped at me.

"I beg to differ since this stalker situation and anything that concerns Iain's safety is my business," I replied as I got up in Harlow's face. "Now, either you give him some time to relax before you send him out to those vultures you call reporters, or I'm going to have to ask you to leave."

"Don't threaten me. One phone call to Greg, and you're done."

"That's it!" Iain yelled and stood up. "Get out, Harlow. I mean it, or I will walk out of this venue and fuck ALL the interviews!"

Regan stepped up to us. "What the hell is going on here?"

"Get your guard dog in line," Harlow sneered and pointed at me. "He's butting in where he doesn't belong."

"And you're insulting a member of Bandit's team by refer-ring to him that way, showing disrespect for his position and yours." Regan motioned for Quinn. "Have a safe trip back to the hotel."

Regan turned to walk away, and Harlow muttered, "Uptight bitch."

She turned slowly on her heel and pinned him with a deadly glare. "I'm an expert at hand-to-hand combat, so be very careful with what you say about me."

Then she pivoted again and walked away.

Quinn looked at Harlow. "Let's go."

"Fuck off," Harlow bit out and stomped off, Quinn and Valen on his heels.

The rest of the guys crowded around us, including Van.

"I can't believe he spoke that way to Regan and Dawson. What a dickhead," Iain snapped. "Someone needs to tell Greg about this."

"Don't worry," Brodie replied. "It'll happen."

"Van, do you think you could look over this statement Harlow gave to Iain?" I asked. "I know it's not your job anymore, but given the circumstances—"

"Of course, happy to," he replied, and Iain handed over the notes. "Give me a few minutes to read this over."

A short while later, the guys were ready for their interviews.

The reporters had already gone through a pre-screening check, but I verified their identities again and then passed them off to Valen to keep an eye on. I headed back into the dressing room with Lennie to watch over the guys while Van ushered the reporters into the room, one at a time.

There were the usual questions about the concert, what they were doing in the city in their free time, and who they were dating. I still didn't know how they kept smiling after answering the same damn questions over and over for two hours, not to mention the cheesy jokes and several blatant come-ons. Van had to intervene a few times to cut off questions or to redirect.

I watched Iain's body tense as time wore on.

The last interviewer shuffled in, a journalist from Entertainment eNews. Once he was settled in, he wasted no time getting to the story.

"Holloway, you just released a statement about a stalker harassing you, and the case is being investigated as we speak. What can you tell us about this situation and how are you coping?"

Iain leaned forward. "I've received some disturbing messages, but that's all I can say. My security team is investigating."

"And how will this affect your current tour?"

"I have full confidence that our current shows will continue without incident."

"Have the police gotten involved?"

"No comment."

"Could it be a former boyfriend?"

"I haven't had any, so the answer to that is no."

"But what about—"

Van stepped in. "No. That's it. Thank you for your time."

The reporter sighed and signaled for his cameraman to stop taping. "Really, Van? That's all you're gonna give me? Come on."

"You're lucky we said anything," Van replied.

"Why are you here directing this show anyway? Didn't you quit your role as Wayward Lane's manager months ago?"

"Off the record, the band's rep is currently detained. I simply filled in temporarily."

The reporter rolled his eyes. "Well, thanks for the bare minimum."

"You and every other reporter who walks in here."

The journalist nodded and packed up their equipment.

"Thank fuck, that's over," Iain sighed when the reporter was finally gone.

"Everyone did great," Van assured them. "Especially you, Holls. I'm sorry you had to talk about it at all, but—"

"I know and thanks for your help, Van. I hope Greg doesn't come down on you too hard."

"If he so much as tries to breathe on my husband, I'm not talking to another journalist for the remainder of our contract," Brodie stated.

And I believed him.

"Time to hit the road," Ronin announced and clapped his hands together. "Forget the interviews, forget this stupid ass stalker, and forget Harlow, our stupid ass manager. Let's go party and fuck!"

"Hell, yes!" Faise agreed and gave Iain a side hug.

"Me and Van are gonna head back to the hotel. My throat is kinda sore, so—"

"Stop giving your husband so many blow jobs," Ronin quipped.

Brodie gave his friend two choice fingers in response.

"Iain?" Faise asked.

"I'm heading back to the hotel too."

"What?" Ronin exclaimed. "Come on, Holls, you love going out."

"Tomorrow night, okay? I'm kinda drained after those interviews."

Iain looked exhausted, something that was rarely said. The man was usually a ball of energy.

"Lennie, send Geoff, Petyr, Quinn, and Valen to accompany Ronin and Faise," I ordered. "You, me, and Will can head back with Iain, Brodie, and Van."

"You got it."

We gathered up the guys' personal stuff from Bibi and split into two groups.

Iain was uncharacteristically quiet on the way back to the hotel.

"You okay?" I asked.

"No. I looked at my socials, and fans are freaking out about this stalker situation."

"I told you; don't—"

"And I need to know what people are saying," Iain snapped. "I'm not going to bury my head in the sand! That's not my way."

"I'm not telling you to do that, just until the news settles."

Iain scoffed. "It never settles, Daws. There's always something else."

As soon as we entered his room and I'd checked everything over, he headed for his bathroom without saying another word.

I guess that was my cue to leave him be.

Opening the connecting door, I sauntered into my room and placed my phone on the charger.

I needed a long, hot shower and a good night's sleep. Not what I wanted, but what I needed. And Iain, too, even though I'd rather have him sleep in here with me.

I headed to the bathroom and started the shower, stripping off my clothes.

And fuck, just thinking about Iain close to me got my dick so hard so fast, I was lightheaded. I stepped into the shower and braced myself with one hand on the wet tiles and the other wrapped around my dick.

I'd gotten off several strokes when I heard a door slam. It sounded like it was coming from my room.

Talk about timing.

CHAPTER 23

DAWSON

S tepping out of the shower, I grabbed a towel and wrapped it around my hips.

I walked cautiously out of the bathroom to find a wet, naked Iain standing beside my bed, his back to me. All that smooth golden skin was just inches away. And the sight of his long, taut body, especially his biteable ass, had my knees fucking weak.

"Iain?"

Then he turned around, and my gaze didn't know where to look first.

He was so beautiful, slim but strong, with defined pecs and pale pink nipples. My eyes fixed on the sexy trail of blond hair that started on his chest and abs and followed down to his cock. His dick was just as pretty as I remembered.

Except this time, it was all for me.

Mine.

I glanced up at his face, at those big brown eyes, and I was a goner.

"You're so fucking beautiful, Iain," I admitted.

He took a long look at my body, the towel doing nothing

to hide my arousal.

"Jesus, Dawson," Iain moaned and stepped up to me, undoing the towel. It fell to the floor, and my heart took off running when he gave me a thorough once-over. He looked up into my eyes and slid his arms around my neck. "You've got that the wrong way around."

I bent down and devoured his mouth, taking his lips in a mauling kiss.

Everything that had been building between us for days, weeks, fuck, maybe even years, finally erupted.

Our kisses were frantic, desperate, as I pulled him in tight to my body. I plunged my hands into his hair and tugged, angling Iain's mouth. He swirled his tongue around mine, and every nerve ending in my body ignited.

If this was my reaction to one kiss, I could only imagine how it would feel the moment we finally came together.

I managed to tear my mouth away for a moment. "Are you sure you want this? Because I'm not just gonna fuck and run. One night isn't going to be nearly enough with you. And I can be kind of intense."

"When are you not?" He smiled at me, his lips wet and swollen from my kisses.

My heart took off running again.

"I mean, I like control in the bedroom, sweetheart."

Iain shivered and licked his lips. "I'm ready if you are."

Now, it was my turn to tremble. I rubbed my thumb over his soft lower lip and leaned in to whisper in his ear. "Get on the bed, hands and knees."

Iain groaned and slowly stepped away from me. He turned and placed one knee on the bed, then the other, climbing up until he was in the middle.

I walked to the nightstand, opened the drawer to search for condoms and lube, and threw them on the bed. Then, I took a moment to appreciate the sight before me.

Having Iain in my bed was never possible. Until it was.

And now, I couldn't picture anyone else.

"I don't want to use condoms," Iain whispered, and I stopped moving. "We get tested quarterly, and so do you. I'm negative."

"Me too. Are you sure?"

Iain growled and turned his head. "Yes, I'm fucking sure! Now hurry up."

Since he was sassing me, I gave his pert ass a firm slap in response, and the loud smack of my hand hitting his damp skin reverberated in the room.

"You're not in charge here, sweetheart. Now spread those gorgeous legs for me."

Iain lowered his head to the mattress and let out the filthiest moan I'd ever heard.

"God, please, please fuck me. I need you so bad. It feels like you've been edging me for ages."

I let out a dirty chuckle.

Oh, I just knew that finally watching Iain give in to me was going to be the most satisfying thing in the world.

"All in good time, sweetheart. First, I'm going to worship this beautiful ass with my tongue. Then, my fingers. Then, if you're good for me, I'll pump you full of my cum and eat you out."

"Oh fuck." Iain reached between his legs and grabbed the base of his dick with his right hand.

"You'd like that, huh? You enjoy dirty talk?" I leaned over and whispered against his bare ass, giving him a teasing lick and a gentle bite.

He was delicious, musky, and so fucking addictive.

"I like dirty action," Iain whimpered. "More."

"Not until you put both hands on the mattress. And don't touch your dick again. It's all mine."

Iain let out a deep groan—of frustration or desire, I didn't know. But he did as he was told.

I rubbed his ass cheeks and spread them, then spat on his tight pink hole.

I could've teased and tortured him for a long while, but both of us were too amped up. This first time was going to be fast and dirty.

Leaning down, I licked a path from his taint to his tailbone, making sure to tease his asshole with quick flicks of my tongue. Iain pushed back, trying to get more, but I gripped his cheeks tight and continued with featherlike strokes.

I wanted to spend all night eating him out, but my own arousal was threatening to unleash. Sitting back, I reached for the lube, and I slicked up my fingers, gently pushing one into his hole.

"I need your cock," he moaned out and gripped the duvet in his hands. "I need more."

"You're gonna get everything you need," I murmured, adding another finger and pushing slow but deep. "I told you before, I'm going to take care of you."

Iain shuddered, and I stopped.

"Tell me if I need to go slower or stop."

"You're not hurting me, and don't you dare fucking stop! Just, ngh," Iain's frustrated growl filled the room. "It's so good, I love the burn. I want it. I need more."

I added more lube and finger fucked him, pumping deep and fast as Iain's moans and cries for more got louder. Sweat trickled down my face, my neck, my chest. My aching cock desperately wanted attention, but I ignored it in favor of pleasuring Iain.

He came first. Always.

Judging by his pleas and moans for more, I knew he was getting close, so I withdrew my fingers and poured more lube on them, then slicked up my cock.

"You ready?"

"Yes! God, yes."

With one hand on his hip and the other on his shoulder, I

pushed my hips forward and slid into his hole, one slow inch at a time. And shit, it had been so long since I'd fucked without a condom that I forgot just how intense it was. Holding my breath, I was mesmerized by the sight of his tight pink hole taking my cock.

Fuck, I was inside Iain, bare. I never wanted to leave.

"Look at you, so damned good for me. Taking all of me."

"More. Please. Fuck me."

I pumped my hips until my heavy balls slapped his ass.

Sliding one hand from Iain's shoulder around to his pec, I sat back on my heels and pulled him with me until he was seated on my lap, his back to my chest. His head rolled onto my shoulder, and I took his mouth in a possessive kiss while he moaned and writhed, our bodies locked tightly together, nothing between us.

"Baby," Iain whispered against my lips, his deep brown eyes staring into mine.

I don't know if he realized what he'd called me because he was so blissed out. But the shockwave that ran through my body from that one word was white-hot lightning racing in my veins.

This was so much more than fucking.

But I knew for sure I was screwed.

Iain

What I thought would be a quick and dirty fuck with Dawson turned into the hottest, most sensual sex of my life.

And then I had to ruin it all by calling him "baby."

Where the fuck had that come from? Not that Dawson seemed put off by it.

If anything, his grip on my body tightened as he thrust his hips and gyrated against my ass like he couldn't get deep enough inside of me. And I pushed back, the feel of his hard, bare cock in my ass the most incredible pleasure and pain, exquisite.

I wasn't the only one whimpering and gasping and moaning in pleasure.

Suddenly, it was too much. I wasn't prepared for the swell of emotions that overwhelmed me. I needed him hard and fast; I needed oblivion.

"Oh God, Dawson, it's too much…I need—"

Fuck, I couldn't even explain it.

But Dawson, like always, could read me without any words.

"I'll give you everything you need," he whispered in my ear.

Next thing I knew, I was pushed back on my hands and knees, facing the headboard, and he began to pummel my ass. Hard.

Every time his massive cock hit my prostate, I nearly jumped off the bed.

He gripped my left hip and gently used his right hand to squeeze my neck, and oh fuck, I liked that a whole lot.

"Good?" Dawson asked with a deep grunt as he squeezed again.

Good didn't even begin to describe it. He was so in tune with my body, and it made me hot all over.

"Yes." My moan was low and desperate.

Dawson squeezed my throat again, and I gasped. Combined with the intense fucking, my climax was building faster, higher, almost frightening in its intensity.

Then, the hand gripping my hip slid around over my stomach in a long, slow sweep that had goosebumps popping up on my skin. Finally, he gripped my leaking cock and began to tug in time to his thrusts.

"Dawson," I whispered, barely getting the word out.

This. This was what I needed.

No face-to-face, no soft touches. Just pure, primal fucking.

"You don't come until I say so," Dawson panted as he pounded into me. "Understood?"

I think I grunted in response, but I was so far gone I didn't care.

Dawson quickly moved his hand to the back of my neck and pushed my upper body to the mattress. The change in angle meant that he nailed my prostate with every thrust.

"Right there! Don't stop!" I screamed, the sound muffled by the duvet.

I could barely swivel my hips in this position since Dawson was in total control of my body. The freedom of giving myself over to him in this way set my blood on fire.

I didn't trust my hookups to dominate me in this way.

What did that say about me, about him, about us?

And then, all thinking was obliterated by pleasure.

Between the fullness in my ass and the heat of his rough hand shuttling up and down my throbbing cock, I was so close to coming.

"Oh God, I'm almost there," I whimpered.

My balls tightened as Dawson's thrusts became frantic. The bed creaked and groaned almost as loudly as the two of us.

"Look at you, so fucking beautiful. Need you to come for me, sweetheart," he demanded hoarsely. "Come for me."

He thrust again, and when he rolled his palm over the head of my cock, I was done.

I screamed his name as wave after wave of explosive pleasure rippled through my body. I came all over his hand and the bed, shaking and sweating and panting for air. Dawson's body jolted, my name erupting from him in a husky roar. His dick twitched in my ass as he flooded me with hot cum.

Fuck, he owned me in that moment, and I didn't want to think about why that was the hottest thing ever.

Incredibly, I came again, another gush of cum leaking out of my spent dick.

Dawson collapsed on top of me, and we lay on the bed, a gasping, shuddering, sticky, sweaty mess.

I hadn't felt this relaxed and happy in... I couldn't remember when.

Music was my first love, but sex with Dawson?

That came in a close second.

CHAPTER 24

DAWSON

was dead.

Gone. Finished.

I'd literally fucked my brains out and left them in Iain's ass.

I had promised to eat him out, but I could barely breathe, let alone move after that intense round of fucking. So, licking my cum out of Iain's ass would have to wait until the next time.

If there was a next time.

Please, God, let there be a next time.

Another shiver coursed through my body just thinking about how hard I came and how satisfying it was to hear Iain scream my name when he climaxed. I wanted to mark him again, rub my cum all over his body, to make it evident, without words, that he was the only thing I wanted.

I hoped to hell this wasn't a one-off.

Fast and furious wasn't the only way I wanted to touch him. But I knew Iain's skittishness, especially when our sex felt like more than fucking, and I was prepared for his withdrawal.

I thought for sure Iain would do a runner once I pulled

my cock out of his ass, but he surprised me, rolled over onto his back, and fell asleep. Was I offended that he knocked off so quickly? Fuck, no. I followed him.

Then I woke up a few hours later, around five in the morning.

Iain was softly snoring beside me, one long, sexy leg thrown over my hip. Despite what his mouth was probably going to say when he woke up, his body sure as hell wanted to be near me and not just for fucking.

I enjoyed the peacefulness of the moment and the opportunity to watch him unguarded.

He was so unforgettably gorgeous to me, his pink lips swollen from my kisses, his body still flushed and warm. His blond hair was a tangled mess on my pillow, and I took a moment to drink in the heady sight of him in my bed.

I realized then and there that tonight wasn't the culmination of the passionate tug-of-war between us.

It was just the beginning.

And since Iain didn't do the overnight thing, that meant I was one of the rare men fortunate enough to earn his trust. Just thinking about waking up next to him had my heart thrumming wildly and my blood racing hot.

I stroked one finger over his flushed cheek, memorizing the feel of his smooth skin and dark blond stubble until I reached his lips. So full and tender, I was aching hard to kiss him again.

I never knew what temptation was until now. Until him.

But I held back.

Because the next time I kissed him, I wanted him to see me with eyes wide open. I knew there would be fear there, trepidation, and uncertainty. But I also knew something special sparked between us, and as crazy as it might seem to anyone on the outside, I wanted him for more than one night. He could run, he could brush me off, but I wasn't going anywhere.

I knew my heart, and it was reaching for Iain. And my gut told me he was reaching for me, too. Whether he acknowledged the magnetic connection between us or shattered my heart into a million pieces, well, that was a worry for another day.

I slid my arm around his waist and cuddled up as close to him as I could get, then closed my eyes again.

Until I heard the faint rumbling of his husky voice.

"Dawson. Baby."

No, I wasn't teasing Iain when I said he talked in his sleep.

It was adorable, and I couldn't help but smile when he said my name. It gave me that flicker of hope that maybe, just maybe, I wasn't alone in my feelings.

Since I didn't need to be up at the crack of dawn, I closed my eyes again and drifted off to sleep.

The next time I woke up, Iain was on his side, and I was spooning him. The sun peeked through the edges of the curtains and cast the bed in a soft glow.

A deep sense of satisfaction settled in my bones, something I hadn't felt in ages.

Iain and I weren't perfect by any means, but this moment sure felt like it.

My phone buzzed on the nightstand, and I reluctantly rolled away from Iain and reached for it. It was just after eight, so there was no rush to get out of bed. The guys didn't need to be at the venue until noon.

The first message was from Jaxon, courtesy of my mom (I didn't allow him to have a phone yet), wishing me a Happy Valentine's Day and accompanied by a funny GIF of dancing hearts.

Shit, I'd all but forgotten about the holiday.

I texted Jaxon back with a promise to call tonight. Then I remembered that his class was going to exchange cards and have a party. I'm sure he'd have all sorts of stories to tell me when I called. I made a mental reminder to pick up a gift for him before we left the city. Jaxon loved to read, so maybe there was a nearby bookstore I could pop into.

The other messages were work-related but nothing urgent, nothing that couldn't wait another hour or two.

After I sent my reply to Jaxon, I put the phone aside. I rolled back over and pulled Iain into my arms again, letting out a sigh of contentment.

Iain turned his head toward me and blinked, his blond lashes fluttering. The warmest brown eyes stared back at me.

"Happy Valentine's Day," I whispered and gave him a languid kiss.

Surprisingly, he kissed me back. No hesitation, pure passion.

But when I pulled back, and he blinked again, I nearly burst out laughing at the sheer panic that washed over Iain's face.

Instead of letting his shock get to me, I reached for the pillow under my head and playfully whacked him in the face with it.

"Oh, it's on," Iain growled and retaliated, yanking on his pillow to whack me on the side of the head.

"You want to grapple again, sweetheart? Come and get me," I replied, getting on my knees and taking another swipe, this time at his abs.

"Show off," Iain chuckled and ripped the pillow away from me, then tackled me until I was lying on my back, and he was straddling my waist.

Okay, so I let him tackle me.

Naked wrestling with Iain was my kind of wakeup call.

All laughter was forgotten as Iain threw the pillow aside and attacked my mouth, biting my lower lip for entry and tangling his hot tongue with mine.

Just like that, playful turned scorching as we ate at each other's mouths, hungry and desperate.

I rolled him over and pumped my hips, our hardening cocks brushing against one another.

"Yes, fuck yes," I groaned as I attacked his neck, biting and licking my way down to that tender spot near his shoulder. I bit down and sucked on his skin, and he moaned and writhed beneath me.

"Just like this," Iain whispered and met me, thrust for thrust, reaching down with those talented fingers of his to squeeze my ass cheeks. "Dawson."

Frotting was fun and dirty and just what we needed.

Until I looked into his eyes. The intensity in them was unmistakable. He dropped his head back, shuttering his gaze, but I gripped his jaw with one hand and kissed him, holding him there while our bodies undulated against each other.

"Look at me," I demanded, and Iain's eyes popped open. "Look what you do to me."

We pumped our hips faster and faster, both of us frantic in our need to come.

"Beautiful," I whispered as I stared into his eyes.

Iain's face flushed a darker shade of red, and then he leaned up to kiss me, our kisses as desperate as our lovemaking.

"I'm close. Oh God, Dawson," Iain moaned, and when his body jolted, I felt the rush of his hot cum all over my dick and abs.

I was right behind him, shouting his name, my body jerking hard with the force of my orgasm. He ran his callused hands up over my back and cupped my neck, bringing me in for another devouring kiss before I could catch my breath.

Who needed to breathe, anyway?

When we did come up for air, I stroked my thumbs over his cheekbones, peppering the rest of his face with soft kisses.

And when he smiled at me, the sight made my heart clench so hard in my chest I was winded again.

I didn't want to leave Iain or this bed. God, I was drunk on him.

"That was the fastest, but hottest, frotting in history," Iain teased and gave me another kiss. "We came like frantic, horny teenagers."

"It's all your fault," I replied, nuzzling his neck.

I didn't miss his sharp inhale.

"My fault?"

"Yes, you. You're too goddamn sexy, and you ruin my control."

Iain chuckled. "You like me."

"No shit."

That response got me a hard pinch on the ass.

"Shower time," I suggested. "Before we become permanently glued together."

"You wouldn't want that. I'd drive you nuts."

I shook my head. "You already do, and yet, here I am."

Before he could retaliate, I took his lips again.

The shower would have to wait.

CHAPTER 25
IAIN

should leave. I should leave now.

I must have told myself that at least two dozen times in the past hour.

Just get up out of Dawson's bed and leave. Go back to your room and act like nothing happened.

It's just sex.

So why, then, did I let him guide me to his shower? Not only that, but when he held my hand, interlocking our fingers tightly, Christ, it was more intimate than fucking. And I never imagined I'd ever be shaken by such a simple gesture.

Touching that led to sex was fine, but anything else was a no-go.

As a guitarist, my hands were a powerful tool. One I didn't share lightly.

Dawson took charge, ushering me into the glass enclosure and cleaning me from head to toe. Then quick touches grew sensual, and we got dirty all over again. And fuck, the way that man kissed me? I was hungry for more, more, more.

Okay, so maybe this wasn't a one-time thing.

Maybe we needed a few days to get it all out of our system. But it would let out.

I mean, that's the way it was, right?

I didn't do relationships, and he didn't want to risk his career.

So while part of me was freaking out, the other was going along for the ride.

And by ride, I meant whatever this was between me and Dawson.

Once we'd used up all the hot water, he slapped my ass and told me to go back to my room and get changed.

Bossy fucker. And yeah, I liked it. But only with him.

Not that I would ever admit it.

Still, I did as I was told, got out, and started drying off. But I was unsteady on my feet, punch drunk from so many orgasms.

"You all right?" he asked me, concern etched on his face as he stepped out of the shower.

I nodded quickly and watched him grab a towel. It was a damn shame to cover up that body.

The thought of anyone else—man or woman—eyeing up Dawson in this way made me irrationally moody. Beyond his muscle mass and bossy attitude, the man was caring and sensitive. Sexy as hell.

And I wanted him all to myself.

"I'll order breakfast while you're getting dressed," Dawson announced. "What do you want?"

Instead of answering him, I gave him what I hoped was a dirty grin.

Dawson shook his head. "Oh no. Go on, get. I need a break, rockstar. You've depleted every last ounce of my energy."

"What about all your training? We're going to have to work on your stamina, baby."

Dawson's mouth dropped open, as did the towel he was holding.

That didn't help matters at all.

Despite my exhaustion, my cock began to fill.

"Go get dressed. Save that for later."

"Yes, sir," I quipped.

Dawson moved lightning quick, backing me up against the wall. His mouth hovered over mine, teasing, just out of reach. I longed to reach up and run my hands over his red stubble, but I held back. I was getting too caught up in my emotions, and touching him like that would surely only feed into it.

"Get dressed, sweetheart," he murmured against my lips. "Then we'll eat and go out for a bit."

"Out?"

"Play tourist for an hour or two before we head to the venue."

"Any particular reason?"

"I want to get Jaxon a gift. There are a couple of bookstores nearby."

"So sweet."

Dawson shook his head, and that telltale flush crept up onto his cheeks.

Fuck it, I couldn't resist. Dawson's shy smile had me reaching up to kiss him softly.

"Grab a hat to cover your hair, and wear a pair of sunglasses," Dawson added. "I'll text Lennie to join us."

"Sounds like a plan. And I'd like crepes with strawberries and an omelet. And pain au chocolat."

"Are you sharing any of that?"

"Nope, it's all for me," I replied, my breath catching as he cupped my face in his hands. "See, I worked up quite an appetite. I had this incredibly hot night with a sexy bear of a man. He fucked my brains out and then some."

"Lucky guy."

"I'm feeling pretty lucky myself."

Dawson gave me one last kiss and then stepped back to

open the bathroom door. I finally forced my feet to move and headed back through his bedroom to my adjoining suite.

First things first, I reached for my phone.

There were texts from the guys, of course, and one from Zoe asking me to call her today about the stalker headlines. Ugh. I'd do that later. I wanted to stay in my happy little bubble a while longer.

I checked the forecast, and while it was sunny today, the temperature was hovering around fifty-five degrees. I slipped on a pair of dark jeans, my biker boots, and a forest green turtleneck sweater. My leather jacket and scarf were a must. Then I tied my wet hair up in a bun and grabbed a black beanie and my favorite pair of wayfarers.

As I looked around my room to see if I missed anything, I fought the strange urge to grab all my stuff and move it into Dawson's suite.

Man, I must really need food because I was starting to hallucinate.

Me wanting to share a room with a man I was sleeping with?

Ha. No. Not happening.

Okay, maybe just my guitar. I always kept one with me in case inspiration struck. And because playing was my form of therapy.

Without further thought, I grabbed my guitar case and hauled it into his room. I placed it on the chair opposite the sofa. Hopefully, he wouldn't make a big deal of it. I mean, given that we weren't nearly done with each other, chances are I'd be staying here tonight. It just made sense to keep my baby close to me.

Thankfully, Dawson was still in the bathroom. I could hear something buzzing.

I walked down the hallway and peered around the door. Dawson was standing in front of the sink, with a white towel around his hips and an electric razor in hand. He gave me a smile when he spotted me.

"Please tell me you're not shaving that off," I teased.

"Just trimming."

"Good."

"Any other demands?" he quipped as he looked at me in the mirror.

"Next time, you better eat my ass out like you promised."

The trimmer fell out of his hand and crashed into the sink. "Fuck, Iain! Save that talk for later."

"Why? I want you to eat me out, and you want to eat me. And I want to feel that beard on my ass. Fuck, you can rub it all over my body."

Dawson closed his eyes and took a deep breath. "Please stop talking. I'm trying not to get another hard-on."

"Why?"

"Because you have a show tonight, and I don't want to be the reason you collapse on stage."

"You can die from too much sex? That's a real thing?" I asked with a smirk.

"Out," he ordered.

"But I like to watch."

Dawson let out a deep groan. "Iain."

I shivered despite the warmth of the room and my sweater. "Do you know how sexy it is when you say my name like that? Like I'm driving you out of your mind?"

"That's because you do." He shook his head and picked up the trimmer. "Out. Before I swat your ass so hard, you'll be squirming on stage all night."

Instead of responding, I turned around and bent over.

"You just have to be a fucking brat, don't you?"

I wiggled my butt and chuckled.

Until Dawson made good on his threat.

The slap of his firm hand hitting my denim-covered ass was loud, and the sting had my dick jerking hard. Fuck, I wasn't into that kind of thing, but with Dawson, it turned me on.

"I liked that way too much," I admitted. "More."

Dawson laughed softly and pulled me against his body.

He nuzzled his face in my neck and slid his arms around my waist, pulling me in tight.

"Our breakfast should be here any minute," he chuckled. "Let me get changed."

"Sure, but you have to let go of me first."

Neither one of us moved.

Until there was a knock at the door.

"I'll get it," I offered.

"Nope. Not protocol."

"I don't think kissing me is either."

Dawson grunted and grabbed his sweatpants from the nearby hook. Once he slipped them on, he walked out of the bathroom. Without a shirt on.

"Uh, you forgot something," I grabbed his arm, holding him back.

"What?"

"How about a shirt? You want to give Georges a heart attack?"

"Oh, please."

He stepped away and headed out to answer the door, and I followed.

Except it wasn't Georges standing on the other side of the door with our order; it was some other guy—a young guy staring at Dawson like he was on the menu.

They were exchanging pleasantries in French, and the longer the guy talked, the more irritated I became. When Dawson finally closed the door, I glared at him.

"What?" he asked me, shrugging his shoulders.

"Don't 'what' me. You know damn well what."

"No, I don't."

"That guy was drooling over you."

"No, he wasn't."

"Uh, I know a thing or two about flirting and attraction. Hello, sex appeal is part of my job. And yeah, he was eyeing you up like his next meal."

"You're ridiculous. Come on, let's—"

His words cut off suddenly, and then I realized he'd spotted my guitar. He froze, practically tripping over the trolley cart.

"I brought my guitar in here because, well, I figured it was safer in here. If I'm in here, you know, overnight. Again. Sometimes, I like to get up in the middle of the night to play. But maybe I shouldn't have assumed. I can just put it back—"

"No. Leave it." Dawson turned and smiled at me. "It's good."

It was better than good. And I knew it.

CHAPTER 26

DAWSON

Once I got over the shock of seeing Iain's guitar in my room, we finally sat down to eat.

After the necessary calories and caffeine, I texted Lennie.

I hadn't heard anything more from Regan about the stalker. I don't know if that meant good news or bad. Cases like this tended to take a long time to figure out. If ever.

We texted the other guys to see if they wanted to join us, but they all begged off. I figured Brodie would, given he had to rest his voice.

Lennie knocked on my door around ten, and we headed out to do some shopping.

It was nice to have this time alone with Iain. Or almost.

Lennie looked at the two of us and shook his head. I didn't think we were that obvious, but Iain did have beard burn. Still, Lennie said nothing. And I was grateful.

There was no problem. I had everything under control.

I wasn't compromised.

If anything, I was even more aware of my surroundings now that Iain and I were lovers. Still, I knew I was walking a fine line. A dangerous one. If this thing between us continued, I'd have to tell my boss.

But I pushed that thought aside for now.

I'd asked Iain where he wanted to go, but he was keen on checking out the bookstore with me.

The shop was located in a historic building with high ceilings, ornate moldings, and crystal chandeliers. It felt more like an art gallery than a bookstore.

"What kind of books does Jaxon like to read?" Iain asked as we wandered through the store.

Iain's question surprised me. And, despite my usual reticence on revealing personal stuff, even to a lover, I was warmed by his curiosity. Most people I'd dated in the past were either put off when I revealed I had a son or they didn't show much interest. Either way, bringing a boyfriend or girlfriend into my life was not easy. If Jaxon didn't approve, that was it.

"He loves anything about animals, outer space, adventure, and, of course, music."

The children's section was on the second floor of the shop. We found a section for readers aged nine to eleven, and they had a good selection of both French and English books. We began to sort through some of the bestsellers. I thought for sure Iain would be bored and beg off, but he looked through more than two dozen books, giving me his input.

"How about this one?" Iain asked. "Anne of Green Gables. It's a classic and one of my favorites. The heroine is a spunky redhead, just like Jaxon. Or at least, that's my first impression of him."

I stared at him, surprised and warmed by his comment.

"He is all that. Spunky and more."

"My… my mom used to read that with me," Iain whispered. "She loved books, and music, and art. After she passed, I didn't have the heart to read it again by myself. I was hoping that my dad would, but he found anything associated with her too painful to deal with. Me included."

"I'm so sorry, Iain."

My heart ached just thinking about what Iain went through. It made me incredibly protective of him and angry on his behalf since his dad checked out. I knew exactly how he felt given what happened with my father.

When Jaxon's mom died, I was determined to ensure my child never felt alone.

"I guess I shouldn't complain. Dad provided for me and brought in a nanny to take care of me. She was a kind woman, but it wasn't the same. I missed my family." Iain shrugged. "Anyway, reading is one of the few happy memories I have of my mom."

"It's important to hold onto those memories. And this is the perfect book for Jaxon, thank you."

Iain nodded and swallowed hard. I slipped my arm around his waist. He tensed, but that didn't discourage me. Iain wasn't that different from me. We both had trouble showing our deepest feelings. And when we did, it left us with a vulnerability that we tried to brush off.

He removed his sunglasses and wiped his eyes.

Fuck me, this man.

I wanted to kiss him and take away all his hurt. Then I remembered that Lennie was nearby, watching us. Iain must have thought the same because before I knew it, he slipped his glasses back on and pulled away from me.

"What about a gift for your mom?" Iain asked.

I stared at him, frozen in place.

"Dawson?"

"Yeah," I finally shook myself out of my trance. "She loves to cook."

"Non-fiction is downstairs. Come on."

We headed back down to the ground floor and picked up a book on French cuisine for my mom. Iain also selected a couple of books for himself—a biography on Jimi Hendrix and a book on learning to play the guitar.

"I think you've already read that one," I quipped, pointing to the *Guitar for Beginners* book.

"Haha. It's a gift," he explained as we stood in line to pay.

"For?"

"For Jaxon. Duh. You mentioned his birthday's coming up."

I smiled and tried to ignore the tightness in my chest, not to mention the way my heart fluttered.

"I'm going to have to soundproof my house, aren't I?" I asked.

"Oh, yeah."

Once we'd paid for our books, we headed outside.

"Is there any place else you'd like to go? We have a half hour before we need to get to the venue."

"I'm done," Iain replied. "I'd rather get there early. I need to call Zoe anyway."

I texted my team, and we arranged to meet at the concert venue.

We were the first ones on site. I left Iain in his dressing room with Lennie so he could make his call while I did the rounds and met up with Regan for an update.

"The stalker is messaging Iain's old phone every hour. Take a look."

Regan passed me the phone.

Unknown number: How could you call our love such an evil name? After all we've been through?

Don't keep ignoring me. If you can talk to the press, you can talk to me.

The flowers were just the beginning. There's more to come.

I'll be waiting for you when you get home.

The last message made my stomach clench painfully.

"Waiting for you when you get home," I repeated. "Do you have someone monitoring Iain's house?"

"Of course. We got the security company to add extra cameras. If anyone tries to breach his property, we'll find out."

"What about the PI?"

Regan shrugged. "They're working on it, but it's going to take time. Stalkers are sneaky bastards."

"I wonder if there's a way we can trip this person up."

"Like?"

"Like replying to the messages. Getting them to talk and reveal more about themselves."

Regan nodded. "I'll talk to my police contact in cyber and see what they think. It might be risky."

"What about the fan page?"

"Zoe is monitoring it. Anything suspicious, she'll flag me."

"And the police?"

"My contact has the information, but until a crime is committed—"

"There's nothing more we can do. For now."

"As you said, there might be an opportunity to catch the stalker in the act, so to speak, when we head back home."

"I'm with you."

"Other than that," Regan murmured, "how was Iain's night?"

"He slept well." Shit. I couldn't help the blush that seared my cheeks. "I mean, he was well rested this morning. Seemed like."

Regan shook her head.

"Dawson, take my advice. Don't ever play poker."

———

Iain

After my call with Zoe—which consisted of her telling me not to look on social media and to avoid reporters for the foreseeable future and me telling her about our dealings with Harlow—I headed back upstairs with Lennie for soundcheck.

But my usual concentration was fucked. All I could think about was last night. And this morning. Being with Dawson. And not just in bed. Now, whenever he moved, even from a distance, my eyes inevitably followed him. I'd never been so aware of another person and the synergy between us.

Someone nudged my shoulder, and I startled.

Ronin.

"Are you okay, bud? You look out of it. Are you stoned?"

"No, I'm not stoned," I replied.

"Drunk?"

I rolled my eyes. "It's noon."

"Since when has that stopped you?" Faise quipped.

"I'm not twenty-five anymore. And I'm not drunk or high or anything," I snapped.

"Ah, then you must've gotten laid." Brodie smirked. "You have that relaxed glow about you."

"Not to mention the beard burn," Faise added.

Ronin eyed me up and down. "But you're distracted as fuck. What's that about?"

I gave Ronin my best finger.

"Come on, Holls, spill the deets," Brodie whispered. "It's just us."

"No."

"No?" Ronin shook his head and laughed. "Someone check to see if this really is Holls."

"Funny. I'm just tired. And worried."

Yeah, tired from fucking and worried that it was more than that.

"It's the stalker, right?"

No.

"Yeah."

"It's gonna be okay," Brodie assured me. "We've got the best security team."

"I know."

I heard a movement behind me and turned to find Dawson chatting with Van. Nothing unusual there, but my awareness of Dawson was. How was I gonna concentrate when all I wanted to do was walk over there, tackle him to the ground, and kiss him senseless?

Dawson looked up at me and gave me a decadent smile. I began to sweat under the stage lights.

"You finally fucked Dawson. That's so hot," Brodie growled.

"Dee—" I warned.

"Come on, we're not going to tell anyone. It's just us here."

I faced my friends. "Okay, all right. Yes."

"And?" Brodie asked.

"And what?" I shrugged my shoulders. "It happened. Nothing else to say."

"That bad, huh?" Ronin goaded me.

"I don't wanna brag and make you guys jealous. Besides, it's a one-time thing, so not much else to say."

Then I remembered where I'd left my guitar. Oops.

"Doesn't seem like it's a one-time thing. Dawson looks like he's going to throw you over his shoulder any moment now."

I sighed. "Okay, so theoretically, we might sleep together again. It's no big deal. Once we burn this out, we go back to our usual roles."

"Did you just fuck, or was there a sleepover?" Faise asked.

"Um—" I paused, biting my lip, and everyone chuckled.

"You never stay the night." Brodie shook his head. "Holy shit, I knew it! Iain's in love."

"Don't even go there, Dee. I was exhausted after the concert. It was just convenient."

Faise chuckled. "Did you conveniently snuggle all night long?"

"Snuggle?" Ronin scoffed. "Have you been reading romance novels again?"

Faise gave Ronin a choice finger. "So what if I have? Maybe you should try reading one. Might give you some desperately needed pointers."

"Hey, I've got no complaints from the men I fuck. But there's no snuggling involved."

"Oh yeah, you save that all for me, baby." Faise waggled his eyebrows.

As usual, when the topic of our sex lives was brought up, we reverted to our teenage selves.

Brodie put a hand on my shoulder. "I like him for you. But there's the matter of your security. If he's distracted—"

"He's not. He knows me, and he knows that this is just a one-off. It's fine. No big deal."

I said the words, but I didn't believe them. Everything about me and Daws felt like a big fucking deal and so far from a one-off. My heart told me to run with it, but my head had reservations.

And for someone who avoided intimate relationships, it was scary as fuck to consider that maybe, just maybe, I was gonna break my rule for Dawson. He'd already broken his rule for me.

"I don't believe a word you just said," Brodie replied.

I turned and looked my friend in the eye.

"I'm not sure I believe me either."

CHAPTER 27

DAWSON

I watched Iain during soundcheck, knowing the guys were talking about us.

Not that I was close enough to hear what they were saying, but I knew them. And Iain was fooling nobody. Neither of us were. At least, nobody who'd been around us long enough.

For him, that wasn't such a big deal, but for me?

It was a problem.

I didn't want to be taken off his detail, but if I couldn't focus when it came to his security, I needed to tell Regan. Not that she didn't already know what was going on.

But if Iain decided that's it, he and I weren't going to fuck again, there would be nothing to tell. So, for now, I held off.

My phone rang, and I glanced at the screen: *Unknown Number*.

I had that awful feeling in the pit of my stomach again.

I stepped away from Van.

"Dawson Everly speaking."

Silence. I quickly tapped *record*, just in case.

"Hello?"

"Leave him alone."

The voice was low and raspy, but I didn't recognize it.

"Leave who alone? Who is this?"

Then the line went dead, the telltale beep of disconnection. Shit.

Regan was talking to Ace, and I waved her over.

"I think Iain's stalker just called me again. They told me to 'leave him alone' and hung up. I recorded it just in case, but I didn't recognize the voice."

Regan regarded me with concern. "It's not much, but we'll take it. Send the recording to the PI."

"Will do."

"By the way, I talked to Greg about Harlow—about his comments to you and to me last night. Harlow apologized and said he'd be here today. Just a heads up, he's arriving around seven."

The rest of the day passed without incident. I put Lennie on Iain's detail while I followed up with the PI back home. It made for a productive day. Iain could focus on his work and me on mine.

See, we could do this.

And maybe Lennie would turn out to be a permanent solution if Iain and I kept doing what we were doing. Admittedly, I wanted to be exclusive with Iain while we were together, but I didn't know how Iain would react to that suggestion.

Only one way to find out. But that conversation would have to wait until we were back at the hotel, alone.

The concert got underway at nine, with Brodie and the boys doing their bit to get the crowd excited. Not that the fans needed it; they were already pumped up, as evidenced by the volume of their screaming and clapping.

"Is everyone extra horny tonight because it's Valentine's Day?" Brodie asked the audience.

The crowd yelled back, and articles of clothing were thrown on stage.

"Yeah, me too." Brodie smirked and ran a hand through his curls. "What about you, Holls?"

Iain replied by strumming the opening riff to 'Ruined.' It was one of their raunchiest, loudest songs, and the crowd responded by screaming Iain's name.

"I guess that's a yes," Brodie remarked and walked along the edge of the stage, touching people's hands. "Well, all right then. This song is for all the lovers out there."

Halfway through the show, Brodie called Van out on stage, and they sang Filthy Pain together. Iain was his usual high energy, wowing the crowd with his guitar solos and backup vocals.

Harlow arrived near the end of the show and got the interviews sorted. Unlike last night, he was subdued, almost apologetic. Not to me, but whatever. If he was mindful of Iain, that's all I cared about.

While the guys were working their PR, with Lennie and Quinn on duty, I texted my mom and then video-called my son.

"Hey bud, Happy Valentine's Day. Did you have a good party at school?"

"It was awesome, Dad. We had pizza and cake and exchanged cards. I'll show you when you're home. I made a card for you."

"I can't wait. And I have something for you, too."

"How many more days?"

"One more week, bud. I promise."

After I gave my son virtual hugs and kisses, I said goodbye.

Then, I got our entourage ready for the next event of the night.

We escorted the band to an afterparty held by one of the tour sponsors. It was set in a swanky fashion boutique near the venue, with pink champagne flowing and plenty of stunning Parisians in designer outfits. The guys were inundated with enthusiastic fans and did their bit, posing for selfies and signing autographs for almost two hours.

Iain drew attention from a ton of admirers, and as usual, he seemed to enjoy being in the spotlight. He hadn't so much as made eye contact with me since we'd arrived here, and a horrible feeling in the pit of my stomach sat like a heavy weight.

Maybe last night was all we'd have? And really, what did I expect?

Chastising myself for falling for the one guy who wanted nothing more than fucking, I forced my jealousy aside.

As soon as we got back to the hotel, his guitar was going back in his room.

If this was it, I didn't want any reminder of him in my bedroom, or I'd never sleep.

Thank fuck we'd be checking out in two days. I didn't want to see that bed again, either.

"Everything okay?"

I turned to find Brodie standing next to me.

"Fine."

"He's just doing his thing, you know. It's part of the job."

"Sure. Right."

Ha.

"Look, we all enjoy the adulation; it's part of what drives us to perform and why we put up with all the other shit. But he's not really interested in any of those guys he's talking to. I can tell. It's just second nature for him to flirt. It doesn't mean anything."

"Why are you telling me this?"

"Because you look like you're about to rip someone's head off. And we don't want to scare off our sponsors, yeah?"

"I'm monitoring the room as I normally would. Nothing else."

"Don't give up on him," Brodie whispered.

"Excuse me?"

"I see the way he looks at you, Daws, and it's more than a fuck. I know it, you know it."

I took a deep breath. "Maybe Iain's not ready for that."

"Maybe. But I can also tell that you more than like him. Am I right?"

I nodded, suddenly unable to speak with a lump the size of a boulder in my throat. Even though I knew I was heading for heartache, I couldn't help it.

Something about Iain just called to me.

"Iain's dad gave up on living when his mom died. He gave up on Iain. So naturally, my friend tries to keep people at arm's length. He doesn't want to get hurt again."

"I would never willingly hurt Iain," I murmured.

"Iain will deny this, but he's got a big heart and a shitload of love to give. He just needs to feel safe enough to let you in."

"I'm worried." I paused and licked my lips. "If I tell him I want more, if I stake my claim, he's gonna run."

"Yeah, he probably will."

"And then what?"

"If he runs, you do what you do best—go after him."

I glanced at Brodie and nodded. "Thanks."

Brodie patted my shoulder. "My pleasure. Now, I gotta go and find my husband before some beautiful man or woman tries to steal him from me."

I snorted. "Yeah, right. Like Van looks at anyone but you."

"Yeah." Brodie gave me a cocky grin. "I know. I'm a lucky SOB."

Brodie sauntered off into the crowd, and I finally caught Iain's attention.

He was staring at me with a strange expression on his face, and before I knew it, I was cutting through the packed floor and heading right for him.

"Everything okay?" I asked as I reached him.

"I'm done. Can we go back to the hotel?"

"Course. Let me just check in with my team."

The rest of the guys were staying at the party, so it was just me, Lennie, and Iain who returned to the hotel.

We said goodnight to Len at his door, and once Iain and I were alone, I gently placed my arm around his waist. "Is this all right?"

"Yeah," Iain whispered as he looked up at me.

I was highly aware of the security cameras in the hallway, so I resisted kissing him. But I held onto him until we reached my room.

When I finally got us inside, I leaned back against the door.

"I want to ask you something."

"Anything." Iain slipped his jacket off his shoulders, then toed off his boots.

When he reached for his sweater, I held his arm to stop him. If he got naked right this minute, any conversation that didn't involve "yes," "harder," or "more" would cease.

"I don't want to sleep with anyone else," I blurted out.

Iain's blond eyebrows nearly hit his hairline. "Okay."

"I mean, while you and I are doing… this… I want to be exclusive. That's the way I am. I'm monogamous. I don't share."

Iain pulled away from my touch, and I felt my heart drop down to my stomach.

Until he reached for his sweater again, yanking it off and throwing it away, then quickly unzipping his jeans.

"Are you going to get naked too, or just watch me?" Iain quipped. "Not that I'm opposed to the latter, but I do prefer partner participation."

"Did you hear me say I want to be exclusive?"

"I did. And yes, I want that too."

I was too shocked to move.

"Didn't expect that, did you?" he asked, teasing me with a sexy grin.

I shook my head. "Why?"

"Let's see," he licked his lips and gave me a slow once-over. "I can't think about anyone but you. I don't see anyone but you. I don't want to fuck anyone but you. It all comes back to... you."

"Are you sure?"

"No. I'm scared shitless. But I'm trying anyway."

My heart pounded so hard that I could barely think.

"A word of warning." I grinned. "I'm possessive as fuck. I nearly pulled you out of that party tonight."

"That was business."

"That's what Brodie said."

Iain shook his head.

"No more talking. I need you to touch me."

Then he shoved his jeans and briefs down, his hard cock jutting out. Before I knew it, I pushed off the door and reached for him, slamming my mouth over his, taking what was mine.

I swallowed his surprised groan and sucked on his tongue, the need for him so overwhelming in its intensity that I began to shake.

"Take my clothes off," I demanded, my voice hoarse with desire.

Iain reached for my shirt and teased my abs with his fingers before removing it completely. Then he reached for my jeans, unzipping them and pushing them down. When he grabbed the base of my throbbing cock, Christ, the feel of his callused hands on my body was better than good. Unreal.

"Kneel and suck my cock," I growled.

Iain moaned and obeyed my command, dropping to the carpeted floor, never losing eye contact.

I pushed my hands into his thick hair and pulled it out of the bun, letting it fall all around his shoulders. He leaned forward and licked the crown of my dick, swiping around the head.

"That's it," I urged, guiding him forward.

He swallowed me all the way down until my cockhead hit his snug throat. He gagged once, and I paused. Until Iain moved one stealthy hand to my ass and gripped my cheek hard, urging me on. Then he sucked and licked my cock, torturing me with every swipe of his talented tongue.

"I want to fuck your face," I panted as Iain's muffled groans grew louder. "If you need to pull off, tap my thigh."

I gripped his head and pumped my hips harder, faster. And fuck, the tight, wet heat of Iain's mouth was so addictive that my eyes rolled back in my head.

He cupped my heavy balls with one hand and ran one of his skillful fingers over my taint, then my hole. His insistent touch sparked the nerve endings in my ass, and I groaned out loud. Iain could play with my ass any time he wanted.

"Fuck, every time with you… I… I can't last. What are you doing to me?" I moaned as the pleasure spiraled higher and higher.

Iain continued to tease my ass and my balls as he sucked harder, pulling me under.

I jerked hard as my orgasm imploded, and I unloaded in his mouth. He continued to swallow, and I could only pant and stare as my cum dripped out of the sides of his mouth and down his face.

I was lightheaded from coming so hard, so fast. Like I had no fucking control.

My spent cock slipped from his pretty lips, swollen and covered in my cum. He licked them as he panted for air.

Iain stood up with my assistance, and I pulled him in for a long, possessive kiss.

"Dawson?" he whispered.

"Yes?"

"Make love to me."

CHAPTER 28

IAIN

Words I never imagined thinking, let alone saying, came rolling out of my mouth.

And it was too late to take them back.

Dawson simply smiled and then kissed me with such passion that I forgot about the rug burn on my knees and the fact that my mouth was swollen and sore. Or the fact that I'd asked for something I never dared imagine I would need.

He walked me back and urged me to lie down on the bed.

"Face to face this time," he whispered. "I want to watch you come apart. I want you to see exactly what's happening between us."

He slid his big body over mine, holding me down and ravaging my lips. God, he could kiss me forever. I never put much stock in it. Don't get me wrong, kissing was hot, but it was more of a means to an end.

But Dawson's kisses were next level. Deep, devouring, and fucking delicious.

Addictive.

As he made his way down my body with heated kisses and tormenting nips, he took his time finding all of my sensitive places. When he licked over my nipples, I cried out and tugged his head closer. He gently bit one nipple then sucked on it, and my body nearly came off the bed.

"Oh God, more."

He gave the same amount of attention to my other nipple, teasing me until I was a writhing mess. Then he rubbed his beard over one pec and the other, and fuck, that was even better.

He licked every inch of my body, making his way down my abs and, finally, over the head of my cock.

"So goddamn gorgeous," he whispered, as he spread my legs and pushed my knees back.

I gripped my legs and watched his darkening eyes as he lowered his head and lapped at my balls.

"Fuck, yes!" I squirmed, shoving my ass in his face, needing more.

"This time, I'll make good on my promise."

Oh God, he was going to fuck me and eat me out afterward. My balls tightened, and I panted, trying to calm myself down. I didn't want to come yet. I was already close, nearly blowing my load when he came down my throat.

Then Dawson spread my ass cheeks and ate me out, licking my sensitive rim and then plunging his tongue in my ass, fucking me with it. The pleasure was so intense I squeezed my eyes shut, willing myself not to come.

"Iain," Dawson whispered against my skin. "Your taste is so fucking addictive."

Then he rubbed his beard against my ass, and fuck, yes, the roughness against my overheated skin made me moan out loud.

Dawson leaned back and reached for the nightstand, grabbing the lube.

"See what you do to me?" he asked as he slicked up his hard cock. "I just came, and I'm ready for you again."

I watched, mesmerized, licking my lips, tasting him on my tongue. His fat cock was red and leaking furiously. I couldn't wait to feel him inside me again.

Sliding closer, he notched the head of his dick to my hole. I swallowed hard, glancing down to watch as he entered me, slow and steady, as my ass took him in. The intense fullness made my breath catch. I full-on shivered as he pushed into me, one tormenting inch at a time.

"Look at you, Iain, so fucking good for me. Taking all of me."

"More, Dawson. I need it all. I need you."

I glanced up at his face, and he was staring at me with such heated tenderness in his eyes. Like I was something special.

My heart clenched, and I reached for him, pulling him down for a kiss, his wicked tongue tangling with mine. When he pushed his cock all the way in, I finally let out the breath I'd been holding onto.

"You belong to me," Dawson growled against my lips. "Say it."

"Yes! I'm yours."

"Only mine."

Dawson rocked his hips, and I met him thrust for thrust. His movements were long and languid, fucking into me oh so slowly, watching me the whole time. It was almost too much, and I fought the urge to look away.

"Don't. It's me, sweetheart. I'm right here. I'm gonna catch you."

I gripped his neck tighter as my emotions took hold of me, building up like the wave of my climax, higher and higher. He pumped into me, faster this time, harder.

"More, more," I chanted and threw my head back.

Grabbing my legs, he slid them over his shoulders and sat up, pulling me onto his lap and changing the angle of his thrust. I reached for the sheets to get leverage and nearly ripped them off the corners of the bed.

The next time he pumped his hips, his cock nailed my prostate, and I couldn't help the loud shout of pleasure that ripped from my throat.

His hands squeezed my thighs as he fucked into me with fast, hard strokes, sweat trickling down his body, over every beautiful inch of his massive frame.

"That's it. Let go, sweetheart, give yourself to me. I want all of you," he panted.

"Dawson, Oh God. I need you."

His slick hand gripped my cock, tugging on it firmly, and I lost it. I tipped over the edge.

I swear, part of my soul left my body as I came hard, my vision blurring. I screamed his name and shot all over his hand, my abs, my dick. Dawson's pace was frantic as he fucked into me, shouting my name in return and spilling inside me.

Christ, why did I love that so much? Knowing that he'd claimed me in such a primal way was hot as fuck. Not just hot, but it made my intense feelings for him turn feral. Like, if he so much as thought about doing this with someone else, I would have none of it.

He was mine, and that was it. I wanted him, I needed him, I fucking loved...him?

Ah, shit.

I didn't know whether that realization should make me laugh, cry, or both.

Dawson gently lowered my legs and slid out of my body as he gasped for air. Wiping the sweat off his brow, he gave me a saucy wink and then scooted down the bed.

Oh, Jesus, I knew what was coming next.

As soon as I felt his hot breath on my ass, I began to shiver. His cum was dripping out of me, sliding down my taint and ass cheeks. He swiped at my tender hole with his skillful tongue, tasting me, tasting his cum.

It was dirty and tender at the same time.

Fuck, this man was going to ruin me for anyone else.

"You and I taste damned good together, sweetheart."

Between his touch and his words, I was floating.

"Fuck, I'm going to come again," I blurted out in response.

He slipped one finger gently in my ass. "Are you sore?"

"Yes, but I like it. I love it. Don't stop."

Crooking his finger, he hit my oversensitive prostate, and I shuddered. I wanted more.

"Will you come for me again?" he asked, his voice hoarse.

"Yes."

"That's what I want to hear."

"Baby," I moaned as he teased me again.

Incredibly, I came a second time. My body shuddered as another pulse of cum leaked from my dick.

Sliding his finger out of me, he rubbed my hole in soothing circles while I tried to come back down to earth.

Then he crawled over me again, and I pulled him down to share a possessive kiss.

We were both sweaty, messy, filthy with cum.

As I stared into his dark green eyes, I knew.

I relented to the incredible shift happening inside me, even if I still didn't know how to put it into words. It was overwhelming and frightening in its intensity.

"Don't be scared," he whispered. "It's you and me."

I nuzzled his jaw, his neck. Letting myself be vulnerable with Dawson was different. Still scary, but I knew, in the deepest part of me, that he was right. I was safe with him.

"I'll be right back. Don't go anywhere."

He smiled and slowly rolled off me. I admired his beautiful body as he walked away, his stride confident, his high, round ass on display. I lay there, unable to move a muscle. Too fucked out.

When he returned with a warm washcloth and cleaned me off, I all but purred.

Throwing the cloth aside, he slipped back into bed and spooned me, our bodies touching from head to toe. He let out a deep hum of pleasure, and yeah, I agreed. I could get used to this.

What I couldn't fathom with previous lovers, I wanted with him.

"You all right?" he whispered in my ear, giving it a quick kiss.

"Yes. I love being with you like this. Don't get me wrong, I'm a fan of the bickering, too," I teased. "But this is better."

"I love being with you, too," he replied and hugged me tighter.

The serious tone of his voice and the possessive way he held me spoke volumes. It was as close to an admission of what was really going on between us as we were going to get. For now.

I drifted off to sleep, but not for long.

Inspiration struck—at four in the morning, no less.

I slowly extricated myself from Dawson's hold and walked over to the chair in the corner of the room.

Taking my baby out of the case, I sat down and began to play the tune circling in my subconscious like an earworm.

As I played, I stared at Dawson's sleeping form, and words began to float to the surface. Searching for a pad of paper, I grabbed a notebook and pen from the coffee table and scribbled down the basic notes of the riff. It was probably gibberish at this point, but I rolled with it.

Brodie and Van created most of our songs, but lately, I'd been inspired myself.

I didn't believe in my song writing ability as much as Brodie did his. I considered myself a guitarist first and foremost. But hey, it was always good to try new things.

I was already doing that with Dawson. Why not songwriting?

Once I'd written all I could, I switched it up and started to play a familiar song that soothed me.

"I love that," Dawson whispered.

I looked up, and he was lying on his side, staring at me with a smile.

"Shit, I'm sorry I woke you."

"Don't be. I love watching you, remember?"

I continued playing "Sideline," singing the words to Dawson, my audience of one.

It was funny because I started to sweat, nervous about how I sounded. Me, the guy who played concert halls and stadiums all over the world, was scared to sing for my... boyfriend? We were exclusive, so, yeah, boyfriend sounded right. I'd never had one before, so it would take some getting used to.

Then I thought about all the ways I could fuck this up. My hands trembled, and I missed a note.

"Come back to bed," Dawson commanded when I finished the song. "I miss you."

"I've only been gone for half an hour."

"Why do you think I woke up?"

I held up my guitar in response.

"Nope," Dawson replied. "As soon as you left my arms, I woke up."

"You've been playing possum all this time?"

Dawson smiled. "I didn't want to interrupt the muse."

"I was just fooling around at first." I shrugged.

"Sounded like the start of another Wayward Lane hit song to me."

"I don't know about that."

"Yes, you do. You're incredibly talented, Mr. Holloway."

I smiled and shook my head, placing my baby back in the case. Then I ambled back over to the bed.

As soon as my ass hit the mattress, Dawson pulled me into his arms.

"Happy Valentine's Day," I quipped.

"Thanks," Dawson chuckled in return. "But it ended four hours ago."

"Doesn't feel that way to me."

CHAPTER 29

DAWSON

I woke up to another surreal morning.

With Iain in my arms.

Why did something that seemed improbable only a month ago turn out to be everything I ever wanted?

There was a lot said between us last night, but for Iain, was that the heat of the moment, or was he all in? It felt like he was ready to take that leap with me, and I prayed he would give us a chance.

But there was still so much that Iain and I needed to talk about.

One thing I knew for sure—now that this was not a one-time thing—I'd have to be taken off his detail. I wouldn't put his safety in jeopardy.

And there was also the matter of my son.

I'd had a few major romantic relationships in my life. And only one after Jaxon's mom and I split, a boyfriend. But I was cautious about introducing Jaxon to a partner. That was a big step for him, for me, and for the person I was dating. Jaxon and I were a package deal, and anyone who would be a part of my life would be part of Jaxon's, too.

"You're thinking hard. Are you having second thoughts?"

I leaned in to nuzzle Iain's neck. "What? No."

"Your body tensed up so—"

"Roll over."

Iain turned over in my arms to face me. "Yes, boss."

"Smart ass," I quipped as I gave him a soft kiss. "I'm not having second thoughts. But there's a lot to talk about."

"You're going off my detail," Iain said matter of factly.

"Yes."

"I can live with that. And?"

"Jaxon. I'd like to tell him we're seeing each other; I want to be sure he's okay with it."

Iain nodded. "He comes first."

"He does. His happiness before mine."

Iain reached up to kiss me back. "And?"

"There's the media. I have some idea what you deal with, but if we eventually go public, we need to have a plan. And again, there's my son to consider."

This time, Iain was the one who tensed. "Yeah. Honestly, I never gave it much thought before because, well, I've never had a boyfriend to consider. But you're right. For now, we only tell our inner circle. There's no point going public until we see how your son reacts. If he's not happy, I guess there'll be nothing to worry about. That'll be the end of it. Of us."

I rolled on top of Iain and cupped his face in my hands. "Boyfriend, huh?" I couldn't help the smile that graced my face.

"Maybe we shouldn't use that word." Iain's big brown eyes looked up at mine, his worry evident.

"Have a little faith, Iain."

"Are we crazy?"

"Probably."

I devoured his lips and any further words. I would live in the moment and enjoy the now.

And yes, there was a lot we had to deal with going forward, but my gut never steered me wrong.

Iain wrapped his long legs around my waist, and my hard cock brushed against his. He ran his hands up the back of my neck and gripped my short hair tightly.

"Your kisses are dangerous," he whispered against my lips. "I didn't stand a fucking chance."

His comment made my dick even harder and made my heart nearly claw its way out of my chest.

However, the sudden knock on my door made my heart take off running for very different reasons.

"Are you kidding me?" I bit out as I reluctantly pulled away from Iain. "This better be an emergency."

I grabbed my jeans and slipped them on, and Iain threw a T-shirt at me.

"No answering the door half naked anymore," Iain reminded me, his gaze lusty and possessive.

Fuck whoever was just outside my room; I was going to crawl back over to Iain and…

"Open up, Dawson. I need to speak to Holls."

Brodie was here? Christ. I needed caffeine for this.

I pulled on the T-shirt and ambled over to the door, checking the peephole first. Habit.

Then I threw open the door and glared at the man who was interrupting my perfect morning.

"What?" I bit out.

Brodie smirked. "Nice hickey."

The singer leaned against the doorjamb in tight jeans and a black hoodie, and his eyes rimmed with smudged eyeliner. Probably from the night before.

I rolled my eyes. "Nice try. What's so urgent that you're knocking on my door this early?"

"Early? It's almost noon. I guess time flies when you're having fun. Or, when you're doing Iain."

I grabbed his arm and dragged him inside the room. "Keep your voice down."

"Why? There's only the band and your team on this floor."

I slammed the door and glanced over at Iain. He was still lying in bed, the sheet riding low on his lean hips, barely covering his body. The sexy sight made my breath catch and did nothing to calm the erection in my jeans.

"Don't you look cozy in Dawson's bed?" Brodie cackled.

"I am, and you're interrupting." Iain sat up and ran a hand through his messy hair.

"Sorry, but I texted you two hours ago and got no response. Then I texted Daws, and same thing. I was worried."

I walked over to the nightstand and reached for my cell. Shit. I had missed several texts this morning, including one from Regan.

I quickly texted her back, telling her I'd call in ten minutes.

And this was why I needed to be taken off Iain's detail.

"My fault," I said. "But it won't happen again. I'm going to ask Regan to remove me from Iain's security."

"Permanently?" Brodie asked as he sat on the sofa, making himself at home.

"Yes." I sat on the bed next to Iain and reached for his hand, interlocking our fingers tightly. "We're together, so things will change."

"I'm so happy for you guys," Brodie exclaimed and ran over, tackling both of us and pushing us back on the bed.

"Get off, Dee!" Iain laughed and shoved Brodie.

Brodie simply rolled off Iain and lay beside us, waggling his eyebrows.

"Can I watch?"

"No," Iain and I replied at the same time.

"Oh, that's how it is, huh? What happened to my fuckboy? Does Dawson have a magic dick you want to keep all to yourself?" Brodie taunted.

"Out," I ordered. "Go back to your husband."

"He's still sleeping." Brodie snorted. "I wore him out last night. Rode him like a—"

Iain groaned and covered his eyes. "TMI, Dee."

Brodie chuckled. "So, I'm the first to know about you two?"

"Obviously," I replied.

"And?"

"All in due time."

"What does that mean?"

"It means we need to keep this private for now," Iain responded.

"Now get," I urged Brodie. "Iain needs to shower and eat."

Brodie finally got off the bed and nodded. "You take care of my best friend, understood?"

I saw the warning in his gaze. I nodded.

"All right, then. I'll see you guys at the venue in an hour."

Brodie sauntered out of the room and shut the door behind him, and I turned to Iain.

"I'll order room service; you hop in the shower."

Iain kissed me and headed for the bathroom. I admired his taut body and the evidence of our lovemaking in the form of beard burn, bite marks, and faint bruises on his golden skin.

"Hey," I called out, and Iain turned around. If we were gonna do this, I need to give him full disclosure. "You should also know that your stalker called me yesterday. Again. The first time was before we left home. Regan and I think it's someone at Bandit, because how else would this person have access to your number and mine, right? Anyway, you don't need to be concerned, but you have a right to know."

Iain froze, staring at me with wide eyes.

"Sweetheart?" I asked when he didn't respond.

"You're just telling me this now?!" Iain roared.

"I didn't want to worry you."

"That's not for you to decide!" he snapped and placed his hands on his hips. "Is there anything else?"

"No. That's it. I swear. You know what I know."

Iain bit his lower lip. "Do not keep shit like that from me. I don't need that kind of protection."

"I promise. And I'm sorry."

Iain shook his head. "This just makes things a whole lot more complicated."

"Meaning?"

Iain crossed his arms. "Jaxon. If you're at risk, he's at risk."

I got up and walked over to Iain. "I'm not at risk. And we're going to catch this person. And that will be that."

"You can't guarantee anything. Some of these celebrity stalker cases go on for months, even years. Jesus Christ."

"Is this it?" I whispered. "Should I bother telling Regan about you and me, about removing me from your security detail?"

Iain gripped my biceps and pulled me in close. "I don't want to walk away, but baby, you already said it. You gotta think about Jaxon first."

"Chances are, if I'm off your detail, the stalker won't bother with me anymore."

Iain sighed and relaxed his grip. "Maybe. But still, you and I need to keep this under wraps. If the stalker finds out we're in a relationship, how do you think they're gonna react?"

I grimaced. "It'll probably set them off."

That was an understatement. Someone obsessed, determined, and pissed off was a volatile bomb just waiting to go off.

I pulled Iain into my arms and ran a hand down his bare back. He clutched me just as tightly. Then I gently kissed the top of his head.

"But we're doing everything we can to find this person. Please, just trust me."

"I've known you for four years. Trusting you isn't the problem. It's everything else."

I didn't let go of Iain. I couldn't.

And that right there told me all I needed to know.

I was falling hard, ignoring any and all warning signs that were flashing in front of me.

CHAPTER 30

DAWSON

Regan stopped by my room a half hour later.

Iain and I had showered, changed, and were eating breakfast when she arrived.

She took one look at the room—Iain's clothes mixed up with mine, his guitar case on the chair, the rumpled bed—and shook her head.

"I need to be taken off Iain's detail effective immediately," I said before she could even sit down.

"No shit."

Iain laughed at Regan's reply, but I gave him the side-eye. Of course, it had no effect on him. He reached out and squeezed my thigh, leaving his hand there. The gesture was intimate and possessive, and I felt my body heat begin to rise again despite our audience.

"We're keeping our relationship private for now," I continued. "Brodie knows, and Iain's going to tell Faise and Ronin. I'm also going to tell Lennie and Zoe. We don't want Harlow to know yet, given everything that's happened with him on this trip."

"That makes sense," Regan murmured as she reached for the pot of coffee on the table and poured herself a cup. "But

I don't know how comfortable I am that you're on the band's security at all at this point. Are you going to be able to focus on your new primary, or will you be concerned about Iain?"

"I trust all my team members to look after Iain. Without reservation."

Regan sat back and nodded.

"Okay, you're on Faise from here on out, along with Valen. I'll put Lennie and Quinn on Iain. But if I see any hint that you're not one hundred percent focused, you're on the first plane back home."

I nodded.

"And I agree with you about Harlow," Regan continued. "Talk to Zoe first and see what she says. She'll want to get a plan prepared for if and when you guys go public. And when that happens, I *will* have to re-assign you."

"I understand."

"I don't," Iain interrupted. "Does that mean he's off the team entirely?"

"If you go public, yes," Regan replied.

"But—"

"It's okay," I reassured him. "And probably for the best. I've been doing a lot of thinking lately, and these long trips are difficult. Being away from my son, given his age. I'll need to find another job with more regular hours."

Regan nodded. "Now's the time to start planning."

"I will. Also, I told Iain about the stalker calling me."

"What are you going to do to protect Dawson?" Iain demanded. "And don't tell me nothing."

Regan smiled. "He's got Valen with him. He'll be fine. Besides, there's no threat to him."

"The stalker called him, so I disagree. And I'm also talking about when we go home. You guys think this person is local. What then? Dawson has Jaxon to think about."

Regan took another sip of coffee and nodded. "He does.

We'll ensure his home security is updated and provide a detail should it be deemed necessary."

"I say it's necessary," Iain bit out.

While I appreciated my lover's concern, he was making this a bigger deal than necessary.

I placed my hand over his.

"I have an idea," Regan murmured and put her coffee cup down. "But you might not like it."

Iain and I both looked at each other and then back at her.

"What is it?" I asked.

"If you decide to go public when you get home, maybe you could all stay at Iain's place? He has the new cameras, motion sensors, and the electronic fence. No one is getting in there. It's probably the safest place in the entire city."

"Uh, I don't know. I mean, look, Jaxon hasn't even met Iain yet, and if that—"

"What Dawson is trying to say is this is brand new," Iain replied and looked at me. "But I'd be willing—that is, if you want to. I mean, for you and your family's safety. Not because of us. It's a big house, with plenty of room. And it's not far from your place, probably in the same school district, right?"

My mouth was hanging open, but no words were coming out.

Move in with Iain? Even if it was temporary, my heart was saying, "Hell yes."

But what happened to his earlier reticence and our plan to take things slow?

"Daws, are you okay?" Iain asked me.

No. No, I was not.

Regan's chuckle broke me out of my head space. "I think you've shocked him. Fuck, you've shocked me too, Iain. I was kinda joking."

"Oh." Iain tried to pull his hand back, but I wouldn't let him.

"I'd have to talk it over with my family first." I looked at him. "But I'll take the idea into consideration."

Iain's face flushed, and I smiled at him. Before I knew it, I was leaning forward to kiss him.

Right in front of my boss…

"Okay, then, I'm off," I heard Regan exclaim. "I'll see you guys at the venue. Last day in Paris, and then it's on to the UK. I'll send Lennie and Quinn up here shortly. Remember, no touching, no flirting, no shenanigans of any kind while you're on duty."

"Yes, boss," I replied when I finally tore myself away from Iain.

I got up and walked Regan to the door.

She turned quickly. "I'm happy for you, Dawson. You two make a great pair."

"Really? I thought you'd be telling me I'm nuts."

She laughed. "That too. I mean, he is a rockstar. And with a hit-it and quit-it reputation. But the way he looks at you? I've never seen Iain look at any man that way. He trusts you. And I know Iain doesn't trust easily."

"Thanks."

"See you shortly."

I breathed out a huge sigh of relief. One difficult conversation down.

Three more to go.

———

Iain

Prior to showtime

After hair and makeup, it was just me and the guys shooting the shit before showtime. And Lennie, of course, stood guard near the dressing room door.

I'd quietly told Ronin and Faise about Dawson and me,

and after their expected razzing, I reminded them to keep their yaps shut.

Lennie smiled at me, and I knew he knew. I guess Dawson had talked to him this afternoon.

"Okay, so, I think I'm in trouble—" I started.

"How many times do I have to tell you to use condoms? STDs aren't fun," Brodie quipped.

I flipped off my best friend. "Seriously, I think I may have put my foot in my mouth."

"That's too kinky, even for me," Ronin offered.

"Will you be serious for a sec?" I hissed. "So, before we told Regan about, you know—"

"You and Dawson boning," Faise replied as he mimed jerking off.

I sighed. "As I was saying, before we told her about our relationship, Dawson mentioned that he's getting calls from my stalker."

"Shit, for real?" Brodie murmured and leaned forward. "Since when?"

"Since our charity concert. So, Regan suggested that, when we get back home, Dawson and his family could, you know, move in with me. Temporarily. Because my security is next level after the break-in. Just for their safety. If it should become an issue. I mean, if he and I are still, you know, together by then and if we go public. Or even if we don't and—"

Fuck, was I rambling. And all three of my band brothers stared at me for a moment and then burst out laughing.

Full-on, bent over, hysterical, uncontrolled laughter.

Faise doubled over, fell off his chair, and onto the floor. Brodie and Ronin had freaking tears rolling down their faces.

"You and Dawson… moving in together… and his son?" Faise hiccuped as he picked himself up off the floor.

"And Dawson's mom," I mumbled.

"Oh my God," Brodie shook his head, laughing so hard he

was barely able to speak. "You go from the proudest manwhore of our group… to a… to a… family of four, just like that. Only you, Iain. Only you. All or nothing, baby, all or nothing."

"I'm so glad that you guys find this fucking amusing. I'm freaking out over here! First of all, this thing with him is, like, a few days old, and now this! Plus, I'm worried about him. And I haven't even met Jaxon yet; what if he hates me?"

Brodie wiped his eyes and smeared his eyeliner. "It's only natural that you're concerned. And he's not going to hate you. From what you told me, the kid already wants to meet you."

"His name is Jaxon. And he wants to meet his musical idol, not me, the person."

"Holls! What the fuck, man?" Brodie smacked me on the back. "You're a great person. Don't talk shit like that."

"You just said it, Dee. I'm a manwhore. A fuckboy."

"A typical rockstar," Ronin added. "So?"

"And I should be the person Dawson wants to introduce to his son? As his boyfriend? Goddamn it, I don't know what the hell I've just walked into!"

Faise shook his head. "First off, just because you enjoy an active and varied sex life doesn't make you unfit in any way."

We all stared at Faise.

"What?" Faise grumbled. "It's true."

"You guys are doing the exclusive thing, right?" Ronin asked and looked around. "I can't even believe the words coming out of my mouth right now."

"Yes," I muttered, my face heating.

"He's blushing again. Shit, this is too freaking adorable," Brodie teased.

I gave my best friend my two best fingers in response.

Ronin tapped my hip. "Are you happy?"

"With Dawson? Yeah. But we're, like, a minute old, for Christ's sake."

Ronin rolled his eyes. "Please, you two have been bickering and flirting for years. Everyone witnessed your foreplay. You were already a couple; you just didn't know it."

"Ronin's right," Faise added. "Just go for it. See where it takes you."

"But I'm not a family guy, I—"

"Yes, you are. We're a family," Brodie stated.

"Dee—"

"Are we not?"

His sharp tone dared me to question him.

I finally nodded.

"Well, then? Go enjoy your man," Brodie gripped my neck and gave me a kiss on the cheek. "Now, are we done with all the emotional revelations for the night? Are we ready to rock our last night in Paris?"

"Fuck yes!" Ronin shouted.

I still didn't know what the hell I was doing, but I felt a lot better after talking with my boys.

Dawson was right. I needed to have a little faith.

Not just in him but also in me.

CHAPTER 31

IAIN

After our Paris concerts, we flew to London. And one week and three sold-out shows later, we headed back home.

And I was ready.

I was used to long days on the road, but the past two weeks felt more like two months. Like I rarely was, I was eager to get back home and get in the studio again. More than anything, I wanted to be able to spend more time with Dawson.

We made good on our promise to Regan. We were our professional selves during the day. But as soon as we returned to the hotel, he'd wait a while, then knock on my door.

And fuck, every night I spent in his arms left me wanting more. I wasn't a romantic person by any means, but I was so far gone for this man. I looked at my face in the mirror and hardly recognized my happiness.

In the mornings, Dawson would sneak back out again like a naughty teenager before Lennie was on duty.

It wasn't ideal, but I'd take whatever time with Dawson I could get.

And the longer I was with him, the more I knew this was it.

I was falling in love.

My band brothers were right. I'd probably been falling long before Dawson and I kissed, but hey, I'm a guitar prodigy, not a relationship expert. I didn't realize that bickering was our foreplay. And I didn't realize that, by trying to escape from Dawson, I was really only drawing us closer together.

As much as I was looking forward to going home, the closer we got to Nashville, the more anxious I became. And no, it wasn't because Dawson and his family were moving in with me temporarily. That wasn't happening. At least, not yet.

It was going back to that ginormous house of mine all alone. It left me feeling unsettled. It always took me a while to adapt to being back home and not living out of a suitcase, but usually, I was so busy going out at night and recording or rehearsing during the day that I didn't think twice.

But now? I didn't feel like hitting the clubs or bars when we got back home. Not at all. Fuck, I'd truly fallen from my rockstar ways.

All it took was one sexy bodyguard.

And now, I just wanted to sit on the couch with Dawson, watch a movie, make out, and then fuck in my bed until I was too sore to move. Or until I needed a new mattress. Whatever came first.

I wanted him to spend the night, the next day, the one after that...

Huh. I couldn't quite believe my train of thought, but hey, there's a first time for everything.

But it wasn't just the thought of returning to an empty house that left me uneasy.

There was also the matter of Jaxon.

Dawson had arranged for his son to stop by our studio in a few days. It would be our first meet and greet with the rest of my band brothers, which I thought was easier on all of us. Then I was taking Dawson and Jaxon out for lunch. That would give us time to gauge Jaxon's first impression.

My mind began to spin with all the what-ifs. My brain was working overtime, so sleep didn't happen for me.

Our plane touched down at just after eight in the evening. Dawson was careful to keep his distance and avoid any contact with me. He was busy anyway, whisking Faise to the arrivals gate after he went through customs.

I went with Brodie and Van and our bodyguards.

Ronin and Faise shared a ride as usual. Ronin recently bought a house on the same street as Faise, a one minute walk from each other. And yeah, we teased them about it mercilessly. They could've saved a shitload of money if they'd just bought one house together. They were with each other twenty-four seven anyway.

When I was finally seated in the back of the SUV, my phone vibrated.

> Dawson: I'll call you first thing tomorrow. I miss you already.

> I miss you too. I'll be waiting.

> What are your plans for tonight?

> Eat, shower, and hopefully, sleep. The jet lag is hitting hard.

> I noticed you didn't sleep much on the plane. You okay?

> Overthinking. And I thought you weren't watching me?

> We were safe on the plane, so yeah, I was watching. And everywhere you are, I want to be.

My heart flipped over when Dawson said stuff like that. I didn't dare admit I loved it, but, like everything about this man, I did.

> It's been over nine hours since you kissed me. I'm not sure I'm going to last a few days.

> I'll make it worth the wait.

> I'm counting on it.

A sharp elbow to my ribs had me looking up to find Brodie giving me that know-it-all grin of his.

"What?" I asked.

"Sexting?"

"No."

Not yet.

"Do you want Van and me to stay with you?"

"What? No. I'll be fine. They've added more cameras, and Lennie will be on site. No worries."

"Call us, day or night, and we'll come over. I mean it, I don't want you alone with that weirdo still at large."

"It's been quiet this week, so maybe whoever it is has found someone else to annoy."

"Still—"

I held my hand up. "I'll reach out regularly and let you know if I need company, all right?"

Brodie nodded and slapped my thigh. "If not, you can

always go with plan B and move Dawson and his family in with you."

"Will you shut it?" I hissed, hoping no one around us heard.

"You meeting up with your man?" he whispered.

"Not until the studio on Friday."

"Two days apart." Brodie sighed. "I don't think I could do it with Van."

"No kidding. The last time your husband went out of town for a weekend, you were a grumpy pain in the ass."

Brodie shrugged, no denial.

"I hear you got a new song for us."

I startled. "Who told you that?"

Brodie just smiled.

"He did?" I asked. "Really?"

"Your man admires your talent, not just your sexy body," Brodie teased. "And apparently, you've been holding out on us."

"No, I haven't." I waved him off. "Most of the time, I prefer to focus on my part. I'm a guitarist first, you know that. I'm not even sure I know what I'm doing when it comes to songwriting. It's just something I've started brainstorming lately."

"Well, Van and I are happy to review what you've got and go from there. I'm looking forward to it. It means our sound can continue to grow."

"You haven't even heard the song yet, Dee. It's barely that. Just a few chords and some lyrics I wrote down in the middle of the night."

"Gotta start somewhere."

We pulled into the long, circular driveway of my house.

Like many of my fellow musicians and celebrities, I'd chosen the Forest Hills area to call home.

I bought the place mainly due to the size of the land. I had the crumbling cottage that sat on it razed. In its place, the contractor built a modern ranch house. The home was all one level, in a U-shape, and sat at the highest point of the property. The central area was the living room, dining, and kitchen. One wing was for my living quarters, including a main bedroom and bath, and the other wing consisted of my music room and three guest bedrooms. A large pool and a massive firepit in the backyard completed the space.

All in all, it was a peaceful retreat. Rustic and minimalist, it was my little bit of zen in the country.

I reached over and gave Brodie a hug, then Van, and promised to call if I needed anything.

Lennie and Quinn did the house tour first, ensuring the place was secure.

Once we were given the all-clear, Quinn told Lennie he'd be back to change shifts at eight tomorrow morning.

I waved goodbye to my friends as the SUV headed back out to the main road.

"You got food in the house?" Lennie asked as we entered the front door.

"Bibi arranged for a delivery this morning. I should be stocked up. If there's anything you need, let me know. I'll show you to the—"

"No need. I know where the guest rooms are. I'll just drop off my stuff."

"Okay, then. Thanks."

Lennie wandered off to the east wing while I headed west.

I wandered down the hall to my bedroom and dumped my suitcases on the floor.

Too tired to unpack, I decided that a shower was in order, then food.

I texted Bibi and asked if she could call me tomorrow. I had resisted, in my independent way, the label's offer of a full-time personal assistant, but maybe it was past due. Our schedules were busier than ever, and anything that could save me time was worth it.

As I made my way past the bathroom, the click of my boots on the reclaimed hardwood echoed loudly.

When I stopped at the foot of my bed and looked at it, I immediately pictured Dawson lying there.

I shook my head, still in shock that thoughts like that belonged to me.

But it was almost painful to be alone again. Strange how I'd gotten used to Dawson and his presence in my life.

It also gave me an insight I never expected.

I always knew that my dad loved my mom. Why else would he have been so destroyed by her passing? And hell, watching him fall apart was my reason for avoiding relationships in the first place. Who wants to go through that kind of pain?

As my mind began churning, I wondered if he ever regretted falling for her. Did he regret me, too?

Questions I hadn't dared to think about for over two decades were rising to the surface again.

I called my dad once a month to check in and see that he was okay. It usually consisted of a two-minute phone call and uncomfortable pauses between "How are you?" and "Fine."

Without thinking of the how or why, I pulled out my phone and sent a follow-up message to Bibi.

After I pressed send, I stepped back into the here and now.

Stripping down, I headed to my bathroom and enjoyed a long shower, too exhausted to jerk off. I wrapped myself up in a big, white terry cloth robe, grabbed my phone, and padded barefoot to the kitchen for a snack.

My body clock was all over the place, but if I didn't eat, I wouldn't sleep.

Lennie was already behind the center island, cooking.

"Smells good, whatcha making?" I asked.

"Pasta puttanesca. Quick and delicious. You want?"

"Spicy carbs? Fuck, yes. Thank you."

Lennie nodded and plated up two dishes of steaming hot pasta.

"Wine?" he asked.

"Nah, it'll mess with my sleep. Just water, thanks."

"Who the fuck are you right now?" Lennie chuckled as he pulled a bottle of sparkling water from the fridge and poured two glasses.

"I honestly have no idea. Ever since Brodie got with Van, everything's shifted. First him, now me. What's next?"

I swirled a forkful of pasta and shoved it in my mouth. It was so damn delicious.

"Speaking of you, I mean, you and Dawson... what's up with that?"

I chewed and swallowed my mouthful of food and took a sip of water. "I'm as surprised as you are."

Lennie shook his head. "I'm not totally shocked after watching you guys for months. But I am concerned. I know it's not my place, but I consider him a friend. And I don't want to see him get hurt."

I heard the warning in Lennie's voice and saw it in his blue eyes. But it didn't change anything.

"I can't guarantee that. All I can say is that I've never felt like this about anyone."

Lennie looked down, stabbing his pasta with his fork. "I don't know if that's a good enough answer."

I should've been annoyed. Who was he to judge my new relationship with Dawson?

But I knew Lennie was only saying what any friend would. I'd do the same if the situation were reversed.

And frankly, he wasn't wrong.

On paper, I was a risky bet for any man.

But for Dawson Everly?

I wasn't sure I could beat those odds.

CHAPTER 32
DAWSON

"Now remember, don't—"

"Dad, I *know*." Jaxon sighed. "I'm not a baby anymore. I won't run through the studio or break their instruments."

I glanced at my son as he sat beside me. I'd managed to snag the last remaining parking spot at Wayward Lane's recording studio in downtown Nashville.

"You gotta chill out," Jaxon continued, unbuckling his seat belt.

"Chill out?" I repeated.

If this was Jaxon at eight going on nine, the teenage years were going to be brutal.

"Yeah. You're so nervous, like when you drink too much coffee. You changed clothes three times, and we're already ten minutes late. And it's weird because you already know the band, not me, so why are you anxious?"

I listened to my son's reasoning and stifled a laugh.

I wasn't on shift today, and the studio tour was purely a personal visit.

A very personal visit.

And yeah, it was true. I was nervous about seeing Iain. Was he still all in, or had he changed his mind about us? I was pretty sure that, given the massive number of texts and late-night calls between us, Iain was feeling the same as me. I missed him something crazy, and I didn't expect to feel so on edge—like if I didn't touch him soon, I was going to go out of my mind.

So, yeah, I spent extra time getting ready, trying to look my best in new jeans, a dark grey button-down, and a beard clip. Not to mention I had my fauxhawk trimmed.

I wasn't the only nervous one, but my son was better at hiding it.

Jaxon had also carefully selected his outfit—black jeans, a matching T-shirt, and his down jacket. Oh, and his new neon orange running shoes.

My kid had more street style than me; that I knew for sure.

I reached my hand out to rub his bristly red hair and smiled.

"I'm not on duty, so it feels kind of strange," I told him. "But I'll be fine. Let's go."

A lot was riding on today. If Jaxon's impression of Iain wasn't positive, I, well, I didn't want to think about that. I swallowed hard and took a deep breath before I exited the truck.

Quinn was at the front door, waving us in, and I knew Lennie was already inside. He'd texted me as I was en route. By Regan's order, he was still at Iain's house, trading shifts with Quinn and Valen.

Everything with Iain's stalker had been eerily quiet since we got back to town, but Regan and I weren't convinced it was over. Greg thought it was done with. But until the investigator gave us some answers about who might be behind the messages, I wouldn't be letting my guard down.

My sixth sense told me we were as secure as possible, but

that didn't prevent me from looking around. I was always aware of my surroundings.

I rounded the hood of the truck and placed my hand on Jaxon's shoulders, guiding him to the door.

"Jaxon," I squeezed his shoulder, "you remember Quinn?"

Jaxon waved. "Hey, Quinn!"

"Nice to see you again, Jax. Cool shoes," Quinn replied.

The former cop-turned-bodyguard was usually a wall of ice, so seeing him smile was strange.

"Thanks. I like your new tattoo. Did it hurt?"

"This one?" Quinn replied as he pointed to the Celtic knot on his left hand. "Barely a pinch."

"Are you sure? My friend Casey's dad got a tattoo on his wrist and said he was never getting another one ever again."

Quinn shrugged. "I'm used to it. I got a lot of them. So, is this your first time meeting the band?"

"Yes! And Dad's nervous. He's been pacing all morning."

Shit.

"He's joking. Not nervous," I said to Quinn, who was giving me a confused look. "Are they all here?"

"Yup, head on back. Have fun."

We slipped past Quinn and down the hallway. The recording studio was at the back of the building.

When we reached the end of the hallway, I knocked on the heavy wood door.

Bibi answered with a big smile. "How y'all doing?"

"We're great, Bibi. I'd like you to meet my son, Jaxon."

"Well, it's wonderful to finally meet you in person, Jaxon. I'm Brodie's assistant," she explained. "Love your outfit! You excited to meet the guys?"

"Thanks, Bibi, and yeah, I'm so excited! But Dad's nervous."

Bibi gave me a knowing smirk.

"Jax—"

"Sorry, Dad."

I could tell from his grin he wasn't sorry at all.

"Come on in. The guys are working on a new piece and have their headphones on, so we'll stand in the editing booth for now, and watch."

Bibi led the way as we headed down another narrow hallway and turned left.

My heart was beating so loud at this point you could've recorded it for the drumbeat on one of the band's songs.

Bibi let us into the booth, where Ace and the other engineers and producers sat. The wall of glass that separated us from the band allowed us to see the entire studio.

As Bibi mentioned, the guys were all sitting in a circle, playing a new piece. It sounded a lot like the tune Iain had been strumming that night in Paris.

Faise was at his drum kit, facing us with Ronin and Brodie on either side, and Iain had his back to us, guitar in hand. Iain's right foot was tapping out a rhythm. Whether in time with the song or his usual nervous tell, I couldn't decipher.

Iain's hair was tied up in that messy bun that I loved, and he wore jeans, cowboy boots, and a blue T-shirt. As always, the man had all my attention.

Brodie looked over and spotted us, then motioned to the rest of the guys to stop playing. When Iain turned around, I saw both delight and hesitation in his expression. He looked as nervous as I was, and knowing that, I calmed—a little.

Iain placed his guitar on the stand, slid his headphones around his neck, and quickly got up, opening the door to let us into their session room.

"You guys are finally here," Iain exclaimed, almost breathless. "Come on in."

I wanted to lean over and kiss him so badly, but given our audience, our reunion would have to wait. With my back to the booth, though, I felt bolder than usual and held Iain's gaze for much longer than was polite. His answering grin told me he knew exactly what I was feeling.

Iain cleared his throat and held out his hand to Jaxon. "How are you, Jaxon? It's so nice to finally meet you in person."

Jaxon shook his hand slowly, staring up at Iain like he was seeing Santa Claus for the first time. "I can't believe I'm meeting Iain Holloway. Can I call you Iain?"

"Of course."

My heart warmed, and I squeezed Jaxon's shoulders.

"Are you guys recording a new song?" Jaxon asked him.

"We're not recording it yet; we're still working on the hook," Iain replied.

"Is that the one you started in Paris?" I asked.

Iain bit his lip and nodded. "Come on in, Jaxon, and meet everyone."

Iain introduced Jaxon to Brodie, Faise, and Ronin, and then my son got to walk around the room and admire their instrument setup.

"Cool kicks, Jaxon; I have ones just like those but in green. Think maybe we could trade?" Brodie asked with a smile.

"Thanks, but that wouldn't be fair. There's no way your big feet could fit into my shoes."

Everyone laughed at Jaxon's blunt statement, and I mouthed "sorry" to Brodie. He just laughed it off.

"But maybe you could autograph them for me?" Jaxon added with a grin.

"You got it."

Brodie motioned for Jaxon to pass over his shoes. All four guys signed them, two signatures on each shoe, and Jaxon was beaming with pride when he put them back on his feet.

"These are so cool! Wait until I show everyone at school!"

I pulled out my phone. "Is it okay if I take some pictures? We wouldn't post anywhere, obviously."

Jaxon looked excitedly at the guys, and they nodded. I took several pics of Jaxon's signed shoes and then him with the band. His smile was so big and beaming that my chest tightened.

"Jaxon, you want to play guitar with me?" Iain asked.

My son nodded and happily took a seat beside his idol, staring up at him and peppering him with question after question. Iain was more patient than I had imagined, getting up to grab one of his prized guitars lined up on the periphery of the room and placing it on Jaxon's lap.

"You told me you play piano, but have you ever played guitar?" Iain asked.

"At my last lesson, my teacher showed me a few chords on her acoustic. But that's all I know."

Iain crouched down in front of Jaxon and guided his hands so he was holding the instrument correctly. They began to talk about chords, E, A, D, etc., and I was lost.

My son, however, was absorbing every word that came out of Iain's mouth, nodding and asking more questions.

Iain sat down beside him again, picked up the guitar he'd been playing earlier and they started playing. Or, Iain played, and Jaxon watched, mesmerized.

When Iain looked over at me again, I startled. The smile he gave me should have been illegal.

A strange lump formed in my throat as I watched the two of them—the son I loved with everything in my heart and the man who had somehow found a way in there, too.

I was so overwhelmed that I turned away and caught Brodie staring at me, his telltale smirk in place. But he didn't say anything snarky. In fact, quite the opposite.

"It's crazy but true," Brodie leaned in to whisper to me.

"What is?"

"Every rockstar has their day."

I hoped that Brodie was right.

Because I wanted to be Iain's.

And I sure as fuck wanted Iain to be mine.

CHAPTER 33

IAIN

"Who's ready for lunch?" I called out.

I looked around the room, trying to act casual, but really, there were only two people I was talking to.

"Van's stopping by in a bit," Brodie explained. "I'm gonna wait for him."

"Me and Faise are gonna hang here too," Ronin responded with a knowing grin. "You go on with Dawson and Jaxon. Have fun."

"I will."

I would. I hoped. If Jaxon liked me.

Fuck.

I'd been a total wreck in the studio today. Anxious as fuck to meet Dawson's son, and the guys sure had their fun watching me pace the floor and carry on.

Brodie's large family of nieces and nephews was my only experience being around kids. As an only child, I was used to being on my own, and now, as an adult, most of my friends were still single like me, with no partners, never mind children.

But thank God for the bond of music.

Jaxon was just like me at that age, inquisitive and soaking up every bit of knowledge he could grasp. I recognized his gift as soon as I saw the way he strummed my guitar. He flubbed a bit because yeah, he was nervous too. But for his age, he caught on quickly. He tested out every instrument we had in the studio—drums, bass—but by the end of the tour, he came back to the guitar.

At least we had one thing in common.

Besides Dawson.

But when it came time for me to head out with Dawson and Jaxon, just the three of us, I began to sweat profusely.

I grabbed my jacket and phone while that self-doubting bastard in my head snuck up on me again.

What the fuck are you doing, Iain? What kind of man wants a rockstar for a partner?

Especially a man who has a young son. Half the songs on our albums weren't even fit for Jaxon to listen to at his age, never mind all the media shit that surrounded my life. What kind of role model could I be?

I started to slip on my leather jacket, but I hesitated until I suddenly felt Dawson standing behind me. Like a perfect gentleman, he helped me get my jacket in place and gave my shoulders a comforting squeeze. My heart skipped a beat, and my stomach dropped out. Why did such a gesture thrill me? And did he somehow know just where my mind had wandered?

When I turned, I caught Dawson's dark green eyes staring at me knowingly. I did the only thing that felt right at that moment.

I moved towards him.

The fear was hovering over me like a bad hangover, but I did my best to ignore it.

"You ready?" Dawson asked.

I nodded and turned to Jaxon. "What do you feel like eating, Jax?"

"Mexican!" he replied enthusiastically.

"I knew I liked you," I quipped. "How about El Corona? Best tacos in the city."

Dawson leaned in and whispered in my ear. "And maybe a margarita or two. Quinn can drive us home."

"Yes. I think today definitely calls for a celebration." I winked.

Jaxon was silent, staring at the two of us. Shit. Was I flirting?

Jaxon took Dawson's hand in his left and then reached out to me with his right. When I got over my surprise, I took his little hand in mine as all three of us headed out of the studio.

I turned my head just before we reached the door to find everyone—my band brothers, Ace, and our producers—smiling at me like idiots and shaking their heads in disbelief. Brodie had his phone out, taking pictures, undoubtedly, to record this day in history.

I just knew I was never gonna hear the end of it. But honestly? I was too happy to care about whatever razzing was coming next.

Lennie escorted us out of the building, with Dawson handing over the keys to his truck to my security lead.

The restaurant I had in mind was my favorite. No one paid me any mind there, and that was part of the reason I was a repeat customer. Occasionally, a fan would stop by and politely ask for an autograph or a selfie, but it wasn't relentless, which I appreciated.

Ten minutes later, we managed to snag a booth at the back of the place, with Dawson and Jaxon sitting across from me and Lennie.

Jaxon was just as chatty now as he was in our studio, peppering me with questions about our trip to Paris, our tour schedule, and what I did in my free time.

"Do you have a dog or a cat?" Jaxon asked me when our drinks arrived.

Watermelon margaritas for Dawson and me, ginger ale for Jaxon, and sparkling water for Len.

"Nope, but I might get one soon. My house seems kinda big for just me. But I'd probably get a cat. If I got a dog, I'd have to take them on the road with me. And I'm not sure how that would work out. I don't want to be a shi… I mean, a bad pet parent."

"You might have to bring your cat, too," Jaxon suggested as he sipped on his ginger ale. "You don't want to leave them with a stranger for weeks."

"Uh, well, I wouldn't leave them with a total stranger. But I think a cat wouldn't mind being watched by someone else. They're pretty independent."

Jaxon nodded. "Maybe you could get two? Then they'd have each other."

I nodded, considering that idea, as I sipped my drink.

"Jax—" Dawson glanced at his son.

"I'm not saying *we* have to get two cats, Dad, but Iain's all alone. He doesn't have a boyfriend or girlfriend or anything. He could use the company."

I coughed and nearly spat out my mouthful of margarita. Lennie was trying to stifle his laughter.

Dawson looked mortified, but I reached under the table and gave his knee a reassuring pat.

Once I was able to swallow, I let out a loud laugh.

"You're so right, Jaxon. I could use the company. I'll have to check out some local animal shelters. Maybe you guys could come with me and help me out?"

"Are you serious? Could we, Dad?" Jaxon asked.

"We'll see," Dawson replied, and then smiled at me. "You sure?"

I nodded in return.

Thankfully, our food arrived—one platter of birria tacos and another with loaded nachos—and we got busy stuffing our faces. I hadn't eaten anything all morning, given my nerves, so I was famished.

Dawson, Jaxon, and Len all had good appetites too.

Between mouthfuls of crunchy, salty chips and saucy tacos, we talked about Jaxon's school and his plans for his upcoming birthday.

"Can you come too?" Jaxon asked me, his blue eyes earnest.

"To your birthday party?"

"Yeah, that would be awesome! I'm going to have a paint-ball party."

"It sounds fun, but it will depend on your dad. He's the one in charge."

I looked at Dawson.

Dawson swiped a tortilla chip with a scoop of guacamole off my plate, and before I could protest, he made a big show of shoving it in his mouth.

"That's right," Dawson murmured between bites as he stared at me. "I call the shots."

Were we still talking about the party? Because suddenly, the room felt like it was over a hundred degrees.

"Please, Dad."

Jaxon's plea brought me back to the present.

Dawson nodded. "If Iain has time in his schedule, then yes, we would be honored for him to join us. Then I can whoop his butt at paintball."

I wanted to reach across the table and kiss Dawson, but I gave him a salty smirk.

"Whoop my butt, huh? Tell me when and where. And what you want for your birthday, okay, Jax? Can I call you Jax?"

Jaxon nodded.

"Not a cat," Dawson warned, giving his son a gentle side hug. "Or a guitar."

I chuckled. "Noted. What are you guys up to this afternoon?"

"Since it's a professional development day at Jax's school, he doesn't have class. I'm dropping him off at his friend Casey's for a play date."

"And a sleepover," Jaxon added.

"That's right. And a sleepover."

Dawson gazed into my eyes.

Did that mean he was free to come over after this? Stay over? Fuck, please, please say yes.

"What about you, Dad? Are you and Iain going to hang out?"

Lennie coughed into his fist, and I turned to find my bodyguard trying not to laugh again.

"Um," Dawson replied, rubbing his beard. "Maybe. Would that be okay?"

Dawson was testing the waters.

"You don't get out much, and Iain needs the company, so I think it's a good idea," Jaxon replied matter of factly.

Lennie and I both laughed at that comment, with Dawson joining in.

"Ouch, Jax. But noted," Dawson teased his son.

"Does anyone want dessert?" I asked. "They've got a chocolate cinnamon lava cake that's so fu… freaking amazing."

Not swearing in front of Jaxon was as challenging as not flirting with Dawson.

Jaxon shook his head. "Thanks, but I'm stuffed."

"Me too," Lennie replied.

I looked at Dawson, and he licked his lips. "How about we order one to go?"

Suddenly, I was picturing him and me in my bed, feeding each other that cake and making all kinds of messes.

Oh God, two days was far too long to be separated from this man.

"I like that idea."

Dawson flagged down the server, and once we had our cake in hand, I paid for lunch, much to Dawson's protest, and we headed out.

"Thank you for lunch and for letting me play your guitar. It was so cool. And for meeting the guys and the autographs on my shoes and coming to my party!" Jaxon exclaimed.

"Well, thanks for dropping by. It was my pleasure."

Jaxon leaned forward and gave me an earnest hug. I was surprised, my heart warming at his gesture.

This kid was too cute for words.

Lennie opened the door, and Jaxon hopped up into the back cabin of the truck.

"What's the plan?" Len asked when he closed the door. "Drop off Jaxon at his friend's and then on to your place?"

Dawson looked at me, and I nodded.

"Perfect," Dawson replied.

Yes, it was.

CHAPTER 34

IAIN

After Lennie dropped off Jaxon, Dawson got into the back seat so we could sit together.

Alone. For the first time in forty-eight hours.

He slid his right hand into my left, interlocking our fingers tightly, and I fought the urge to jump over his lap and kiss the fuck out of him.

Our legs brushed, and I began to squirm until he pulled his hand out of mine and gripped my upper thigh firmly. Then he began to rub and squeeze, up and down, and it was the most delicious kind of torture. My dick was so hard there was no way I was going to hide the bulge in my jeans when I got out of this truck.

Not that I cared if Lennie saw. Since he was staying in my house, and Dawson was with me, he would probably see—and hear—a hell of a lot more.

It didn't matter.

I just needed to be alone with Dawson as soon as possible.

When we pulled up to my driveway, I was ready to bolt to the front door, but Dawson gripped my hand again.

"No. Lennie has to check the house first."

Shit. I forgot.

"Sorry, lost my head for a second," I whispered in Dawson's ear. "I'm too fucking excited to be alone with you again."

As soon as Lennie stepped out of the truck and the door slammed shut, Dawson manhandled me. My back hit the leather seat, and I was held down by the only fucking man I wanted.

"Your reaction is the biggest goddamn turn-on," Dawson moaned before he took my mouth in a fierce kiss, ravaging my lips and sucking on my tongue like a man starved.

I kissed him back, every taste and touch of our lips more desperate than the last.

Until a knock on the door startled us.

Dawson lifted his head and let out a string of curses, then slowly sat back up, taking me with him.

After a few deep breaths, Dawson opened the door and stepped out first. Then he held his hand out to me, his eyes imploring mine. Instead of ignoring the gesture like I had in the past when we were bodyguard and client, I readily took his hand.

And this time, I didn't let go.

Not even when my boots hit the gravel.

Not that I felt the ground below me, because I swear to God I was floating on air.

Was this what Brodie was going on about when it came to Van? And why he couldn't keep his hands off his husband? This whole falling-in-love thing was more powerful than I'd anticipated. The way Dawson held me, the way he kissed, every single touch was protective and possessive, and I was there for it.

I was standing in Dawson's spotlight, soaking up his desire. He made my knees weak and sparked a passion I'd never believed I was capable of.

I thought I knew everything about my needs and wants, my sexual desires. Lust was simple, easy, and fun.

This, what was happening with me and Dawson, was anything but.

And fuck, I still had a difficult time wrapping my head around the changes that were happening, not just to me, to him, but to us.

We were ready to tear into each other only a few weeks ago. Now, all we wanted to do was tear our clothes off.

Lennie walked ahead as usual, ignoring or not caring that Dawson and I were still holding hands.

I didn't give a fuck. If Lennie didn't like it, that was his problem.

Then I imagined what it would be like if Dawson and I were a public couple. What would have made me run far and fast a month ago now filled me with a sense of longing and a wish for things to come.

We entered the front foyer, and without saying a word, Dawson dragged me down the hallway to my bedroom.

"I'd give you the full tour, but you've already been here," I teased.

He stopped halfway to my room and suddenly turned.

"I shouldn't have just assumed—"

I grabbed his face in my hands and reached up to take his lips. The kiss was as devouring and heady as the one in the truck, leaving no room for doubt or pause.

"Are you kidding me? Consider this your open invitation to my bedroom," I whispered against his lips. "And every other room in this house."

"Every room?"

"Each and every one."

"Christ, it's been two long fucking days," Dawson groaned.

Next thing I knew, he bent down and threw me over his shoulder, carrying me in a fireman's lift as he continued on down the hallway.

He swatted my ass for good measure, and my dick grew so hard it was damn near painful.

"You're the first guy to literally sweep me off my feet." I chuckled. "And why is it the sexiest thing ever?"

My eyes locked on Dawson's round ass, flexing with every step.

Question asked and answered.

"What kind of men have you been fucking?" he bit out. "Wait, don't answer that."

"Don't need to. I can't remember anyone else."

He rubbed and squeezed my ass as he entered my bedroom, using his foot to shut the door behind us. "Smooth talker."

"No, that's you. I'm the needy, whimpering kind."

Dawson's husky laugh filled me with happiness.

I couldn't ever remember being so at ease with any other lover. And on the other hand, feeling so desperate for his touch.

He swatted my ass again, then threw me down on my California king.

I bounced once, and then he was on me.

Our kisses were deep and drugging. And interrupted only by our haste to get naked as soon as possible.

Dawson tore my T-shirt off, and as I struggled to unzip my jeans, he slid down the bed and yanked my boots and socks off. Then he stood up, toed off his boots, shed his button-down, and shoved his jeans and briefs to the ground, stepping out of them. My hands paused as I took in the sight of my gorgeous bear of a man. I was suddenly so overwhelmed —not only by my want for him but by everything that was happening between us—that I was shy like I never was.

"All right, sweetheart?" Dawson whispered as he stared back at me.

"Yes. Just taking a moment to appreciate you."

Dawson's face flushed as he stepped closer. He pushed my hands away, unzipping my jeans and revealing my black jockstrap.

"Fuck, you are the sexiest thing I've ever seen," he groaned. "And all mine. Roll over."

I did as he asked and when his warm hands cupped my ass cheeks, I glanced over my shoulder. The intense look on Dawson's face as he looked his fill had me rutting against the mattress, desperate for friction on my cock.

"Judging by the look on your face, I'm going to need to order more lube," I quipped.

His dirty laugh made all the hair on my body stand on end.

"Cases and cases of it," he replied.

He reached over to my nightstand, yanked on the top drawer, and threw the biggest tube of lube I owned on the bed beside me.

"But first, I'm going to feast on your beautiful ass. I've thought of nothing else for days," Dawson declared as he tugged on my jockstrap. I lifted my hips and let him slide the garment down and off my body.

Dawson wasted no time, pulling my ass cheeks apart and diving right in to make good on his promise.

When his hot tongue flicked over my sensitive rim, I reached for one of my pillows and shoved it in my face, muffling my loud moan.

Dawson suddenly withdrew, and this time, I nearly screamed in frustration. "What the—"

I looked over my shoulder at him.

"None of that, now. We're not going to censor ourselves in here," Dawson announced, pulling the pillow out from under me and throwing it aside. He leaned over my back, blanketing my body with his, and whispered in my ear. "I want to hear every fucking filthy sound you make. Understood?"

Ngh. Bossy Dawson was so freaking hot.

"Yes," I gasped, my body feverish for his.

"That's what I like to hear."

Dawson wasted no time sliding back down my body and shoving his bearded face in my ass, licking and fucking my hole with his skillful tongue. I gripped the sheets in my hands for purchase and pushed my ass back, needing more.

"More," I begged him loudly. "Don't stop!"

His hands gripped my ass cheeks tightly, so tight I'd probably have bruises tomorrow.

And I wanted them. I wanted Dawson to mark me, to claim me in any way he wanted.

His tongue continued to tease, licking down over my taint and back up over my hole. Then he plunged the tip of his tongue inside me, fucking my ass with tormenting strokes. The pleasure was so raw that I was rocking my hips back and forth, wanting more tongue in my ass and more friction on my leaking cock. My climax was building higher and higher as he ate me out, and I chanted his name.

Fuck, I was going to come already. Hands-free.

"So close," I panted, and he reached between my legs to cup my balls. I was about to sneak my hand underneath to tug on my cock, but Dawson pushed my hand away.

Then he withdrew his tongue with one last lick and pulled back.

"Stay."

"What? Wait, where are you going?"

Dawson calmly padded over to my walk-in closet and opened the doors. He disappeared for a moment and came back out, holding up two long scarves.

"Just what do you plan to do with those?" I asked, curious and curiously turned on by the intense expression on his face.

His cock curled up against his stomach, the head red and leaking pre-cum.

I licked my lips as he stepped to the bed and smiled at me. "I want to see how good you are at taking orders."

"Only the sexy kind. And only with you."

"I wouldn't have it any other way, sweetheart. I don't want to dim your fire. I want to make it burn brighter."

I swallowed hard and nodded.

"Now spread your legs again."

"Not my arms?"

Dawson shook his head. "I won't risk your hands."

I was so far gone I hadn't even considered that. And even in this, Dawson was always looking out for me, caring for me.

I did as he asked. I looked over my shoulder and watched as he deftly tied one end of the scarf to the wooden bedpost and the other around my left ankle. Using the second scarf, he repeated the steps with my right foot.

"Not too tight?" he asked with concerned eyes.

I shook my head. I could pull my knee up close to my hip, but no higher.

Believe it or not, I'd never indulged in this type of play before. And yeah, I know, what the hell? And I called myself a rockstar?

I mean, I'd had threesomes, foursomes, and enjoyed an occasional orgy. But this kind of thing required trust, and no stranger would ever tie me down this way.

I was vulnerable like I never was, and the rush of emotions couldn't be contained any longer.

"Only you," I repeated.

Only him.

My heart and mind and body were all on the same page.

The only thing I needed was Dawson.

CHAPTER 35

IAIN

Dawson finally slid back onto the bed, taking his time running his hands up my calves, over my thighs, and, finally, cupping my ass cheeks again.

Then he was all over me, covering me with his body, rubbing his cock over my ass, and pulling my hair aside to nuzzle my neck.

He kissed his way up my jaw and then took my lips in a teasing kiss that was delicious and yet not enough. I couldn't kiss him deeply at this angle, and my frustrated moan made him smile.

Next thing I knew, his slick finger was circling my hole, teasing the rim and then pushing inside. I pulled my left knee up as high as the binding would allow me, and his knee followed suit.

"Slow and easy, just you and me," Dawson moaned as he slowly finger-fucked me.

"More, please. Please," I begged. "Fuck me. I don't need much prep."

He withdrew his finger and pushed his cockhead into my hole. Thank fuck for the rimming and the lube because Dawson was a big fucking man, and his cock was no exception. I felt like he was splitting me in two, the pain and pleasure so intense that I shuddered with every movement of his hips.

"Baby, that's so fucking good," I gasped. "I need you. All of you."

Inch by inch, slow but steady, he pushed inside me. I was so full, and when his balls hit my ass, I groaned out loud. With Dawson's weight on me, and his bare dick in my ass, this was it; I was done. I could die happy right here and now.

"You're mine, sweetheart," Dawson gasped. "All fucking mine."

"Dawson."

His hands slid along my arms and over my hands, interlocking tightly.

Raising our left hands, he brought mine up to his mouth and pressed languid kisses on my callused palm. Playing as much as I did, my hands weren't as sensitive as they used to be. But when he kissed me like that, so unexpectedly sweet, a shiver rolled through my entire body. The gesture was sexy, intimate, and words I never imagined saying, never mind feeling, longed to be let out.

My eyes welled up, and I tried to blink the tears away.

But I didn't succeed.

Sweat slid down over my face, mixing with the tears that slipped out of the corners of my eyes. I felt the rapid tempo of his heartbeat against my shoulder blade.

"You're not alone, sweetheart; I'm right here with you," Dawson murmured.

He was warm and real and all mine in return.

"Don't stop, baby," I pleaded.

Dawson placed my hands back on the bed as he lifted his chest up and rocked his hips. Rocking into me.

I was surrounded by his heat and musky sweat as he fucked into me with short, hard strokes.

God, I needed to come. My climax kept building, higher and higher.

I tried to move my leg up, but the scarf tightened around my ankle. Shit. Fuck. That was frustrating.

"Give yourself to me, Iain. Let go. I will give you every fucking thing you need," Dawson growled as he pistoned his hips harder, faster.

I relaxed my body, and Dawson took control again.

He kneeled and took hold of my hips, pulling me back and fucking into me with powerful strokes. With my upper body on the mattress, my legs restrained, and my ass in the air, I was too blissed out to do anything but whatever Dawson wanted.

"That's it, sweetheart," Dawson panted as he pounded my ass. "Look at you, taking my cock so good. I'm going to mark this pretty ass with my cum, inside and out, so you know exactly who you belong to."

"Yes. Please, please fucking take me!" I whimpered.

His slick hand tugged on my dick, stroking in time with every thrust. He nailed my prostate over and over, and the tormenting pleasure spread through my body until I was begging, pleading to come.

"Who do you belong to, Iain?" Dawson demanded. "Say it."

"You. Only you," I gasped. "But you belong to me too."

"Fucking right, I do."

His hips thrust into me in a frantic rhythm, and with one more stroke on my cock, I came long and hard. I shouted his name as wave after wave of pleasure consumed me, pulling me under until I could only gasp for air.

Dawson's body tensed, and then he moaned my name, unleashing his cum in my ass.

He continued to rock his hips, slower now, and after-shocks rippled through my body.

When he withdrew, he untied my ankles and rolled me

over. I was rubber at this point, happy to move wherever he wanted to place me. On my back, still panting, I stared up at him, a fucked-out smile on my face.

The shimmering green of his eyes was bright, almost feverish in intensity.

I reached for him at the same time he lunged for me, taking my lips in a hungry kiss. It didn't matter that he'd just fucked my brains out. I wanted him again, now.

I wrapped my legs around his waist, holding him as close as possible.

He paused and leaned back, cupping my face in his hands.

"Why are you looking at me like that?" I asked, my voice hoarse.

"Like what?"

"Like I'm something special."

"Cause you are, sweetheart. Beautiful, talented, sexy, stubborn, sweet—"

"Sweet?" I scoffed and tried to look away, but Dawson's grip was firm.

"Yes. You. Sweet and sensitive and a million other things. You're incredible. And I am one lucky man."

"I think you have that mixed up."

Dawson raised one eyebrow. "Do I need to tie you to the bed again? Didn't you hear what I said?"

I smiled and licked my swollen lips. "You can tie me to the bed anytime you want. And I heard every word. I just... I still can't believe it."

Dawson reached down and kissed me again.

"In that case, I'll just have to tell you every fucking day. I want you, and I want us. And seeing you today with my son, I...I want more. I want to tell him about us."

I waited for the fear, the panic to rise up inside me.

But it never came.

"I want that too," I admitted. "I don't want to hide."

Dawson's answering smile knocked the remaining breath right out of my body.

———

Dawson

An hour later, after a long shower and with our stomachs rumbling for sustenance (tacos don't last), Iain and I made our way down to his kitchen.

He was wearing my button-down with the sleeves rolled up, and a pair of grey sweatpants. The shirt was long on him, but like everything the man wore, he was sexy as hell. Especially when he had his long hair pulled up in a messy bun and the shirt started slipping off, exposing his shoulder. I was tempted to haul him back into his bedroom and start all over again, but we both needed a break. After all, we had the rest of the night.

I threw my jeans on, and since he had my shirt, I borrowed one of his. The T-shirt was tight on me, but Iain insisted. And hey, if he was happy, so was I.

And that's how we strolled into the living room of his house, hand in hand.

Lennie was sitting at the dining room table with his laptop open, working. He glanced up at us, smiled briefly, nodded, then grabbed his laptop and headed for the guest wing. The privacy was appreciated.

I headed for the freezer since I was craving ice cream.

Then I remembered the cake.

My sweet tooth was in full force now that my other appetite had been sated.

Well, sated for now.

But I didn't stray far from Iain. And he was the same, affectionate in a way I hadn't anticipated, outside of sex. Whether it was a gentle touch on my back, a heated look, or simply holding my hand, the synergy and ease between us went well beyond the bedroom.

Part of it was because Iain and I had been around each other for the past several years. There was a familiarity there, and a comfort that made the transition to lovers a bit easier. I'd seen different sides of him, not just at work but here in his home, things that only someone who knew and worked with him closely had access to.

Trust.

In and out of the bedroom.

A gift I didn't take lightly. And even though the same couldn't be said about Iain's access to my life, up until this point, at least, I was ready to let him in. We'd already started that today. Him meeting my son was a huge step.

I just hoped Jaxon would be all right with this turn of events.

I'd been open with my son about the fact that I liked to date men and women. But knowing that and having my boyfriend around were two very different things. And me having a boyfriend who was a famous musician to boot was a lot to handle.

That was probably true for me, as well as Jaxon.

Lost in my head, I stared at the contents of the freezer while Iain grabbed a bottle of water from the fridge.

Then he leaned up and kissed my cheek.

I was suddenly wide awake again.

I pulled out two containers of ice cream: mint chocolate chip and caramel fudge brownie.

As soon as I turned around, Iain raised an eyebrow at me.

"What? We burned a lot of calories."

Iain sighed and gave me that heart-stopping smile of his. "Okay, but you're lucky I love you. I don't share mint choco-late chip with anyone."

He what? He loves me?

I dropped both containers on the floor.

Iain slapped a hand over his mouth, his brown eyes wide with alarm.

"I don't share caramel fudge brownie, so you're lucky that I love you too," I admitted, my smile so wide that my face fucking hurt.

Then I reached for him, one hand around his waist, pulling him in before he could backpedal.

I ignored the containers of ice cream near my feet and the fact that both of us were breathing so hard we'd probably pass out, and did what the circumstance called for.

I kissed Iain.

Hard.

CHAPTER 36

IAIN

Had I really just told Dawson I loved him?

Those three little words held a fuckton of power.

And I'd rarely spoken them.

Sure, people in the music biz used the term all the time. Record moguls told us they loved us; fans screamed "I love you" when they spotted us, but that was different. That was adulation.

But this?

Nothing else in my life felt like me and Dawson. A tornado of emotions that knocked me flat on my rockstar ass.

And the words just flowed out of me. Right there in my kitchen.

As natural as strumming my guitar.

"Did you hear me?" Dawson asked as he held my face in his hands.

"What?"

"I love you too, Iain. I've probably been falling in love with you for ages, but I was too stubborn to let myself even imagine—"

This time, I placed my hand over his mouth. "Don't even

go there. I'm just a musician, baby. A famous one, yes, but outside of the paps and the fans and the tours, it's just me. You know me."

Dawson nodded, and I felt his smile against my palm. He gently kissed my hand.

"Now, the ice cream is starting to melt on the floor," I added. "But we still have that lava cake we can share."

Dawson removed my hand and placed it around his neck.

"If you're sharing chocolate cake, I know for sure that you love me," Dawson teased.

"I said so, didn't I? And I always mean what I say."

I reached up and kissed him.

"You get the cake," Dawson ordered and swatted my ass. "I'll clean up the floor."

I walked to the end of the island and grabbed the container, then popped it in the microwave to warm it up while I searched for two bowls.

Dawson lifted the ice cream containers off the floor; thankfully, not all of it had exploded. He grabbed a paper towel, wiped up the mess on the hardwood, and then grabbed a couple of spoons.

I split the round cake in half and added it to the bowls, then Dawson added a scoop of the remaining ice cream.

We made our way to the living room, sinking into the teal velvet sectional. I clicked on the gas fireplace for good measure.

Dawson spooned a piece of cake and offered it to me.

I took the mouthful and groaned as soon as the intense chocolate flavor hit my tastebuds.

"I swear you make the same exact sound when you perform Filthy Pain."

"I just sing back up." I chuckled and licked my lips.

"Your voice is distinctive. You've got this throaty purr that—"

"Throaty purr?" I interrupted.

"Yeah," Dawson waggled his eyebrows. "Your voice is pure sex, sweetheart."

I kissed him soundly.

"Speaking of sex… you seem to know what you're doing, tying me up like that."

"I've been to a few sex clubs, but I'm certainly no Dom—"

"Whoa, one bombshell at a time. Tell me about the clubs."

Dawson smiled and scooped another mouthful of cake and ice cream into his mouth.

"I started going with Nadia. She was curious, and I was happy to explore that with her. I've always enjoyed being the more dominant partner in the bedroom, so it felt like a natural fit."

"And?"

Dawson sighed. "While I learned a thing or two, the whole lifestyle was not for me. I mean, I appreciate parts of it, but I'm not into having a submissive partner in all aspects of my life."

I nodded. "Yeah, I know what you mean. I went to a BDSM club with Ronin once, but it was a little over the top. I'm far too stubborn to be submissive. And I've been to my share of private sex clubs, but only because I enjoyed the anonymity."

"I can see that." Dawson cleared his throat. "And is that, I mean, is it something you still want to do?"

"With you? Maybe? But I'm not sharing."

Dawson looked relieved. "That's good because I sure as fuck don't want to share either. But watching others and them watching us? It might be hot."

"Oh, it is." I kissed him soundly. "What else do I not know about Dawson Everly? What do you do besides guarding irresponsible rockstars and being a super dad?"

Dawson took another mouthful of cake and shook his head. "Not a super dad, but thanks. And honestly? For the past two years, my life outside of work has been focused on

Jaxon. The first year after Nadia died was the hardest. Some days, I look back and don't know how I managed. He'd often wake up from nightmares, and there was a lot of therapy for both of us. My mom's been instrumental in helping me cope. I couldn't have managed the past two years without her."

"And now?"

"Jaxon's a strong kid. Nadia will always be a part of his life, but we try to focus on the happy memories. Not on the automobile accident that took her life. And thankfully, he's doing well."

"I can see that. And what about you?"

"I'm too busy to think most days."

"What do you do just for yourself?"

"I still train at a dojo once a week when I'm home. I'm kind of an introvert, so I prefer to stay in or go for dinner with friends. I'm not a big party guy. But I have two buddies, Davis and Will, also single dads, who I met through Jaxon's school. Once a month, we do a movie night or hit a bar and chill, shoot the shit."

"Invite them to our next performance," I suggested. "We're doing one local show before we take a break."

"Are you sure?"

"Of course, I want to meet them."

Dawson looked as shocked as I felt. Meeting his son and then his friends? It was happening. Like jumping on stage in front of a live audience, there was no turning back.

Until the loud ringtone of a cell phone interrupted our moment.

"That's mine. I left it on the island." Dawson sighed and got up. "Be right back."

———

Dawson

Would it be too much to ask for one uninterrupted day with Iain?

Then again, I should probably get used to it. With my schedule and his, making time to see each other would be a challenge.

I walked over to the island and glanced at my phone. It was Regan calling.

I picked it up and tapped accept. "Yes, boss?"

"Where are you?" Regan asked.

"I'm at Iain's. What's up?"

"I just got off the phone with the investigator. My contact helped him track down that floral delivery payment. It came from a credit card in the name of one Franklin Salich, a former Bandit employee. He was let go a month before the break-in."

"Franklin Salich, I know that name." Then it hit me. "Frankie! He was at the Nashville show on February 4. He said he was a friend of Zoe's. Fuck, he even signed an NDA, and the security team cleared him. I double checked his ID but nothing came up. Everything looked to be in order."

"He's not a friend of Zoe's but he was a coworker. He worked in IT for just over a year, same floor. I've got Quinn liaising with HR. His name should have been flagged in our system as soon as he was fired but it wasn't, because HR never deactivated his clearance. That's a serious breach that needs to be rectified ASAP."

"Why was he fired?"

"His boss found out he was offering information on several Bandit musicians to the tabloids in exchange for money. He had high level access. And what he didn't have access to, he obtained by hacking into company records. Salich was clever but not smart enough. The last time he went searching, he unknowingly breached a firewall. It set off a series of notifications, and he was caught."

"Fucking hell! And he was right there in front of me. But why Iain?"

"That I don't know yet. I'm combing through his email, laptop, and work phone history as we speak. As soon as I know, you'll know."

"What's next?"

"I'm having a call with our legal team. If we can find proof that Salich is behind the messages, we can request a restraining order. But the messages to Iain's old number have stopped, so I have a bad feeling. And there's one other thing—"

"What?"

"A photo of you, Iain, and your son was posted online a half hour ago on a gossip site. It looks like it was taken while you guys were headed out to lunch. Zoe just texted me. I'm guessing that Salich either took that photo and leaked it, or he's seen it, and that's why he's gone dark."

"Shit. And where's Salich now?"

"The PI is watching his place. Said Salich hasn't left his condo since this morning. I'm sending a note to our entire team containing his details and what to do in the event he tries to approach anyone."

"Good. Is there anything I can do on my end? Since I'm off duty, I'm staying at Iain's overnight."

"I'd say keep a close eye on him, but that's a given."

I chuckled at Regan's sarcasm. "It is. Lennie's here, and Quinn will be back to switch in the morning. The alarm is on. We're as secure as we can be."

"I'll be in touch with updates."

"I'll be waiting."

As soon as I was off the call, I texted Zoe to ask about the photo. She forwarded the link.

It was taken as we were entering the Mexican restaurant, but from a distance. I cursed myself for not noticing the pap. Or if it was Salich, not paying close enough attention to who was nearby. Normally, I had good radar for that type of thing, but I guess where Iain was concerned, I was distracted.

I wandered back into the living room, where Iain huddled under a cable knit throw.

"Did you hear all that?" I asked, sitting down beside him and taking his hand.

"Parts of it. I heard you say Frankie. That was the guy I met at the concert weeks ago. Is it him? Is he the one who's been harassing me?"

I nodded. "He worked at Bandit but was fired in December for breaching company data, and for selling private details about several musicians to the tabloids. It wouldn't surprise me if he was also the person responsible for the break-in. He worked in IT and had access to a lot of information."

Iain shivered, and I pulled him in close to me.

"The good news is that we've identified the person responsible. The PI is tailing Salich, and Regan is looking into a possible restraining order."

"And the bad news?"

"Someone got a photo of us with Jaxon. It's on a gossip site, and there's speculation about our relationship. And before you ask, I texted Zoe. She told us to leave it to her. But Salich has gone dark, and that photo might be the reason why. He's not messaging your old number anymore."

"That means you guys are targets now. Christ, I knew this was going to happen!"

Iain pushed away and stood up. Then he began to pace.

"You've got to be with your family," he muttered. "Stay away from me."

"How about we *not* panic and instead do as Regan suggested and have Mom and Jaxon stay here? Your house is safer."

Iain stopped moving.

"Here? Now?"

"If that's okay?"

There was a moment of silence. I thought for sure that Iain was going to tell me to leave.

"Yeah, let's do that," Iain whispered.

An hour later, I picked up my mom and my son. I'd given Mom the gist of what was happening. Trusting in my instinct, she was calm and agreed with my plan. Jaxon was upset about the cancellation of his playdate, but once he found out we were staying at Iain's, his mood turned around.

When I got back to Iain's, and while Mom and Jaxon were getting settled into the guest wing, I went in search of my lover.

I found him sitting in the living room, staring at the fireplace.

"What do we do now?" he asked me.

"Now, we wait."

"You know me. I'm not good at that."

I pushed Iain down on the sofa and gave him a languid kiss.

"We'll just have to find a way to keep you distracted."

CHAPTER 37

IAIN

"How could he lose him? He's tailing one person! This isn't mission impossible."

I rolled over at the sound of Dawson's voice. I was still in bed while Dawson stood at the picture window in front of my bed, his phone to his ear.

He was naked, the early morning light highlighting every curve and ridge of his big, beautiful body. And the freckles that trailed over his skin like snowflakes. His free hand was rubbing his spiky red hair, his biceps bulging.

Then I spotted the scratches on his back and the red marks on his ass.

Turns out, Dawson wasn't the only one with a possessive kink. My need to claim him intensified with every minute. Even now, after a long night of fucking, I was hungry for him again, starving for more, and only too happy to show him he belonged with me.

He had a lot more at stake when it came to this relationship. But his faith in me was humbling. It made me fall that much harder, deeper.

So deep I didn't see any way out.

Dawson turned around to face me, and when our eyes locked, my heart took off again.

My ass was sore, my mouth was aching, fuck, my whole body felt used in the best possible way.

But I still wanted more.

"All right," Dawson spoke into the phone. "The meeting's at head office? Valen and Quinn, right?"

Dawson tapped the phone, walked back over to the bed, and threw it on the nightstand.

Then he slid over me, capturing my lips in a devouring kiss.

"Good morning, sweetheart," he whispered. "Sorry about that."

"It wasn't the wakeup I had anticipated, but I'll take you any way I can get you," I murmured, and gave him another kiss. "What's going on?"

Dawson let out a groan. "The PI lost sight of Salich. He followed him to a shopping mall this morning, and somehow, lost him in the parking lot."

"The guys and I have a meeting with Greg and Harlow at noon. At his office. In person."

"I know. Regan confirmed Valen and Quinn will accompany you."

I nodded. "Now that Jaxon and your mom are here, will you tell them about us?"

"Definitely." Dawson cupped my face. "I hope their reaction is positive, but—"

"I know. With my celebrity status and everything that's going on, it's a lot." I turned my face and kissed his palm, worried about what might happen if Jaxon wasn't on board. And really, could I blame him? "You know, making music and being in the spotlight was the only thing I ever wanted. I never thought I'd have to consider anything else. Or anyone else. And now, the only work I love might cost me the one person I love. Christ, I sound like I'm ready to write another song."

"You can write that song, but don't write me off," Dawson whispered before taking my lips in a heated kiss. "Promise me."

Faith. I had to keep reminding myself.

"I promise. Besides, if it has anything to do with heartbreak, I'm not sure I'd be able to survive it, much less write about it."

"You and me both, sweetheart."

After another deep and drugging kiss, Dawson smiled at me.

"Let's go make breakfast."

"Good idea. I think we burned through an entire week's worth of meals last night."

"And lube," he quipped.

"Thanks for reminding me. I need to place that bulk order."

Dawson chuckled and swatted my hip. "Get up and make your man some food."

"First, it's 'let's make breakfast,' and now I'm the one cooking? Always with the demands." I sighed dramatically. "I told you, only in the bedroom."

"I want to amend that rule. You must, in all circumstances, heed my demands, both sexually and otherwise. But the sexual ones come first."

"I thought I always came first?"

"Exactly."

I grabbed my pillow and playfully whacked Dawson over the head with it. He retaliated, and the next thing I knew, we were making out again. But his stomach growled so loud that sexy time was interrupted.

"Okay, I give in. I'll make scrambled eggs and toast."

Dawson's satisfied grin had me rolling my eyes.

An hour later, after I'd made enough breakfast for ten

people, Quinn and Valen had arrived. Dawson and I said our goodbyes at the door.

"I'll call you as soon as this meeting is over."

"Don't go anywhere without your security. Promise me?"

"Where the fuck am I gonna go?" I asked.

"Iain," Dawson warned.

"I promise. I'm not going to do what I did before. Not with that Frankie guy on the loose."

"Good." Dawson leaned down and took my lips in a tender kiss. "I love you."

"I love you too."

"Text me, call me anytime."

"I will. Text me as soon as you speak to Jaxon."

With the cold winter air swirling around us, I left him standing at the doorway, in my T-shirt and his Philly sweatpants.

Walking toward the SUV with Valen and Quinn, I noticed they were unusually silent.

"What's going on?" I asked as I looked up at them.

"You and Dawson? I thought that was a rumor." Valen's eyes nearly bugged out of his head.

"Nope. But we're not public yet," I replied.

"Wait a sec," Quinn held up his tattooed hand. "So, you and Dawson are a legit couple? Like a couple, couple?"

"Yes." I smiled as Valen opened the back door.

"I knew it!" Quinn exclaimed. "You owe me a hundred bucks, Val!"

I turned and glared at my security detail—both of them.

"You guys were betting on us?"

"Fuck yeah, the same way we did with Van and Brodie. We see it all. The way you flirt with Daws? And how possessive he is with you?" Quinn scoffed. "Please, the pheromones were off the chart. I'm surprised it took you this long."

"Did everyone know we were a thing before it actually happened?"

"Fuck, yeah," Quinn replied. "And we also know who's next."

I didn't want to think about that. Shaking my head, I settled into the backseat.

When we finally pulled into the parking lot of Bandit Music's head office, my stomach dropped.

I hadn't been here for a long time. Greg only called us in for heavy conversations about our contract or something that Brodie did or said to the media.

I was guessing that this convo was the same.

When I arrived at the office on the thirty-fifth floor, Brodie, Faise, and Ronin were already there. Harlow too.

Greg's assistant motioned for us to enter his office while Valen and Quinn waited outside the room along with the other bodyguards.

Greg was sitting at his desk with his phone to his ear.

I heard him murmur, "HR will courier the severance letter," and then he hung up. When he was done, he ushered us forward to have a seat.

"Any guesses as to why I called this meeting today?"

I looked at my friends, and they were as silent as I was.

"First off, what's going on here?" Greg asked, placing his phone on the table in front of us.

I stared at the picture of me, Dawson, and Jaxon, as we were entering the restaurant that day. My eyes zoomed in on the way Dawson and I were looking at each other. I'd never seen myself so happy before.

"It's called lunch. Perhaps you've heard of it?" I snapped.

"Don't be a smart ass, Holloway. If you're involved with your security detail—"

"He's not on my detail anymore. And my personal life is my business."

"No, it's *my* business," Greg replied. "Everything you do is in the public eye and reflects on my company."

"Like you haven't fucked people you worked with?"

Brodie snarled. "And don't even try to deny it. The music world ain't that big. People talk."

Greg's face flushed, and he shook his head. "Watch your mouth, Brodie. I've had just about enough."

"You're not in any position to threaten me," Brodie scoffed. "We're the ones the fans stand behind, not you."

"As I was saying, this doesn't look good. Given that, changes will be made to the security team. Dawson's services are no longer required as of end of day today."

"You can't do that!" I yelled as I stood up.

"I can, and I did. Maybe next time, stick to fucking your usual randos and not someone on your team."

"Why you—" I leaned forward, but Brodie stopped me.

"Don't," Brodie whispered as he pushed me back. "That's what he wants."

I managed to rein in my temper for now, but it was not the end of this conversation. I pulled out my phone and texted Dawson, asking him to call me ASAP.

"Also, I want more press coverage on this stalker situation, especially now that we've identified who it is. We'll set up interviews with all the major entertainment channels. We want to milk this story for all its worth. Harlow, what's the plan?"

Harlow leaned forward and was curiously hesitant.

"I talked to Zoe and Regan today. We don't think it's a good idea that we egg this guy on any more. It's a volatile situation."

Greg shook his head. "If you can't follow my directive, you might want to consider updating your resume as well."

"Really? Again, with the threats?" Harlow stood up. "I did your bidding when I was in Europe. I let things slide with the interviews and played the role you wanted, but now this is getting serious. I don't think it's smart to play with this kind of fire."

"Then get the fuck out of my office!" Greg bellowed. "And pack up your desk."

"With pleasure," Harlow snapped, and fled the room.

I stood up, with Brodie, Faise, and Ronin following.

"I didn't mean you guys!" Greg shouted.

"We're leaving anyway," Ronin announced. "We've heard enough."

"Don't you dare walk away from me! We're not done here," Greg warned.

"Oh yes, we fucking are!" I roared.

I turned and headed for the door, my band brothers right behind me.

Once we stepped out into the hallway, our security team gathered around us.

"What's with all the shouting?" Quinn asked. "What's going on?"

"Greg fired Dawson," I explained.

"Fucking hell," Quinn muttered. "When?"

"Just before we got in. He's done as of the end of day."

My phone buzzed.

Dawson: It's going to be okay. I was planning to resign anyway. This is NOT your fault. Just come home to me.

"Is Dawson okay?"

I showed them his text.

"Greg also wants me to go to the press about Frankie Salich."

"To do what? Paint the bullseye on your back?" Valen grumbled. "That's fucking stupid."

"I'm not doing it." I shook my head and looked at Brodie. "I won't."

"We're behind you," Brodie replied.

"All of us." Faise nodded. "Greg can go fuck himself."

"Thanks. I'm going to see Zoe, and then I just want to go home. My head hurts."

The guys left first.

I headed down to the twenty-fifth floor with my detail so I could talk to Zoe in person. When we arrived at her office, though, she was on a conference call.

After waiting for ten minutes, I decided fuck it. I sent her a text to call me later. All I wanted now was to go home.

Quinn and Valen were stoic on the way out, and I felt the weight of their silence. Dawson was their friend and coworker. They had every right to blame me for what happened to him.

"Dawson knew what he was doing," Quinn finally mumbled. "He was talking about quitting anyway. Jaxon needs him at home."

I knew that, but still, I felt guilty. Quitting on your own terms was one thing. Being fired was another.

We headed outside to the parking lot, and walked over to the SUV.

Everything was quiet.

Until it wasn't.

Suddenly, a boom rang out. It was so loud that I automatically covered my ears.

Quinn shouted and fell sideways, grasping his shoulder. Val screamed and pushed me to the ground.

I looked up, utterly shocked and confused at what was going on.

Until I looked up and saw Frankie Salich, only a few feet away.

Holding a gun.

CHAPTER 38

IAIN

Oh my God. Oh my God, what do I do?

Fuck, fuck, was this really happening?

Only an hour ago, Valen and Quinn were joking with me. Dawson told me he loved me…he loved me. And I loved him.

No, this couldn't be happening.

"Look at me!" Frankie roared. "Show me your hands!"

I was still lying on the ground, so I lifted my hands as high as I could in the position. Then I turned my head to look at Valen crouched beside me. He'd drawn his weapon.

"Put the gun down, Frankie! This isn't the way to get Iain to talk to you," Valen yelled.

Frankie fired off another shot that had me covering my ears again. The crash of breaking glass from nearby car windows rained down over us.

"Why didn't you listen to me, Iain?" Frankie demanded.

"I…I'm sorry," I panted.

I was hyperventilating at this point.

"All you had to do was listen. Like the first time we met. Remember?" Frankie asked me with wild eyes.

"The charity concert in February."

"No!" Frankie roared. "No! No! No! I met you last fall! Bandit threw a company event on September 20. Remember? You said hi to me, and you touched my hand. You were the only band member to do that. I couldn't believe it. I'd never felt so…*seen*. Special."

I didn't remember that event—or him—at all. But I rolled with it. "Oh. Y-yes, I remember now."

Frankie nodded and visibly calmed.

I had no fucking clue what he was talking about.

"You're not like the other musicians. The ones I sold out to the tabloids. They were corrupt. Selfish. Rude. Not talented and kind like you. As soon as I met you, I knew you were different. You smiled at me. And I knew then that you loved me. As much as I love you."

I didn't remember any of that. Jesus, I met him once, and he thought I was in love with him?

What the fuck?

I glanced over at Quinn, and the red stain on his pale blue jacket was getting bigger and bigger. Blood was covering his right hand. Shit. Fuck.

We needed the police and an ambulance. Now.

I slowly put my hands down, then reached for my phone in my pocket.

"Don't move!" Frankie shouted and fired again.

I grabbed my head as more glass fell over us. And I prayed that someone nearby had heard the shots and dialed 911.

Then Valen spoke so low that I barely heard the words. "I hit the SOS alert; police are on the way. Keep talking to him. We need to distract him so I can get a clear shot."

"Frankie! Stop! Please," I pleaded, and Frankie focused on me again. "I r-remember. I remember m-meeting you. All of it. I remember how special you were. Are."

"I knew it!" Frankie shouted as he stared at me, holding

the gun with two shaky hands. "I knew you loved me! And you got my messages? And the flowers?"

"Yes, I did. T-thank you," I managed to reply, my voice shaky.

"That's just the beginning. Now that you're back, we can be together again. We're meant for each other. Right, Iain? The last time I saw you, you felt it, too. You invited me back-stage after the show. You wanted me."

"Yes, t-that's right. I did."

My stomach was churning with nausea and fear, thinking about how close I came to being alone with this man.

"But then you brushed me off!" Frankie yelled. "Why didn't you take me home? That's all I wanted!"

I heard the wail of sirens in the distance. My phone began to ring.

"And then I saw that picture of you and him! That stupid bodyguard!" Frankie roared. "He wants you. But he can't have you. He can't. He's not here, and I am. Me!"

"Yes, you are," I choked out, my body shaking so hard my teeth rattled.

"Come here, Iain. Right now! Or I'll kill both of your bodyguards!" Frankie screamed. "And shut that fucking phone off!"

"Okay, I'm going to sit up and take out my phone. Then I'll walk over to you. Okay?"

Slowly, I got off the ground and reached for my phone. My hands were shaking so hard that after I managed to get the phone out of my pocket, I dropped it. The phone skidded on the pavement toward Frankie.

Oh shit, now what?

Frankie stared at my phone for a moment, then he reached for it.

It was a split second.

Another shot rang out, and I jolted, shutting my eyes until I heard Valen yelling.

When I finally opened them, I saw Frankie lying on the ground and Valen, with his gun drawn, headed toward him.

Oh my fucking God.

"Iain, put pressure on Quinn's wound! Now!" Valen ordered.

I finally snapped out of my daze and threw off my jacket, pressing it to Quinn's shoulder. Then I noticed the grey pallor in Quinn's usually ruddy face.

"It's okay," I murmured, unsure if it ever would be. "It's okay."

Was Frankie dead?

Fuck, this can't be happening. It can't be real.

"It's all right," Quinn panted as he placed his bloody hand over mine. "Val… got him."

"You're losing so much blood," I whimpered, my vision blurring.

"It's okay...been shot...before...when I was a cop. I'm tougher than I...look."

"You look pretty fucking tough," I replied without thinking.

Quinn snorted, then grimaced. "Don't make...me...laugh, Iain. Hurts."

"How are you so calm right now?"

"Better… calm… than dead."

And then it was chaos again—police cars flooded the parking lot, cops yelled at Valen to show his hands.

My ears started to ring, and my vision blurred.

Suddenly, Regan was there, crouched down in front of me, but I couldn't understand anything she was saying.

I was yanked up and away from Quinn as paramedics arrived and placed him on a stretcher.

Finally, Dawson was there, too, standing in front of me, pulling me into his arms.

I buried my face in his neck and burst into tears, not caring who saw or how I sounded.

"How did you know?" I sobbed against his chest.

"The SOS, Regan called me. It's okay; it's all over, sweetheart. It's okay," Dawson reassured me. I was shaking, and so was he. "You're safe now."

"Quinn?" I asked as I finally leaned back and looked around.

"Quinn's on his way to the hospital. He's going to be okay."

"Is Frankie…is he…"

"He's dead," Dawson murmured. "Now we have to get you to the hospital."

"No."

"Yes, you're in shock. You need to be checked out."

"But—"

"I'm coming with you. I'm not leaving your side."

"I was so scared. And I felt helpless. I—"

Dawson gripped me so tight I'm surprised I didn't crack a rib. But I needed it; I needed his strength more than ever.

I'm not sure what happened after that.

Everything went dark.

———

I woke up to fluorescent lights, the sound of machines beeping, and the smell of rubbing alcohol.

Hospitals. I hated them.

I had a flashback to when I was ten years old, holding on tightly to my dad's hand as we stood in the emergency room. I remember the doctor whispering my mom's name and saying, "I'm sorry. We did everything we could." And then my dad dropped my hand, covering his face while he let out an anguished sob that I would never forget.

And everything was different from that moment on.

There were no more hugs. No holding on to my hand. Nothing.

I blinked and looked over to find Dawson sitting in a chair beside me, typing away on his phone. He was biting his lower lip, and there were circles under his eyes. How late was it? How long had I been in here?

Then it all came flooding back.

The meeting with Greg.

The parking lot.

Frankie.

The shooting. The blood.

"Dawson," I whispered, my voice hoarse and dry.

He got up and reached for my hand, sitting on the bed beside me. "Hey, sweetheart, how are you feeling?"

"Like shit. How's Quinn?"

"Quinn is out of surgery and in recovery. He's going to be fine."

"Thank fuck. What time is it? How long have I been here?"

"Several hours. You passed out from the shock."

"Val? Is he okay?"

"Yeah. Val was with the police for hours, but he's here now, being checked out."

"The guys?"

"All waiting outside to see you. Are you ready for company? Do you need anything?"

I shook my head, my eyes welling up again. Fuck, why couldn't I stop crying?

"Just some water. And I want to see them. Can you send them in?"

"Of course."

Dawson leaned over to hug me, but I held my hand up and shook my head. "Go home. Be with your son. I don't need you. If the guys are here, one of them will stay with me."

"But—"

"I don't want you here. You and me. It just isn't going to work."

His face fell, but he said nothing in response.

I just...I couldn't look at him right now.

This. This was exactly what I was talking about when I told Dawson that my life was crazy.

I wasn't safe. Well, I guess I was, now that my stalker was dead, shot by my bodyguard.

Jesus Christ.

I'm sure the tabloids were all over this. The news would live on forever.

And sitting here in the hospital, with an IV in my arm, I had to face the truth: I wasn't meant for white picket fences, or partners, or kids. As much as I loved Dawson, and he loved me, it wasn't enough.

I was a fuckboy rockstar.

I lived hard. I played hard. I didn't have a normal life.

If this incident didn't prove how unfit I was to be in Dawson's life, I didn't know what would.

I closed my eyes and let the hot tears fall down my face.

I felt Dawson gently kiss my hand. And I listened to his footsteps as he left the room.

Alone again. Which was good. Fine. As it should be.

I had my music and my friends. I didn't need a boyfriend.

"Iain?"

I opened my eyes to find Brodie, Van, Faise, and Ronin entering the room. They all looked like they'd aged a decade.

"Fuck, am I glad to see you guys," I croaked as I wiped my eyes.

They all crowded around me, hugging tightly.

"Dawson just told us to stay with you. When's he coming back?" Brodie asked.

"He isn't. I told him to leave. For good."

"Iain—" Brodie started.

"Don't, Dee," I interrupted. "Just don't. Look at where I

am, at what just happened. Frankie tried to kill me, and he nearly killed Quinn! This is a whole other level of crazy that Dawson does not need. I can't even imagine what's going on with the news and—"

Brodie sighed. "Zoe is handling it, but yeah, there's a lot. But you know as well as I do that these things will eventually pass."

"It doesn't feel that way right now. I can't even imagine Dawson would want to be around me. Or want his son around me."

"Don't you think you should let Dawson decide what's best for him?" Faise asked.

"No. I'm not cut out for a relationship."

Ronin patted me on the shoulder. "Maybe you just need time to process. I'm sure once you calm down—"

"I am calm!" I yelled, obliterating my statement.

I took a deep breath, and the tears welled up again. "I made the right decision. I'm fine. It's better this way."

My heart was aching like a motherfucker.

"Close your eyes and rest," Brodie insisted. "We'll be here when you wake up."

I leaned back and did as Brodie suggested, but I couldn't sleep. I couldn't stop my mind from spinning.

Minutes or hours later, I heard another set of footsteps entering the room, and a familiar scent wafted over me.

"You're back," Ronin announced.

My eyes snapped open.

Dawson was standing at the foot of the bed, holding two trays of drinks. "I thought decaf was best; help yourself."

"What the hell are you doing here? I asked you to leave!" I snapped.

Dawson ignored me and passed out the coffee to my friends.

"Thanks, Daws; appreciated," Ronin murmured.

Brodie and Faise also offered their thanks.

"No, it's not. Get out!" I yelled.

Dawson shook his head and stared at me. "I'm not leaving you. You can throw one of your rockstar tantrums if you want, but it won't work. I've been chasing you for years, sweetheart, so bring it on."

I sat up again, my heart pounding furiously. "I don't want you here."

"Bullshit! You're trying to protect me by pushing me away. But it won't work. I love you, end of story," Dawson announced as he calmly sipped his coffee.

My band brothers were staring at Dawson, then me, with their mouths wide open.

"Be reasonable—" I started.

"*You're* telling *me* to be reasonable? How much meds did they give you?"

I looked at my friends. "Do something!"

"Sweetheart, you've been through a lot today," Dawson continued. "Close your eyes and rest. Getting upset isn't helping."

What was happening right now? Why wasn't Dawson leaving? Maybe *he* was the one who needed medical attention.

A nurse walked into the room and glared at everyone. "Only one visitor in the room at a time. I don't care how famous you are."

My band brothers chuckled, gave me a reassuring pat on the shoulder, and left the room.

The nurse stepped up to my bed and checked my IV. "How are you feeling, Mr. Holloway?"

"Upset. Exhausted. Wired."

"That's understandable. Another dose of sedative should help you sleep. The doctor will be by in a few hours."

"Can you get him out of here?" I pointed to Dawson who was sitting in the chair again, watching me.

"Nope," he replied. "I'm staying right here with my boyfriend."

"Aw, that's so sweet," the nurse cooed at him.

Her reaction made my temper spike again. I'm pretty sure I'd need blood pressure meds to go along with that sedative.

She checked my vitals and IV and left the room as quickly as she had come.

"I love you. I'm not leaving you," Dawson repeated and reached out to take my hand again.

Tears threatened as I held on to my fear.

"But—"

"Now, here's what's going to happen. You'll be discharged tomorrow morning, and we're going home, and I'm going to look after you. Then, we'll go see a therapist to talk through what happened today and anything else needed to move forward. And we'll also sit down with Jaxon and my mom and figure this thing out."

Hot tears lashed my cheeks again. Dawson got up and cupped my face, wiping them away.

His green eyes implored mine, and I so wanted to believe.

"You've always been fearless on stage, Iain. The way your hands bring that guitar to life? Fuck, you're a musical force of nature. I know you're strong enough to get through this, too. But don't push me away. I want to love and support you. My heart knows, sweetheart, and yours does, too. Please."

Despite the IV in my arm, I reached up with both hands and gripped his tightly, pulling it to my chest, over my heart.

And, like always, my hands said everything I couldn't.

He reached down and gave me a tender kiss.

Dawson was right.

His heart knew, and so did mine.

CHAPTER 39

DAWSON

"Anyone want more lasagna?" I asked as I looked around the dining room table.

Iain and Jaxon were sitting across from each other, their half-eaten plates left aside as they got into a conversation about acoustic vs electric guitars. My mom sat across from me, watching the two of them with a soft expression. When she looked back at me, she winked.

Yeah. I was pleased, too. We'd landed at Iain's five days ago and hadn't left since.

Iain had nightmares about the incident, but overall, he was handling it well.

And having him lying there beside me in bed every night was amazing. We talked for hours, and every day, I learned something new.

Besides talking in his sleep, Iain was a blanket hog.

He was a fan of hot baths and hotter coffee. He loved any kind of puzzle, especially sudoku, and board games, too. And man, was he fiercely competitive.

I also learned that Iain had a soft spot for animals, and I

just knew he was already plotting to get Jaxon that cat he wanted.

We hadn't been intimate, but that was to be expected. Ronin was right; Iain needed time to process.

For all of Iain's talk about independence, he sure took to my family quickly. He liked my mom's say-it-like-it-is Philly attitude since he had no problem being just as blunt as she was. I was concerned she might talk me out of staying here, but of course, I should have known better. I'd told her about the entire incident and that I was worried about him. She knew, just like I did, that Iain needed love and protection.

In the least amount of detail possible, I'd explained to Jaxon what had happened to Iain and why we were still staying with him. My son was also concerned, but he also understood that Iain needed us. I'd finally had that talk, explaining to Jaxon that I loved Iain, and he loved me. And that given Iain's celebrity and our relationship as boyfriends, things would be changing.

My son, in his matter-of-fact way, told me it was cool, and he had my back.

I tell ya, eight going on eighteen…

I'd also reached out to a therapist, one that Van had recommended. Someone he'd talked to after the loss of his parents. Iain had his first session tomorrow. I knew there was a lot for him to unpack, not just about the stalker, but about his mom and his strained relationship with his dad. We'd also agreed to go as a couple since Iain was new to this relationship stuff, and I would be new to the media scrutiny that was about to unleash the moment we went public.

And speaking of healing, Quinn was recovering from surgery, and his prognosis was good. His shoulder didn't sustain any permanent injury, so after things healed, he'd be back to work in a few months.

Iain still had a detail, with Lennie and another bodyguard,

Petyr, taking rotating shifts. Thankfully, the house had plenty of room to accommodate.

The media continued to circulate stories about the stalker and Val's role in stopping the attack, with fans calling him a hero. He told reporters that Quinn was the one they should be lavishing praise on, and left it at that.

Regan was working with the police to piece together the events of that day. It turned out Frankie had gotten hold of a rental car using a fake identity. He'd also stashed a hidden camera on the public road just outside of Iain's property that clearly recorded every car that came in and out of the compound. When Frankie saw the SUV leave that day, he made his move and followed them to Bandit's office.

The police also had a look through Frankie's condo and uncovered an alarming number of photos of Iain, most of them taken near his home, out and about in Nashville, and at various Bandit events.

But Frankie was gone. I was sure there would be more disturbing news to come once the investigation wrapped up, but we'd learned enough for now.

I wasn't worried like before.

Now, the only threat to Iain was the press camped outside his property.

Even though I was no longer on the Bandit payroll, I'd texted back and forth with Zoe about the next steps. Iain and I were due to talk to her next week to finalize a plan to make our relationship public.

But one breaking news story at a time…

"Dad?"

I looked at my son. "Yes?"

"Did you hear what I said?"

"Uh, sorry. I guess I zoned out for a moment." Then I looked at the spatula in my hand. "Oh, did you want more lasagna?"

"No, I'm stuffed. I want to go play video games. Can I be excused?"

"You may."

"Not so fast." Mom pointed at Jaxon. "First, you help me clear the table."

"Yes, Nana."

Jaxon's response was so solemn that I bit back a laugh and caught Iain doing the same.

"Dawson, why don't you and Iain go relax on the couch? You know the rules; you cook, I clean," Mom offered.

I'd take any opportunity to get cozy with my man.

I walked over and took Iain's hand, guiding him to the sectional.

Once we were seated, Iain tucked into my side, I slid a hand through his silky hair and kissed his temple. "Do you want us to stay another week?"

Iain let out a contented sigh. "Could you?"

"Of course. I love you, and I love being here."

"I was thinking of doing some renos. Maybe make a bigger kitchen and expand the living room." Iain looked up at me, his big brown eyes filled with warmth. "But only if you design it with me?"

"I'd be honored," I replied, then took his mouth in a soft kiss.

"Good. That way, we can make my house *our* home," he whispered, gently biting my lower lip.

"That's the sexiest thing you've ever said to me."

Iain's husky laughter came a close second.

Iain

A week later

Dawson and I were video conferencing with Zoe to discuss our PR plan.

We were about to go public with our relationship, and while I was used to seeing my name splashed over the headlines, Dawson was not. Now, he appeared to be the one on edge, his knee tapping out a nervous rhythm.

I reached for his hand. He brought mine up to his mouth, placing kisses on my palm.

The man could not stop touching me, and his possessive affection drove me wild. My sex drive, which had been on pause since the incident, had come rumbling to life over the past twenty-four hours. As soon as we were done with this call, and since we had the house to ourselves, it was on.

Dawson reached for the tablet with his other hand, and tapped *accept*. Zoe's face popped up, and she waved at us.

"Hey guys! How are you doing?"

"Hey, Zoe. Better this week," I replied. "I'm seeing a therapist to talk about it."

"That's good. I know it isn't easy, but in time and with support, you'll be feeling better."

I nodded. "I'll be ready for our tour start date in May."

"Okay, so back to you and Dawson… Hi, Daws."

Dawson smiled at her and waved. "Hey, Zoe."

"I've prepared a statement about your relationship; check your inbox. Once you review it, give me your feedback, and I'll post it. Let me deal with the questions and comments, okay? Do not engage in any posts. I'm going to schedule a few interviews with select media outlets. We can discuss the questions ahead of time so you control the information. These will be brief interviews with the two of you. Dawson is no longer working for Bandit, so that's the good news. There will still be questions about when your relationship started and how long you've been together, but you can choose not to comment."

"Can I tell them to fuck off?" I quipped.

"Please, no." Zoe laughed. "I get enough of that with Brodie."

"Are you also taking over my accounts?" Dawson asked.

"You can give me permission to do so, or you can turn off the comments. Either way, don't engage."

Dawson nodded. "I'm worried more about my son. He's almost nine, and even though he can't participate in social media yet, other kids might see and hear things from their family or friends. Any suggestions on that?"

"I think you're best to talk to a therapist about how that might impact him and strategies for coping with any attention. On my end, I would avoid posting any pictures of him. I know people are proud of their kids, but the longer you can avoid it, the better. Maintaining his privacy in that way is essential."

"Thanks, all sound advice. Sweetheart, do you have any more questions?"

I shook my head. "I'm good. As long as the reporters leave Jaxon out of it, I'll be respectful. But Zoe, you need to make it clear that he is out of bounds. Bad enough that picture of us leaving the restaurant is still circulating. I don't want that to happen again. Or I swear I will pull a Brodie."

"I'm with you, Holls. I've got it well in hand. And even though Greg has pressured me to make you tell all, I'm not doing it. So don't be surprised if I'm the next Bandit employee to get axed."

"He better not. And thanks for everything."

"You're welcome. We'll talk soon."

Dawson tapped *end* and closed the tablet.

"Feel better?" he asked.

"I do. How about you?"

"We've got this."

"We've got the house to ourselves and no other plans this afternoon, so, tell me—" I leaned over and kissed him soundly. "Do you want to fuck a rockstar?"

Dawson burst out laughing and shook his head. "Please tell me you've never used that line?"

"Too much?"

"The ultimate cheese," he quipped, and kissed me back.

"Is that a no?" I teased, even though I recognized the desire in his eyes.

Just in case he had any doubt about my intentions, I got up and started stripping down.

Dawson shook his head. "I thought you'd never ask."

CHAPTER 40

IAIN

We hadn't had sex in weeks, and it felt like forever.

I needed Dawson, and I needed him right fucking now.

I was half naked when Dawson stood up, so quickly that his dining chair toppled over. I went to grab it, but he shook his head.

"Leave it," he demanded, pulling off his sweatshirt and jeans in record time. Then he reached for my pants, pushing them down my hips.

Suddenly, he looked up at me and paused. "Are you sure you're ready?"

"Yes! I need you inside me so bad."

His hands were shaking, and so were mine. To prove my point, I stepped out of my jeans and turned around, bending over the kitchen island, offering up my ass.

"Right here, right now."

"It feels like forever since I touched you like this," Dawson whispered as he slid in behind me, his hard cock brushing my ass, his nipples teasing the skin on my back.

"I was just thinking the exact same thing," I moaned, as I tilted my head.

Dawson pushed my hair aside and bit and sucked on my neck in that spot that drove me wild. I reached back to grab his hip, to pull him in closer.

"Need you so much," he growled against my overheated skin.

He stood back, and I whimpered, not wanting the separation.

Until he dropped to his knees, spread my cheeks, and tormented my ass with his hot, wicked tongue.

Fuck, this man knew how to rim me straight to heaven.

I panted, my hands flat against the countertop, while the intense pleasure licked up my spine, making my cock throb harder. My balls were aching, so full and heavy. I hadn't even jerked off lately, but now I was so fucking ready.

I went to slip my hand around my cock, but Dawson grunted.

"Don't touch that. It's mine."

God, I loved when he talked to me like that. So possessive. In the very best way.

I obeyed him because I knew what was coming next was going to blow my mind and my load.

He pushed his face into my ass and continued to eat me out, teasing my asshole with skillful flicks of his tongue. I nearly screamed when he pushed his tongue into my hole and fucked me with it. I tilted my hips back, wanting more. Desperate for all the filthy pleasure.

Dawson swatted my ass, and the sharp sting only made me moan louder, the pain-pleasure an exquisite torment.

When he moved, I protested. "Hurry up."

With one hand, he gently pushed me towards the counter until my chest hit the cool marble, and I was fully exposed to him.

"This olive oil will have to do in place of lube. I'm so fucking turned on I'm just about ready to spill my load."

Fuck, his intense want for me was so hot. "Do it. I need you now."

I heard a bottle cap opening; then his slick hand slid down my crease. He pushed one finger inside me. I was relaxed from the rimming, so I didn't need much prep. I was needy and desperate for him.

"Look at you. So good for me, just begging for me to fill you up," Dawson whispered as he slid a second finger in, pumping in and out with increasingly fast strokes. "You want my cock, sweetheart? You want my cum?"

"Yes," I groaned loudly.

His other hand teased my hip and then slid around to tug my cock.

"So hard for me. But this is mine. You only come when I tell you."

"Yes, fuck yes! Please. Dawson, fuck me."

"I love it when you beg like that," he groaned out. "Who do you belong to? Say it."

"You, only you. I love you."

I gasped as his fingers began to fuck me harder, faster.

"I love you more," he panted in response.

And then his fingers were gone, and I felt the head of his cock push into my hole.

Fuck, the intense burn, the fullness, it was so fucking good I could only moan and plead for more.

Dawson's hips snapped, and he pushed inside me all the way until his balls hit my ass. With one hand on my shoulder holding me down and the other on my hip, I was at his mercy. The only thing I could do was swivel my hips, but even then, I was captive to the punishing pace Dawson was setting.

But hell, it wasn't just my body captive to him.

My heart, my soul, everything I had to give, I gave to Dawson.

And I wouldn't have it any other way.

————

Dawson

I wanted to live inside Iain.

The way this incredible man trusted me, fuck, it was the hottest thing ever.

And after long, stressful weeks, we needed this. We needed to reconnect on this primal level, just me and him, nothing between us but our passion, our love.

I glanced down at Iain's long, lithe back, his skin slick with sweat, his blond hair a disheveled mess. And then back down to his ass, where he and I were joined.

Nothing separating us.

He was mine, and I was his, and this was it.

He was so beautiful—vulnerable and strong in the same breath. Iain had my total and unwavering attention, devotion, and love.

I fucking loved this man so much.

Sweat slipped down my face and neck as I pumped my hips harder and faster, my hand moving in tandem as I tugged on Iain's cock. His gasps and moans grew louder, and combined with the filthy sound of my skin slapping against his, it was heady.

"Baby, right there! Don't stop!" Iain shouted.

I thrust faster, desperate to give Iain everything he needed. As my climax grew stronger, my pace became frantic. My grip on his shoulder tightened as I pounded his ass over and over. I wanted to last longer, but we were both desperate.

That ultimate point of pleasure grew sharper and more intense with every thrust.

"I'm going to give you…everything," I panted. "Everything I have is yours, Iain."

"Dawson, oh God, oh fuck," Iain chanted.

His cock jerked in my hand, and I knew.

"That's it, sweetheart. Come for me. Give it all to me."

Iain shouted my name as he released all over my hand. His asshole clamped down hard around my dick.

My orgasm was just within reach.

Iain was still writhing and trembling in the aftershocks, gasping for air. And when he turned his head over his shoulder and our eyes locked, that was it for me.

I came long and hard, moaning his name and releasing so much cum in his ass that it began to slip out of his tight hole, along with the oil I'd used as lube.

We were a filthy, beautiful mess.

"I never knew," Iain gasped.

I continued to rock my hips, not wanting to stop. The aftershocks rolled through my body, and I ran my hand down Iain's back.

"Knew what?"

"That kitchens could be so sexy."

I laughed and finally pulled out of the warmth of his body.

Watching my cum slide out of Iain's hole was so fucking satisfying. I rubbed his tender ass, and he finally stood back up.

Turning around, he reached up and captured my lips, each kiss deeper and more drugging than the last.

"How about we clean up here and then go back to our bedroom?" he whispered against my lips.

"Our?"

"What's mine is yours and ours."

I smiled at him. "That sounds like a big commitment."

"It is."

"Are you ready for it?"

"Are you gonna chase me if I freak out and do a runner?" Iain quipped.

"Always."

"Then I'm good. But be patient with me."

"I will," I whispered, pulling him in tightly. "You've been strong, sweetheart. But you can lean on me."

"I think—" Iain paused and looked up at me with earnest eyes. "I need to go back home. I mean, Rhode Island, to see my dad."

I nodded.

"Do you want me to come with you?"

Iain kissed me again. "Thank you for the offer, but this is something I need to do on my own. I can't keep letting the past haunt me. I'll always miss my mom, and that will never change, but I think it's time I finally sat down with my dad and told him how I feel. Even if he's not ready, I am."

"Every day, you amaze me," I replied, pulling his body in tighter. "You're brave and strong, and I'm so fucking proud of you."

Iain flushed, and it made my heart clench.

"I don't think I deserve that." He leaned in and kissed my collarbone gently. "I didn't have the courage to face him before."

"You were so young, and you wanted to get on with your life; it's only normal."

"Maybe you're right. Timing is everything. And now it's you and me. Us. I couldn't do this without your support," he returned.

"You would, but I'm honored to stand by your side. I will support you no matter what. And I know you'd do the same for me."

"I would. I will." Iain cupped my face in his hands. "I promise you here and now."

We sealed his words with a tender kiss.

CHAPTER 41

IAIN

flew to Rhode Island as planned.

Not that I wanted to leave Dawson, but he had responsibilities back home.

But I wasn't entirely alone. Lennie was with me.

I'd called my dad weeks ago when the news story about the stalker hit the headlines. As usual, the call was brief, with my dad seemingly more concerned about getting to his tennis game on time than making sure I was all right. It was always the same. I hoped he'd give me something other than formal pleasantries, but I was always left disappointed.

No more.

I knew if I wanted to step into the next phase of my life with Dawson, I needed to face my past.

Over the years, I'd head home, but I stayed with Brodie and spent time with his family. They'd taken me in as their own, which I will forever be grateful for.

And this time, I was borrowing Brodie's cottage.

Okay, it was a mansion more than a cottage, but done in a cape cod style that suited the oceanfront property.

Lennie rented a car and drove me to my dad's place in Providence, about forty-five minutes away.

The closer I got to our old family home, the more unsettled I became.

The house looked eerily the same, a two-story colonial that was the typical suburban dream.

Dad had hardly changed anything over the years except painting the front door. That was new. Everything else, from the rose bushes in the front yard to the wind chimes hanging from the porch, was as it was when I was a kid.

Swallowing down my anxiety, I knocked on the door and waited.

The housekeeper, Mrs. Allen, greeted me.

"Iain, so nice to see you again. Your father is in his office."

"Thanks."

Fuck, even the smell of the place—pine-scented cleaner and lavender—haunted me.

I walked along the hallway to the first door on the right and knocked on the door.

"Come in!"

Opening the door, I walked in to find my father in his usual place, sitting at his desk with his laptop open. As an accountant, he worked both in the office and at home. He should've had a bed put in here since this was where he'd pretty much lived for the past twenty-years.

Stephen Holloway was a man of business, first and foremost.

Looking up, he took off his reading glasses and startled when he saw me.

Every damn time.

Like he was shocked that his only son might want to talk to him.

"Iain, you're looking well."

He motioned to the chair opposite him.

"I'm feeling better. Thanks, in large part, to my boyfriend, Dawson," I replied as I sat down.

I rubbed my sweaty palms on my jeans. "You look surprised to see me. I did mention I was coming here today."

My dad nodded, then ran a hand through his short silver hair. "Sorry, it's just that, when you walked through the door…you look, I mean, your smile. It's so much like her."

I glanced over at his desk and the picture of my mom, the only one in the house, that sat there. In the picture, she was posed on the deck of their sailboat, her long blond hair blowing in the wind, her red lips and matching jacket bright against the blue sky in the background.

I remembered that jacket. And her lipstick. The smell of her rose perfume. Twenty years suddenly felt like nothing.

"That's the reason I'm here. To talk about mom."

My dad shook his head and reached for the glass on the table.

A tumbler of whiskey, neat.

"I can't, Iain; you know that. I just can't talk about her—"

"That's the problem, Dad. You never did. She's been gone for years. We buried her two decades ago, but you never dealt with the grief. And I was the one who paid the price. You shut me out."

"I…I wasn't in a good place. I didn't want to hurt you," he muttered, taking a long sip of his drink. "And why are you saying all this to me now? What brought this on?"

"A stalker nearly killing me, that's what brought this on. And I'm in a relationship. A man I'm in love with. But I want to give Dawson all of me, and I can't do that unless we talk about this. About you and Mom. About the loss of our family."

"I'm still here, and you're here. We're both okay. Isn't that enough?" he snapped.

"No, it's not enough, and it's not okay. You pushed me away when I needed you. I didn't understand why because I was a kid. All I knew was that my mom was gone, and I needed my dad. But you weren't there. Well, physically, you were somewhere here in this house but never looking at me or talking to me. Do you know how alone I felt? She died, but you went right along with her."

Dad stood up and walked over to the window, facing the front yard. Taking another long gulp of his whiskey, he finally turned around.

"I made sure you were always taken care of, Iain. You wanted for nothing."

I scoffed. He still wasn't getting it.

"I'm appreciative of the fact you put a roof over my head and hired a nanny to raise me. But I was your son. Your child. A ten-year-old boy who needed love from the only parent he had left."

Dad ran his free hand over his jaw. "I had to work long hours and—"

"Stop with the excuses. You had enough money, and you could have made the time. Burying your hurt under the guise of work was your choice, but it made you a shitty father. And thank God for Brodie and his family, or I don't know what would have happened to me."

"You've made a good life for yourself. You turned out fine. Lots of money and fame."

"Yeah, I did turn out fine. With the help of my friends, who are my family now. Not you."

"Is that all?" he asked as he took his final sip of whiskey and walked back over to his desk, slamming the glass on the tabletop. "You came all this way just to insult me?"

"No, I came to tell you how I was feeling. I was hoping, foolishly, that you might want to actually deal with Mom's passing and move on. Maybe talk to a therapist. With me."

He shook his head. "Shrinks. All they want to do is ply you with medication, like they did with your mother. Or make you confess your most painful feelings."

"Well, I guess I have my answer." I sighed. "All that's left is to say goodbye."

"Goodbye?"

"We don't have a relationship. And you obviously don't want to build one. So, there's nothing more to say."

My heart racing, my stomach roiling, I stood up and headed for the door.

"Iain."

I turned around and stared at my father's face, at the eyes that were just like mine. But his were colder, harder. Had they always looked like that? I shivered but ignored my fear.

I was nothing like him.

"What?" I bit out.

"She would've been proud of your success, of the man you are."

I stared at him, shocked but also terribly saddened. I nodded.

"I hope so. But she would've been devastated by the man you turned out to be."

Then I walked out of that house, and I didn't look back.

I didn't realize I was crying until I slipped back in the car, and Lennie asked if I was okay. I'd told him all about why I was here on the flight up.

"I'm not," I replied as I wiped the tears off my face. "But once I get back home to Dawson, I will be."

Lennie patted my hand reassuringly, then pulled out of the driveway and headed back to the cottage.

"You sure you want to stay tonight?"

"I guess."

Lennie nodded.

"If it's any consolation, I know where you're coming from. Sometimes, it's better to let go of toxic people. It's the only way to move on."

My phone buzzed.

> Dawson: Jaxon just gave me his very extensive birthday wish list. I'll need your help. Especially when it comes to choosing a cat. I hope everything's all right. I can't wait until you come home tomorrow. I love you.

"On second thought, let's get our stuff from the cottage," I informed Lennie. "I want to fly back home tonight."

"You got it."

A few hours later, we were on our way to the airport.

> Change of plans. We're on the six p.m. flight tonight, arrival close to nine. See you soon. And I love you too.

> I'll meet you at the airport. Text me the flight details.

Four hours later, Lennie and I touched down, and the sense of relief I felt was palpable—not just relief, but excitement.

When we got to the arrivals gate, there was Dawson, standing head and shoulders above the crowd, of course.

He ran one hand over his fauxhawk, and the other held up a sign.

But instead of my name, it read: *Pick Up For: The Sexiest Man Alive.*

I bit my lip to keep from chuckling out loud. People walked past him and stared at the sign, laughing and taking pictures.

"You'd think he was never a fucking bodyguard," Lennie grumbled. "He's drawing a crowd."

My boyfriend hadn't entirely left his security work behind. He'd decided to go into business for himself. Dawson and Quinn were starting their own private investigation agency. It meant he could choose his own hours and, in the summer months, head on tour with me.

But Dawson's security experience was still valuable for us as a couple. Ever since we'd gone public, the press had been following us around. Dawson knew how to evade the press and when to confront them, albeit politely. Especially when it came to Jaxon. We made it clear that his privacy was our foremost concern. Jaxon took the media attention in stride, and with the guidance of his therapist, it was so far, so good.

Most of the media were eager but respectful. In fact, once we'd given our statements, they went gaga over our relationship. Personally, I think it was all because of my boyfriend. I was convinced the press was now in love with Dawson.

But not as much as me.

And they couldn't have him because he was mine.

As Lennie and I drew closer, Dawson spotted me and began to weave through the crowd, meeting me halfway.

Dawson put the sign down and pulled me into his arms.

"It was only two days, but I missed you like crazy," I said as I smiled up at him, so happy to be back where I belonged.

"Tell me about it. Are you okay? How did your talk go?"

I shook my head, my eyes starting to fill for a whole different reason.

"I'm sorry, sweetheart," Dawson whispered.

"I finally said all I needed to say. I feel…lighter. Maybe not better, but lighter."

Dawson hugged me tighter. "From now on, where you go, I go."

"Is that an order?"

"Fuck yes."

He kissed me, and despite our audience, I kissed him right back.

I was home.

And home was Dawson.

CHAPTER 42

DAWSON

"Who's ready to fucking rock tonight?!" Brodie yelled out as he ran across the stage.

The sold-out stadium crowd erupted in cheers and hollers in return.

"Come on, L.A., you can do better than that! I want to hear you scream!"

Another roar blasted through the venue.

"I said louder!! Like you do when you're fucking someone really hot. Or maybe more than one person?" Brodie laughed into the mic.

The boom from the audience this time around was ear-splitting.

I was standing in my usual spot, in the wings, but this time, I could stare at Iain to my heart's desire.

And did I ever.

I was getting so turned on watching Iain strum his guitar as he strutted around the stage, the fans going wild in response. Seeing him in his element always made me so fucking proud. Some days, I still pinched myself that this incredible, talented man was all mine.

The past four months had been a whirlwind for both of us. And I wouldn't have it any other way.

Therapy was going well for all of us, and Iain was more confident than ever. And secure in our relationship, which meant everything.

At the end of May, the band signed with Hardwick, a new label based in the UK. They'd just opened satellite offices in Nashville and LA, which was a perfect fit for the guys. No more dealing with Greg.

Zoe, along with Regan and some of the security staff like Lennie, had also left the label and signed on with Hardwick at Brodie's recommendation. It was great that the guys in the band had familiar faces to work with on this new leg of their rock 'n' roll journey.

That wasn't the only big change.

The renovations on Iain's house were completed. And just prior to leaving on this trip, Iain had asked me, Jaxon, my mom, and, of course, our newest family members, our tabby cats, Jimi and Hendrix, to move in with him.

The answer was a resounding "yes," and his house became ours.

Now that Jaxon had finished school for the year, we had time to organize the move.

I decided to sell my place and use the money to invest in the PI business Quinn and I had launched. The money would enable us to hire a full-time administrative assistant, something we desperately needed (invoicing was not in our skill set). It only took us a few months to get our license, and we had clients from the start. No doubt my boyfriend had a hand in our initial success, given that he referred some of his fellow celebrities. The renovations to the house included a home office for me and Quinn. It meant I'd be around more when Jaxon needed me.

Some might say Iain and I combining households was fast, but we'd discussed it as a family and agreed. Iain and I made it clear to everyone that someday soon, we were going to be husbands.

This was it.

And I wasn't the only one anxious to make Iain a permanent part of our family. At Jaxon's birthday party in April, he told me I should put a ring on it already. When I reminded him that Iain and I had only been dating a short while, he rolled his eyes.

I said it, nine going on nineteen.

The Wayward Lane family was expanding again, and I was so freaking happy to be a part of it.

"Holls looks good tonight," Van murmured beside me.

Good?

My boyfriend was smoking hot in his skintight leathers, ripped T-shirt, and braided cuffs. Wearing black eyeliner, and with his blond locks styled in a 70s shag, I couldn't take my eyes off him.

"Sexy as fuck is more like it."

Van laughed and nudged me with his elbow. I tore my eyes away from my boyfriend to look at him.

"You sure are vocal now when it comes to Iain."

"He's it for me, Van. I'm so fucking in love with him."

"Knocks you right on your ass, doesn't it?" Van sighed, staring at his husband as Brodie began to sing. "What is it with these Wayward Lane guys? We didn't stand a damned chance."

"Tell me about it."

"Iain isn't sneaking off anymore."

"Only with me."

And there would be sneaking off tonight.

As soon as Iain finished on stage, I was gonna haul him back to our hotel and do very dirty things with him.

This was the first weekend we'd had completely to

ourselves in over six weeks. Jaxon was back home with my mom, and Iain and I had two days in California together. Alone.

We were gonna spend every moment (when he wasn't on stage) naked.

Halfway through the concert, and before their third set, Iain took to the mic.

"Is everyone having a great time?" he asked.

The crowd shouted in response, and I heard several people yell at Iain, telling him they loved him.

Forget it, folks. He's taken.

"Alright then, that's what I like to hear." He wiped the sweat off his face. "Before I let Brodie take the mic again, I'd like to give a special shout-out to a very special man. My boyfriend, Dawson Everly."

Oh, Jesus, he didn't.

"Come on out here, baby," Iain encouraged as the band whistled at me and motioned for me to take the stage.

Despite my pounding heart and the cacophony of the crowd surrounding me, I walked out on stage.

"That's right. He deserves all the applause because I tell you, this man," Iain started as his smile unleashed, "this man is my world."

The audience went wild with more shouts and whistles.

"And because he's everything to me, I want to dedicate this brand-new song, one I had the pleasure to write, to him. Dawson, I love you."

He stepped back from the mic for a moment, and I reached out, pulling him in for a possessive kiss.

In front of fifty thousand screaming fans.

I tasted his sweat. And cinnamon, from the gum he liked to chew before he got on stage (no more cigs).

More than anything, I tasted his love.

After one more kiss, I let him go, waved to the crowd, and walked back to the sidelines so he could perform his song.

"All the way, baby. This is you and me," Iain spoke into the mic as he glanced at me, pointing between us. Then, he faced the audience again. "This is called 'Running Start.'"

I laughed out loud at the title of the song until Iain began to sing.

To me.

About us.

Then the tears followed until everything around me was a blur.

And there was only him and me.

And *our* music.

————

Iain

As soon as I stepped up to that mic, my nerves sizzled, and my hands shook.

Only Dawson could have that kind of effect on me.

Keep it together. It's just one song.

A song that meant so much to me.

I didn't know if it was going to be a major hit—a Wayward Lane classic. I didn't write it for that purpose, even though my band brothers assured me it was.

None of that even entered my mind. It was all about capturing a feeling that only Dawson inspired.

Ever since we'd committed to each other, not a day went by that I didn't know or feel how much I was loved.

I always thought a romantic relationship meant heartache and pain and losing a part of yourself.

No doubt there would be ups and downs for us down the line.

Nothing was ever constant.

But Dawson had shown me that, with the right partner, you could be a better, stronger, brighter version of yourself. I was happy and whole before we became lovers, but my life now was so much richer, and none of it had to do with money.

Even if I lost all my fame and fortune overnight, I knew I'd still wake up smiling if I woke up next to him.

And while I sang in front of thousands of fans about running away from my feelings and finally coming full circle, I felt the weight of the gold ring in my pocket.

I'd bought the ring a month ago, and I was searching for the right time to pop the question. I'd already asked his family for their blessing.

And now I didn't want to wait any longer to make that man officially mine.

But unlike my very public declaration of my love on stage, my proposal to Dawson would be private.

Just the two of us.

The hotel room was ready. The champagne was ordered.

I glanced over at the wings where Dawson stood and saw him wiping tears from his face. I smiled and sang the words I'd had etched on his ring.

Always, I run to you.

EPILOGUE

IAIN

"Stop pacing, sweetheart."

"I can't help it," I replied as I pulled on the tie I was wearing.

I hated it. Anything formal made my skin itch. This suit wasn't helping either. But I knew that today, of all days, I had to look polished.

"This is a huge deal. The biggest day of our lives."

"It'll all work out. Just breathe," Dawson encouraged as he pulled me into his arms.

I looked up into his eyes, and all I saw was his devotion.

This beautiful man was all mine.

How the fuck had I gotten so lucky?

"How do you know for sure? What if—"

"Iain, this is us," Dawson whispered. "This is it. We're ready."

I was. I knew it. I just wanted everything to go smoothly.

A tap on my back had me turning around. Jaxon was there, looking sharp in a navy blue suit we'd had made for him for this occasion. He was smiling up at me.

"Dad's right. We're ready."

I grinned at him in return.

A door opened, and a young woman waved us over. "We're set to begin."

I reluctantly stepped out of Dawson's arms but held onto his right hand. I offered my left to Jaxon, and together, all three of us walked through that door, ready to embrace our future.

I turned to Dawson, whispering to him. "I love you."

"I love you too. So much," he returned and kissed me.

As always, Dawson's touch grounded me.

Today was a moment two years in the making. One we would remember forever.

Not only were we coming up on our one-year wedding anniversary, but I was officially petitioning to adopt Jaxon.

Right here and now.

There had been a lot of conversations—with Jaxon, with Dawson and his family, and, of course, with Nadia's parents, Jaxon's other grandparents. And everyone agreed that this step was the best thing for our family.

Fuck, *my* family. Every time I thought about it, I got choked up.

It took me thirty-two years to appreciate that family isn't just the one you're born into. It's the one you create.

When my mom passed, and my dad fell apart, it left me adrift.

But then I had Brodie, Faise, and Ronin.

We became each other's rock, and then we became rockstars.

But now? With my husband by my side and Jaxon as my son, I had it all.

"No escaping us now," Dawson teased me as we stepped into the courtroom.

"Good," I assured him. "Besides, I was only running so you would catch me."

"And how did that work out?"

I looked at Jaxon and then back at my husband. "Better than my wildest dreams."

THANK YOU for reading B-Mine! Read about Brodie and Van in PUNK-IN, and Ronin and Faisel get their story in <u>4-EVER</u>

Find all of my books here

ABOUT THE AUTHOR

Ava Olsen writes steamy and dreamy MM romance with heartwarming characters, sexy banter, and ALL the romantic feels.

Sign up for my newsletter for the latest updates, cover reveals, and bonus scenes: http://avaolsenauthor.com

FOLLOW ME

OTHER TITLES BY AVA OLSEN

Sutton U Crew: MM Sports Romance

Catch

Bar Down: MM College Hockey Romance

Rule Breaker

Play Maker

Heart Taker

Stand Alone (enemies to lovers)

Happily Never After

Wayward Lane MM Rockstar Romance

PUNK-IN

B-MINE

<u>4-EVER</u>

Wayward Lane Backstage

Don't Fall For A Rockstar

Don't Fall For A Bodyguard

Don't Fall For A Dreamer

Voyagers Series

Oh Buoy

Starboard

The Cockpit

Endeavor

Nauti or Nice